Also by D.D. Ayres

Irresistible Force
Force of Attraction
Primal Force

RIVAL FORCES

D.D. Ayres

WITHDRAWN

St. Martin's Paperbacks

This is a work of fiction. All of the characters, organizations, and events portrayed in this novel are either products of the author's imagination or are used fictitiously.

RIVAL FORCES

Copyright © 2016 by D.D. Ayres.

For information address St. Martin's Press, 175 Fifth Avenue, New York, NY 10010.

ISBN: 978-1-250-08695-2

Our books may be purchased in bulk for promotional, educational, or business use. Please contact your local bookseller or the Macmillan Corporate and Premium Sales Department at 1-800-221-7945, ext. 5442, or by e-mail at MacmillanSpecialMarkets@macmillan.com.

Printed in the United States of America

St. Martin's Paperbacks edition / May 2016

St. Martin's Paperbacks are published by St. Martin's Press, 175 Fifth Avenue, New York, NY 10010.

10   9   8   7   6   5   4   3   2   1

To my brother Michael and his wife Marlene.
Love ya, M&M!

PROLOGUE

December 30, FBI Headquarters, Washington, D.C.

"What do you mean he's gone? Gone where?"

"We are unable to provide that information at present." The deputy U.S. marshal in the Phoenix office sounded miserable. "When Dr. Gunnar didn't make his check-in call this morning, we came to the house."

"Any signs of a struggle?"

"No. The apartment is neat and locked up. He didn't pack but his wallet is missing."

FBI task force supervisor Jamal Jackson ran a hand over his sleek dome. Three months in witness protection, and suddenly their key witness was in the wind. This was not good. "Sounds like something spooked him."

"Yes, sir. That's our judgment."

"Find him. Now."

Jackson glanced at his calendar. Missing witness. Hell of a way to start the New Year weekend.

CHAPTER ONE

The high-pitched shriek warned Kye McGarren of an incident taking place on ski slope three. He shifted the view in his field glasses in time to see a female skier plow into a snowbank that formed one edge of the slope and tumble headfirst onto the other side.

"Your turn."

Kye lowered his glasses to find his ski patrol partner for the week, Joe Saunders, grinning at him from their perch at the top of the slope. "I'm cutting you slack, old man. She looks hot. But I've already got a date for tomorrow night's New Year's Eve party."

Kye grunted. At thirty-six, he was hardly old. More-over, it was against company policy for staff to socialize with guests. Not that he would bring that up here. Tech-nically, Joe had seniority. What Joe and the SAR squad members didn't know was that they worked for Kye.

"Call it in. I'll sit second until the EMS guys get

there." Kye adjusted his goggles and then picked up Lily, his SAR K-9, and slung her across his shoulders.

Lily, a forty-pound Nova Scotia duck tolling retriever, often called a toller, confidently straddled Kye's shoulders. Ski patrol dogs often piggybacked with their handlers to their target.

Kye grabbed his poles off the edge of his snowmobile and pushed off down the hill in a silky swoosh.

Lily barked, a bright eager sound that from a distance sounded a bit like a coyote. Often mistaken for small golden retrievers, tollers had bright-red fur but possessed higher energy and intelligence. With a white blaze down her chest, a rosy-pink nose, and a narrow wedge-shaped head like a fox's, Lily looked dainty. But she was as tough as a wolf, with the balance and agility of a mountain goat. No terrain was too tough or too steep. She also had a nose that could pinpoint human scents buried beneath several feet of dirt, mud, water, or snow with equal ease.

He came up on the group of skiers who had paused at the edge of the slope where the female skier had gone off into the rough a little faster than necessary. They were laughing and taking pictures with their cell phones.

"Move back. Now." Kye's commands instantly parted the gawkers.

He lowered Lily to the ground and rubbed her fur briskly with both hands to energize and warm her. "Ready, Lily. Search! Search!"

With her flag of a tail held high, Lily barked twice as she plunged over the berm. SAR dogs worked off the leash in snow. It allowed them to cover search territory much faster than a slower-moving human could. In an avalanche situation, seconds counted.

Even as Kye dug his poles in the ground and kicked off his skis, Lily was barking in a key that meant she had found something.

The skier, in a bright-pink parka, was about ten feet beyond the edge of the slope, skis and poles scattered in the snow. She was kneeling in unpacked powder, and digging. If the volume of her curses was any indication, she was okay.

Kye waded through the calf-deep powder to the skier. "Are you injured? In pain? Any other problems?"

"Your shitty ski slope's the problem. I almost died." She didn't spare him a glance as she continued to paw the snow. "I've lost my Dolce and Gabbana goggles!"

Kye rested a gloved hand lightly on her shoulder. "Are you certain you're okay?"

She quick-rolled her shoulder to shrug off his touch without glancing up. "I'm suing. I swear, if I don't find my stuff, I'm suing."

Kye sighed as he glanced at Lily. "Search. Article."

With the skier's scent in her nostrils to guide her, Lily happily complied. On this gig, it wasn't unusual for her to be asked to find glasses, cell phones, and other gear. A few quick circles and Lily found the spot where something with the skier's scent lay buried. Digging quickly, she produced the goggles.

Kye took a waterproof chew toy from his pocket and tossed it to Lily as reward. "Good girl!" He dusted the snow off the goggles before handing them to the skier.

She shoved a handful of thick blond hair from her face and finally glanced up.

Seeing him for the first time, her gaze widened and her jaw fell open. Then she smiled and held out her hand. "I'm Shari."

"McGarren."

She used his grip to pull herself to her feet then didn't let go. "Did anybody ever tell you you look like that action-movie actor The Rock?"

"No."

"Well, you do. And he's *sooo* hot!"

"Uh-huh." She thought comparing him to some random movie star was going stroke his ego? Thanks but no thanks. Still, The Rock? He hid a smile.

Kye lowered his goggles. "You need to get back and change before a chill sets in."

She touched his arm again. "How about you come along and warm me up?"

Ignoring her, he pointed at the snowplow two EMTs had pulled up. "They'll take care of you."

After a quick conversation with the EMTs, Kye put on his skis, scooped up Lily, and headed for the bottom of the slope.

This assignment wasn't working out as he'd planned. He was here to relax. Sort of. A working vacation. The only kind he allowed himself. Too much time on his hands gave him time to think about what might be missing from his life. That's why he kept busy.

Four years ago he and Oliver Kelly, an Aussie with an appetite for adventure and a keen understanding of K-9 dogmanship, had formed a professional search-and-rescue company. They named it BAR K-9s, short for Bolt Action Rescue K-9 Service. Everyone quickly shortened it to BARKS.

They managed more than two dozen teams of K-9 handlers and dogs who worked every sort of search and rescue, from natural and man-made disasters to war zone recovery and jobs where local law enforcement needed additional expertise in tracking and rescue. Even ski patrol. Whatever kept them in the black.

At the end of his shift, Kye returned to his room and stripped out of his ski gear, every major muscle group protesting the day's effort. Within minutes he was settled into the liquid heat of his personal hot tub laced with a muscle soak that smelled of birch bark. "Ah, sweet."

A huff answered his sigh of contentment. Lily watched him from the doorway with her head kicked over. That was her puzzled look. As much as she liked streams, ponds, and snow, she didn't understand the use of water when it was hot and bubbly. On the other hand, she saw nothing wrong with making a snack out of his worn skivvies. A pair of them hung from her mouth.

"Lil-*lee*." Kye stretched out her name for emphasis. "Drop it. Now."

She looked away, mouthing the tighty whities a few more times before unhinging her jaw and letting the soggy material drop to the floor.

It was her only fault. Lily was mouthy.

Kye decided her fondness for his undies was a form of affection. He'd never met a woman who wanted to chew his drawers. Well, except for that one time. In his thirty-six years, he'd met some wild women.

He picked up and tossed Lily one of the chew toys he kept lying around as preferable to his personal items. "Good girl. Out."

Lily picked it up, glancing at him reproachfully before turning tail and walking out.

"And don't chew my socks or tee or . . . anything." He leaned back and stretched both muscular arms along the rim of the tub to let the heated bubbles work the kinks out. The warmth of the water reminded him of home.

Hawaii born and bred, his full name was Kekoa Alena Maleko McGarren. Kye for short. He'd spent his childhood seeking and riding the smooth rolling curl of a perfect wave. Skiing had its pleasures. Surfing was riding barefoot on the back of a sea god.

He loved nothing better than the feel of a wave beneath his board, undulating like a live thing. Crouched with his arms wide, he felt like a tern swooping along on the flow of a sea breeze. Salt on his lips. The sting of seawater in his eyes. The caress of the wind on his sun-bronzed shoulders. Life didn't get any better.

He opened his eyes and squinted at the bubbling water surrounding him. What the fuck was he doing here when he could be stretched out over the warm undulating body of a smiling wahine who tasted of sea salt and sunshine?

The sound of Hawaiian drummers woke him from a dream of warm salt breezes and a nighttime family beach luau with a perfectly roasted pig wrapped in banana leaves that had just been dug up from its sandy pit.

The smell of imaginary roasted pork lingered as he jabbed the ANSWER button on his phone without bothering to check caller ID. "Yeah?"

"Battise here."

Kye jerked fully awake at the sound of Law's voice. They'd served together in the military police CID overseas but hadn't exchanged a word in years. "I knew I should have turned over instead of answering."

"This isn't a social call, McGarren."

Kye sat up and rubbed his eyes. His ex-buddy's tone was professional, and distancing. Better that way. "Okay. Shoot."

"It's a personal matter." A pause. "There's no one else I trust with this."

Those words put Kye on alert. He would have bet a year's wages that he'd be the last man on earth Law would trust for anything. "What do you want me to do?"

"Check up on Yardley Summers, my half sister."

The answer made the hair on Kye's arms stiffen. "You screwing with me? Yard's your sister?"

"You know her?"

Kye's turn to pause. Everyone in U.S. K-9 law enforcement knew Yardley Summers as one of the top K-9 trainers in the country. He just wasn't prepared to admit exactly how well he'd once known her. But considering her brother's request, he didn't seem to have a choice.

"Your sister and I have a history."

"Care to elaborate?"

"Your sister and I have a history that's none of your goddamn business."

"Then it's not relevant."

Law was letting him off the hook. Kye wasn't sure he should be grateful. Law must have a hell of a job for him. "What's this about?"

"Yard's been seeing this guy for over a year but I only know the bare bones about him. His name is Dr. David Gunnar. He's with Doctors Without Borders. I wouldn't know that much except that he's disappeared, and Yard's convinced he's in some kind of trouble. She called me only because she's gotten nowhere through her usual contacts. My gut tells me if they won't help, something's not right."

"Right." Though they hadn't been in touch in years, Kye knew enough about Yardley's reputation to know her "contacts" included all levels of law enforcement up to and including the FBI. Even so. "Relationship issues sound like a job for big brother."

"It will be if I find out he simply walked out on her. Right now I've got a situation here I can't get away from. Meanwhile, I need to know Yard's not going to go off on her own until I can find out what the deal is with the guy she thinks she wants to marry."

Marry. Kye would pay money to meet the man who thought he could handle Yardley Summers. *Wait.* That's what Law was offering him a chance to do, for free. He was now too curious to hang up.

"I can't get away until late tomorrow."

"That'll work. You'll find her at Harmonie Kennels. Keep her there."

"You're talking about Yard. She'll be doing pretty much what she wants."

With the conversation over, Kye leaned back on his pillows and settled Lily on his chest. She poked her nose into his right armpit and settled in while he lay there thinking.

Yardley Summers. He hadn't allowed himself to dwell on thoughts of her in a dozen years. Sure, she popped up on his radar from time to time. But he'd avoided running into her. Because, hell, he supposed one never forgot a first love.

Kye sighed. He'd never in his life tangled with a woman the way he had with her. Young and beautiful, she had a way with dogs that bordered on spooky. She was also stubborn, defiant, and suspicious of everyone's motives. She had good reasons. That didn't keep him from falling for her harder and faster than anyone with a fully functional brain should.

For most guys first love happened early, at fifteen or sixteen, when they were 90 percent dick and 10 percent reason. He'd been twenty-four. Even so, meeting Yardley had been all about a sudden unexpected heat and wonder that had knocked him sideways.

Kye blew out a breath, feeling the heat of a long-ago craving race across his skin. The memory of Yard's volatile black eyes and feel of her rare dark-red hair sliding through his fingers as their lips clung together still stung like a scorpion.

For about a minute he'd thought he would be her hero, her knight in shining armor. Then reality landed on him like jackboots. At that point in his life, all he'd had was the army and a dog. He wasn't in a position to jeopardize either.

"Shit."

Lily lifted her head and began licking his chin, an indication that she was reading the uptick in pheromones caused by his thoughts. He pulled his dog in more closely to reassure her he was okay.

There was no reason for him to feel sorry for Yard. She'd gotten her happily-ever-after. Her father, the old bastard, had left her Harmonie Kennels—despite what he'd threatened.

Time to put what might have been away. But the deep stirring caused by Law's call continued to swirl in his gut.

He rubbed his sleep-gritted eyes, regretting the lost dream of roasted pig. He should have said no to Law. In fact, he still could. His ticket to Hawaii was practically doing a hula on the bedside table. His mouth began to water with possibilities of *kalua pua'a*. He would text Law. Say *Sorry, bro, my homeland calls.*

But he wasn't going to. He wasn't an immature hot-head rushing headlong to the rescue this time. He was a man with hard times and years of experience behind him. Yard was in trouble. So what if the very idea had those rusty trumpets in his head inconveniently blaring to life? He just hoped they weren't playing taps for his peace of mind.

CHAPTER TWO

"I see a head." Taggart, Harmonie Kennels' senior trainer, sounded like a boy on Christmas Eve. "Here we go again!"

"Easy, girl. You're doing fine." Yardley Summers leaned over the prone body of Loba, a black German shepherd. She gently stroked the thick brindled fur of the bitch in labor, evaluating the contractions through her skin. With five pups already delivered in her first litter, Loba was doing amazingly well.

Panting a little, Loba lifted her head to look back at where the action was going on. A wet glassy-looking knob of a dark head appeared behind her hind legs.

"Are you getting this? Be sure you're getting all of this."

"I'm trying, Yard. But you're blocking the shots." Georgiana Flynn leaned in over her friend's shoulder to get a better angle for her camera. "This isn't my usual fare, you know. Oh, look! It's another boy!"

Yardley didn't spare her friend a glance. Instead she watched intently as Loba nudged the pup out of its membrane and then began licking it vigorously.

"Don't let her hurt it," Georgie said from behind her lens, never stopping the shots that made her camera whir softly.

"She's doing her job," Taggart assured her. "Making the puppy breathe."

"If you say so." Georgie sounded less enthusiastic. That was because Loba was eating the embryonic sac.

Soon, the final puppy—six in all—was placed in a quilt-lined basket covering two hot-water bottles. Yardley bent over and kissed Loba on her dark snout. "Good girl. You're a real trouper, Mama. Your babies are beautiful. So proud of you."

Loba made a nasal sound and licked Yardley's face.

"*Oooh*. Ick!" Georgie commented behind her camera.

Laughing, Yardley stood up and stretched. "Miracle of life, Georgie, in all its messy glory."

When she had cleaned her hands, Yard reached automatically to check her cell phone. A shadow sailed across her expression as she realized she hadn't kicked the habit. She shoved her thoughts another way, to her penchant for meticulous record keeping. Dates and numbers came easily to her.

"That's six pups delivered in five hours and forty-nine minutes. Put that in the records, Taggart."

"You got it, boss." Doug Taggart was a dozen years older than her, having worked first for her father. But he had always treated her with respect, calling her boss even when he didn't need to.

She equaled his five-foot ten-inch frame. But Taggart was build like a Hummer, short legs balancing a massive chassis that made her seem willowy in comparison as they stood shoulder-to-shoulder in identical gear of charcoal-gray cargo pants, long-sleeved polos, and windbreakers with the kennel name embroidered on the back.

Sensing that her ordeal was over, Loba rose and moved to nose about in the wiggly pile of her pups. They were climbing over one another and rooting around in the basket lining, making mewling noises.

Georgie moved in slowly to catch the mother-and-pups moment. "That's amazing. Newborn puppies sound just like newborn humans?"

"Even after seeing dozens of litters being born, it never gets old." Taggart picked up the basket of pups. "I've got it from here, ladies. Happy New Year."

Half an hour and a nearly empty bottle of champagne later, the two friends were huddled together on a pile of quilts before the wood-burning fireplace in the century-old farmhouse Yardley called home. "Here's the new headshot for your website." Georgie held up her tablet, into which she'd downloaded her photos.

Yardley took one look at the photo of her sweaty face and goofy smile and feigned horror. "Oh no! Delete it now."

"Not so fast." Georgie jerked her tablet out of Yardley's grasp. "Let's see. What do I want in return for not releasing this photo?" She pretended to search her mind. "*Hm.* For now, I'll take the rest of the champagne."

"Oh no, you don't." Yardley grabbed the bottle out from under Georgie's reach. "You met Brad because of me. That's got to have earned me a break."

"Won't argue that." The expression on Georgie's face said it all. She was absolutely in love with sexy FBI operative Brad Lawson. Even if their affair had begun with Georgie at the center of an FBI bomb investigation after Brad's explosives-sniffing K-9, Zander, had implicated her. Now, *that* was attraction.

Yardley tried to hide a twinge of jealousy as she filled her own glass. "How is your hunk of wonderfulness?"

"Good, when last seen." She made a motion for the champagne bottle. "He and Zander had full holiday bomb-squad duty in D.C. But he's off for ten days beginning tomorrow. He's been very mysterious about a trip he's planned for us. It better be somewhere tropical. All I've packed are bikinis, sarongs, and fifty-plus sunscreen." The freckled redhead waggled the empty bottle before Yardley's nose. "The question is, why are you alone?"

"More bubbly coming up." Yardley popped up and headed for the kitchen before she could be interrogated further.

When she reached the privacy of the kitchen, she took a deep breath, waiting for the anxiety to subside. She knew her sense of trouble brewing was bogus. She now knew the answer to why her phone would never again ring.

"Crap." She grabbed a chilled bottle and hurried back to join Georgie. She wasn't going to let anything spoil this rare girlfriend sleepover.

"Tell me about your most recent shoot." Yardley sat and handed over the bottle. "Anyone interesting?"

Georgie made a face. "Just A-list celebrities. The worst. Now you answer my question." She loosened the wire holding the cork. "Why are you alone on New Year's Eve?"

"I'm not alone. There's you. And him." Yardley

pointed to the large metal kennel at the opposite end of the long room.

Her simple action was enough to alert the inhabitant. A midsized dog with a thick yellowish-gray coat, pointed snout, erect ears, and the white face mask of a wolf stood up and growled softly.

"That's my exchange student Oleg. He's a Czech wolf-dog."

"Wow. I didn't even know he was there. Why didn't he bark when we came in? Is he shy?"

"Far from it. He simply doesn't like to give his location away."

Champagne abandoned, Georgie grabbed the camera that was always nearby and moved closer. "Look at those slanted yellow eyes. It's kind of unnerving how he seems to be sizing me up. Oh, but he's gorgeous."

"And deadly." Yardley smiled, always in her element when talking about K-9s.

"Silent and deadly?" Georgie's green eyes appeared above the top of her camera. "Are you training K-9 black ops?"

"Classified." The security firm that had imported him wanted Oleg evaluated, but she was to keep her work and his skill set confidential.

Georgie came back to her place and set her camera down. "So, about your guy. You haven't mentioned him once."

Yardley's mouth turned down. The *journalist* side of Georgie's photojournalist personality was tenacious. "That's because there's nothing to say. It was momentary madness. I'm over it."

"You don't sound like you're over it."

"That's because I don't like to lose. He ghosted me.

And I don't know why." Yardley heard the irritation level in her tone and reined it in. "Sorry. You know I don't do emotional intimacy well."

Georgie nodded. "You're a private person. I respect that. But even if I never met him, I know David meant something to you. If only because you never told me about the other men you've dated."

Yardley reached for the champagne. "There haven't been that many. And none of them were serious."

"Until your doctor. You lit up like a Christmas tree when you told me about him."

"My mistake." Yardley bit her lip. She wouldn't, couldn't admit what she'd done when she'd still hoped that David wanted her. Georgie would think she was losing her shit. "It just hurt that he ghosted me without even a text good-bye."

"Then he's an asshole. Forget him. You can so do better."

Yardley smiled in gratitude for her best friend's support. "You're right. Whatever David and I had wasn't real. Not like you and Brad."

She felt Georgie's inspection of her increase. "Don't you want what we have?"

Yardley hesitated. She'd said too much. But she couldn't, this once, keep from voicing the question that had haunted her for her whole life. "What if there's no one out there for me? What if I'm not the type of woman a man can love?"

Georgie chuckled. "Have you looked in the mirror lately? The men who come through Harmonie Kennels on a daily basis trip on their tongues when they catch sight of you. You could have your pick of sexy alpha males."

Yardley shook her head. "I can't be all sexy come-on with a man one minute and the next expect him to appreciate me chewing his ass in public for a mistake on the training field." She shrugged. "Besides, you know what the K-9 handlers call me."

"The Citadel. Unconquerable." Georgie couldn't tease her friend about that. Yard had fought too hard to gain and keep the respect of her male colleagues. Too bad. Every woman needed a man willing to storm her castle. "Screw Dr. Gunnar if he couldn't see what he was throwing away. Someone will come along who's worthy of you."

Yardley smiled, trying to lighten the mood. "You're right. Some random guy will come along soon and I'll screw his brains out to take my mind off this."

"No! You know that's not at all what I meant." Georgie reached up and touched her friend's arm. "You deserve a man who can handle his business and be okay with you handling yours. Yet he'll be there, if you need him. Of course, he'll need an iron constitution and balls of steel. I've got it! I'll notify the cavalry, armored division."

Yardley burst out laughing, feeling the sadness and doubts drift away as she raised her glass. "To the cavalry."

After the toast Georgie looked around for something else to talk about and spied her gift under the tree. "We didn't open our presents. Open yours first."

As Yardley reached for the brightly packaged box, something fell from the bottom. It was a red envelope with sticker wreaths decorating it. She picked it up.

"A card, too?" She faked surprise. "Oh, you shouldn't have."

Georgie smiled. "I didn't. It was on the doorstep when I arrived earlier. I forgot to tell you. Maybe you have a secret admirer."

When she opened it, Yardley's mouth turned down. "Not exactly an admirer."

"What is it, Yard?"

Yardley hesitated, then offered it. "See for yourself."

Georgie gasped softly. It was a cover from a porno magazine featuring bondage. The disturbing graphic picture was of a nude woman tied up in very painful ways. A photo of Yardley's head had been Photoshopped over the model's and her eyes blacked out. "That's disgusting. What are you going to do?"

"What I usually do." Yardley took it from Georgie and tossed it toward the flames in the fireplace.

"Wait." Georgie jumped up and snatched it out. "You might need this. As evidence."

The image had shaken her, but Yardley stuffed down that feeling. "Your FBI boyfriend is rubbing off on you. I don't jump at every insult lobbed my way."

"Have there have been others?"

"About once a year someone thinks it will make them feel better to threaten me with retaliation for my decision not to pass them as certified handlers."

"And you get this?" Georgie held it up with two fingers.

Disgust shuddered through her. "No. Nothing like that."

"You need to tell the authorities."

"Where would I start? My clientele comes from around the world."

"But this was delivered today. Without a stamp. This guy's local."

Yardley rolled her eyes. "I hate having smart friends."

"I hate it even worse when my smart friend doesn't act like one."

"There's no one local I have a beef with. We did have to scrub a Georgia police officer trainee a few weeks back after he deliberately set his dog on another student."

"Sounds like the kind of guy who'd do this."

"Maybe. But I can't accuse anyone without proof."

"Still, you should notify the sheriff. When will your staff be back?"

"First thing Monday morning."

"That leaves you alone tomorrow and Sunday." Georgiana reached for her phone. "I'll ask Brad to come out here when he gets off in the morning."

"No. Don't!" Yardley wrapped her fingers around her friend's phone to prevent her from texting. "I won't be responsible for ruining your getaway. I'll call the sheriff in the morning. Okay?"

Georgie glanced at the front door. "It's not safe to be alone. Promise me Oleg will sleep in your room from now on."

"Done deal." Yardley felt suddenly teary for no good reason she could think of. Then she did something totally out of character. She reached out and hugged her friend, hard. "Thank you for caring. Now can I open my real gift?"

It was nearly eight a.m. but the sun had yet to climb the dark summit of hills to the east. At the moment the frigid gray sky was clear of the thunderstorms that were predicted to precede even colder weather by nightfall.

Yardley adjusted the headband covering her ears to shut out the wind swooping down the shoulders of the nearby mountains. The pink crocheted headband was part of her Christmas gift from Georgie. Otherwise she wouldn't have been seen dead in it. She suspected it was a gag gift because the box had also contained another gift, a beautiful sterling-silver heart necklace with a paw pendant.

She and Oleg had been for a brisk jog. They were still getting to know each other. But now, in the deep shadows on the side of the road, she felt the nagging fatigue of too much champagne and too little sleep. She paused and reached for the cell phone in her pocket.

Her heartbeat quickened as she stared at the blank screen. Only one person had the number. For the past three months, six days, and innumerable miserable hours, she'd carried it with her, as if it were as necessary to her heartbeat as a pacemaker.

She squeezed the phone until the pressure equaled the tightness around her heart. She hadn't expected to fall for David. Hadn't wanted a real entanglement. That's why she'd been so slow to recognize what was happening.

The last time they'd met, in late September, he'd been moody, worried even. He wouldn't say why. But as they were parting at the airport in Antigua, he'd suddenly asked her about the future. Their future. Did she think they could have one? If so, would she be willing to drop everything and just come with him on a moment's notice? No questions asked.

Coward. She stared at the empty screen as if it had voiced that accusation.

She'd choked. Too afraid to say yes to anything bordering on commitment, she'd told him she needed to think about it. So he'd nodded, kissed her a little too hard, and then boarded his flight. She hadn't heard a word from him since.

Opposing emotions Ping-Ponged through her thoughts. For three months she'd worried that something bad was keeping David from her. She'd even called her half brother Law to get his advice, which was embarrassing to think about now. At this point, she realized that kind of worry had no basis in fact. Maybe the truth was that her fear of him being in trouble was easier to accept than the fact that she'd ruined her chances with David because she couldn't commit.

She felt something splash her cheek. Crap. She pushed the offending moisture away with the heel of her hand. She never cried. Ever. Certainly not over a man who had dumped her without so much as a good-bye. Her father would be ashamed of her.

That thought pushed even Dr. David Gunnar from her mind.

Being the daughter of the late Bronson Battise, one of the most famous trainers of military and police K-9s in the United States, had its perks. And drawbacks. The biggest one being that she'd been born female. Battise didn't think women were equal in any way to men. Harmonie Kennels wasn't meant to be hers.

Well, she had it, even if it was by default. Her half brother Law, whom she'd known only slightly at the time, had refused his father's legacy. He'd signed over the hundred pastoral and wooded acres bordering the Blue Ridge Mountains to her and walked away.

Even so, she'd fought harder than anyone would ever know to be worthy of this legacy. But it was a burden, too. This place, these acres, the business was an all-consuming life. Her trainers got to go home for the holidays to families and friends, parties and traditions. Harmonie Kennels was all she had in the world.

Don't feel sorry for yourself, Yard.

Too bad if she wanted more. She knew what it was to have so much less. Maybe wanting to be loved was asking for too much.

So she'd screwed up. She wasn't one of those women who needed a man to feel complete. She wasn't like Georgiana. She'd never known what it felt like to be so in love her brain stopped working because her feelings had taken control.

Liar. She felt her face catch fire as her conscience called bullshit. She had been in love once before. *Kye McGarren.*

Yardley did a mental head shake. Where had that thought come from? She must be more shook up than she thought. McGarren was her first romantic failure.

She wasn't good with people. She was good at being a boss. Everyone looked to her to be strong, make the hard decisions, make it work. She was respected and admired. The only ones who gazed at her with unguarded love and appreciation were her K-9s.

At the moment, Oleg was rotating his head back and forth between her and the road ahead, as if he needed to keep an eye on both. Unlike most of her K-9s, he preferred to keep his distance from his handler. He'd been bred for protection. His job, safety of the pack. She supposed they were a lot alike.

She reached out to brush a hand over Oleg's tall ears. That brought his attention back to her. In his gaze, which she knew better than to hold long, she saw that he accepted her as his alpha. But he didn't adore her, as every other dog she worked with did. "You're my male challenge of the moment, are you, big fella?"

Or maybe she was losing her touch.

Suddenly she was angrier than she could ever recall being. She hauled back and put everything she had into the toss that sent her phone arcing into the undergrowth on the hillside. On Monday she'd get a new phone with a new number. And go back to her life.

"Screw love!" And screw Kye McGarren, wherever he might be, and the memories of a time when she'd wanted more.

CHAPTER THREE

Kye swallowed the last of his extra-large Styrofoam cup of coffee. It was lukewarm, revealing the oily dregs from a convenience store pot that needed cleaning. The liquid hit his stomach and spread acid burn like napalm. Even so, he regretted that it was his last gulp. After a final working day on the slopes, he'd spent New Year's Eve on a red-eye flight from Salt Lake City to Washington, D.C.

Being a big man, flying coach middle seat wasn't his favorite way to travel. But he really couldn't have asked the six-year-old at the window to change with him. Not when she'd been face-glued to the miracle of darkness outside and offering a running monologue about its "awesomeness." On the other side of him the girl's mother, with a three-month-old in her arms, needed the aisle. Lily, down in luggage, had more room in her crate.

No worries. He'd plugged in his headphones, turned

up the volume, and tried to forget that he was wedged in like tuna in a sardine can.

All in all, an IV drip of Red Bull would be welcome about now.

Kye glanced over at Lily, who occupied the kennel beside him on the seat of the rental car. He reached between the bars with his fingers and scratched her snout. "I know this isn't our usual assignment. It's more Lucy and Ricky Ricardo than search and rescue. Your job. Be charming. I'll be comic relief. Oh, and don't get eaten by the locals." The kennel would be full of alpha K-9s happy to assert their authority. "Think you can do that?"

Lily gave a series of high-pitched yips between finger licks, her thick tail beating the bars because it wasn't free to wag.

"That's my girl."

He could do this. Get in good with Yardley Summers. Absolutely.

He was known as something of a goofball among his friends. The big guy with a decent face, he'd often been the target for a certain kind of male who seeks to prove his manhood by taking on the biggest alpha in the room. He was good in fights though he didn't like them, especially stupid pointless ones. In defense, he'd learned to use his sense of humor to defuse those moments.

If Yard didn't know what to make of him, he might get in the door before she blew up.

As he turned onto the gravel drive that led to Harmonie Kennels, he noticed the entry gates to the property stood wide open. The most innocent explanation was that Yard was up and out. But after the global up-all-night-to-have-fun celebration of New Year's Eve, who didn't sleep through the first half of the first day of the new year? Or at least until bowl games began?

He drove on through, checking for signs of life. There were no vehicles parked by the barracks where handlers stayed when they came to train. The only two vehicles he saw were parked close in, near the two-story farmhouse with a wide porch front. One was a well-used Jeep Wrangler. The other a Mazda Miata. Maybe Yard owned both vehicles. Or had she been celebrating the new year with company, after all?

"Aw damn." Maybe her missing doc had made a house call last night in his lame-ass Mazda.

Kye rolled his eyes. If he had flown all this way, in the wrong direction, only to barge in on a love nest, he was going to take it out of Law's hide.

He came to a stop quietly, watching the front of the house for signs of life. No lights on the first floor. Windows were shuttered or draperies closed. The second floor was the same. What now? Knock on the door? Call Law?

The image of a woman and dog coming up the drive appeared in his rearview mirror. She wore a Gore-Tex jacket and leggings, black with flashes of deep pink along the seams, and a matching pink headband with a bow. Pink bow? Yardley?

He sat still, pretending he didn't see her. No point in giving her the advantage of recognizing him from afar. He wanted her in close so he could judge her initial reaction to him. *Shock and awe, baby.*

He had forgotten how tall she was, five foot ten with long, lean legs that moved in an easy stride. A flash of memory of those legs wrapped around his waist surprised him. He shoved it aside.

Her hair was in a loose ponytail, unraveling in the wind behind her. He'd only seen it completely free once before. The memory sent the sensation of hair the color of Cherry Coke spilling over his bare shoulders. He shoved that one away, too.

Yardley had always been a stunner, though she'd seemed not to know that when they met. Dressed most often in jeans, a tailored shirt, and military boots, her tall, lean frame had curves in all the right places. Her elegant cheekbones and full mouth held a hint of sensuality she couldn't quite hide behind her no-nonsense gaze. Eyes, blacker than his, revealed her Native American heritage. Her long dark-red hair flagged the Cajun ancestry of her father. He knew all that.

Yet something he wasn't prepared for tumbled into place as he exited the vehicle and faced her. His last memory of her, sitting on the ridge of a nearby hill while the setting sun painted her profile gold as it sank into darkness.

And then she was staring at him.

That ramrod-straight posture of hers he'd always associated with pride now struck Kye as a defense. She looked braced against all the hurts and slights and pain of the world. Had life been that hard for her? Once, yes. He knew that. But nothing he'd heard about her these last years would make him think that her life was anything less than two thumbs up. Except for her stiff stride as she came toward him. It made him want to put his arms around her. Slide a cupped hand up her spine in a soothing gesture that was also protective. He wanted, for a moment, to shield her. From what? He didn't have the slightest idea.

That protective feeling clenching his gut was as raw

and immediate as it had been the day he left here, left her, a dozen years ago.

Well, hell.

Now he was the one who needed a moment.

Yardley watched the man emerge from his SUV. His back was to her but that didn't delay her first impression.

The stereotype was so dramatic she almost laughed. Tall. Really tall. And dark. Check and check. Handsome? She wouldn't know until he turned around. But the guy drew her eye anyway, like the gravitational pull of the moon. It wasn't only that he wore a bright-red ski parka with black shoulder patches and a large blocky white cross on his back. She recognized them as emblems of ski patrol search and rescue. A little bit out of place in Virginia.

At that moment, he pivoted.

Her first thought was that he was ridiculously gorgeous. Broad face, bold nose, and high-definition mouth. And wide eyes that managed to be open yet intimidating beneath his heavy brows. It was really too much for one man. He had the height, width, and bronze good looks of a Polynesian god. Running up hard against that thought was surprise that she recognized him after all these years.

Kye McGarren.

The shock of recognition hobbled her stride. The only man who'd ever made her believe, if only for three days, that she was in love. That was twelve years, five months, and three days ago. But damn, she wasn't about to admit she remembered it. Not to him. Most of all, not to herself.

Scowling hard, she turned her shock into a minute assessment as she approached. As if he were a K-9 she was considering buying. Yes, distance. She needed it badly.

He was bigger than he'd been a dozen years ago. The sexy lean physique of twenty-four had filled out impressively, if his jacket size was any indication. Gone, too, was the raw new-recruit haircut. His black hair grew in thickly on top though it was short on the sides. Crap. He was now a man in his prime. But none of that mattered. In fact, it only made her angry.

She moved purposefully toward her unwelcome guest. Oleg followed close by her side, in full K-9 mode. The ridge of hair along his spine stiffened as he sniffed the emotional surge sliding off his handler. After a few more steps, he added a soft growl.

Yardley frowned. Any other person facing Oleg should be getting very nervous by now. This man simply folded his arms, leaned back against the door of his SUV, and smiled.

Yep. Nailed it. She still recognized that smirky *aloha* smile after all this time.

"Kye McGarren. What are you doing here?"

His smile widened. Deep curves carved in his cheeks by humor emphasized his wide, perfect mouth. She suspected he was all kinds of pleased that she'd remembered his name, and was instantly sorry she had let him know that.

"*Hau'oli Makahiki Hou*, Ms. Summers. I wasn't sure you'd remember me."

"Don't flatter yourself. I remember everyone."

She looked down at Oleg. His rumble was like a cat's purr, only scary. Even her handlers weren't sure of their ability to keep the wolfdog in check. He was the kind of

K-9 who might get handed from handler to handler as being "too hot" or difficult. She wasn't worried about that but didn't want to test her control with a person she didn't like. Being a jerk wasn't a crime.

"Knoze."

Oleg complied immediately, coming to heel and going silent, yet still wary.

"Your Czech friend runs a bit hot, huh? Or is he feeding off you?"

Damn. He'd noticed her hesitation.

Yardley looked up at him, her face expressionless. Nothing and no one got to her. Everyone knew that. "Why are you here? Dressed like that." Damn, she couldn't resist asking. Despite his ridiculous getup, his sexiness was leaking through into every pore of hers. That had to stop.

He glanced down at his board shorts and flip-flops, his smile holding. "Side trip on my way home." He reached into the open doorway of the SUV and withdrew with an armful of dog. "But first I'd like to you meet Lily."

She glanced at the toller and then back at him. He'd brought a dog to her. Of course. What other reason ever brought people here?

The faint disappointment stirring in her thoughts made no sense. A problem with a dog. That, she could handle. Just not today.

"Call and make an appointment. We're closed for the holidays."

She started to walk past him.

Kye fell into step on her right side but with a respectful distance between them. "Here's the thing. I'm headed for Hawaii and I don't know when I'll be stateside again.

I was at the airport when I thought I could swing by here first."

Yardley shook her head. "My staff's on vacation."

"There's no one here but you?"

Why was everyone suddenly so interested in her solitude? Yardley paused and glanced around, nerves tingling, as she did a perimeter search of her property in one direction and then the other. Finally her gaze came back to him. "How did you know I'd be here?"

"Who said I did? It's a bit chilly out here, isn't it? Can I come in?" He made a motion toward the house.

"No." She made sure there was nothing iffy in her reply.

He watched her a few seconds—unable, she hoped, to read anything in her expression besides disinterest. Why was he staring at her as if she'd grown another ear?

"Then I guess I'll billet right here until I get further instructions." He dropped his backpack—when had he picked that up?—on her porch and sat down on the first step with the toller still in his arms.

Further instructions? What was he talking about? Yardley opened her mouth to ask but then shut it. What he did or didn't do was up to him. Not her problem.

She turned and climbed the stairs.

The front door opened before she reached it. Georgie stuck her head out. "I thought I heard voices." Her gaze moved from Yardley to Kye, her sea-green eyes widening. Unconsciously, she reached up to brush a handful of bed-head red curls back from her face. "Oh, you have company."

"He's not staying." Yardley stepped closer to the door, cutting off her friend's view of Kye, and gave her a squinty stare that said *Back off.*

Unfortunately, her friend ignored her.

"Um, Yard, I'm dying for coffee." Georgie gave Kye the once-over, her bright gaze lingering maybe a fraction too long for simple curiosity. "You look like you could use a cup, too."

He popped up from the step, giving Georgie his best laid-back surfer-dude smile. "I've give my left nut for a cup."

Yardley moved to square off against him as he came forward. It felt strange to be dwarfed by any man. He was bigger in every way. "I don't allow strangers in my house."

"Then let's not be strangers." Kye turned to Georgie and held out his hand. "Kye McGarren. Co-owner of Bolt Action Rescue K-9 Service out of Honolulu, Hawaii."

"Oh." Georgie's expression went blank for a second as she glanced at Yardley.

That's when Yardley realized she'd thought Kye was David Gunnar. Before she could make it clear that Kye wasn't welcome, Georgie's green eyes lit up with mischief. "I'm Georgiana Flynn. And you're our First Footer."

Yardley stared at her friend. "What are you talking about?"

"Hogmanay," Kye and Georgie answered together then grinned at each other.

Georgie spoke first. "Scottish tradition says that the first person to cross the threshold on New Year's Day determines the homeowner's luck for the year. The best First Footer to have is a tall, dark-haired man."

Yardley scowled. "You're Irish."

"McGarren sounds Scots." She grabbed Kye's arm and pushed him toward the door. "Welcome, First Footer."

As he passed Yardley, Kye paused and offered her a smile so wide she felt the warmth of it curl in her stomach. Then he reached up and flicked her headband. "Nice bow. It's so you."

"That's what I thought." Georgie winked at Yardley, letting her know it was a gag.

Lips firmly pressed together, Yardley watched her traitorous friend follow Kye in. Only when they were inside did she reach up and snatch the bow off her head and stuff it in her pocket. She could take a joke. She so could. But what had she done to the universe that it required that Kye McGarren return to her life?

CHAPTER FOUR

Yardley stood uneasily just inside her front door, feeling as if she were the unwelcome stranger. Georgie had moved into the center of the room, her hand still on McGarren's arm, chatting like they were old friends. She'd never seen her friend so animated with a man. Not even with Brad. With Brad she smoldered, a quiet but intense burn. A very private fire for very private emotions. Right now, Georgie was practically giddy. Maybe she was still high from last night's champagne.

"Don't you have somewhere you need to be?" Yardley gave Georgie a meaningful look as she made a wide arch past McGarren, being careful to keep Oleg a respectful distance from the toller he now had on a leash.

"I'm packed. I've got an hour. How about some coffee, Yard?"

"After I feed Oleg." She disappeared into the kitchen, needing a moment to compose herself before her anger got the better of her. She set up the doggy gate to keep

Oleg in the kitchen. It was strictly a reminder. He could jump it with ease.

Yardley's zipper made an angry *zzzzt* sound as she yanked her jacket open. McGarren had no business being here. And Georgie was no friend to do this to her.

When she had wrestled off her jacket, she closed her eyes, reaching for that inner peace she chased twice a week at a yoga class. But after only a few seconds she realized she was straining to hear every word coming from the other room.

As she reached for the bag of dog food she heard Georgie say, "And who is this pretty pup?"

"Her name's Lily. You two have the ginger coloring in common. I hope you don't mind me saying that."

"Oh no. I've been compared to worse things."

Yardley rolled her eyes. Georgiana Flynn hated people making remarks about her red hair, or calling her "Ginger" or "Annie." Right now she was acting like the worst kind of fan girl. *I've been compared to worse things. Pul-eeese!*

She bent to fill Oleg's food bowl, but the wolfdog began noisily lapping water. Her gaze swerved back toward the doorway, wishing he would stop but knowing Oleg needed to drink after their run. After a few moments, the sloshing stopped and she could hear again.

"—the cutest thing," she heard Georgie say.

"Lily can seem a bit reserved but secretly, she loves attention. Take all the photos you want."

"No. Stay in the frame. The shots are better with you two interacting."

Yardley felt the urge to growl as she moved to dump fresh coffee beans into her pot only to realize Georgie had already made fresh coffee. The girl had lied to get that man inside her house. *Can't trust anyone.*

Belatedly, she gave Oleg the signal that he could eat.

In his hungry surge to clean the aluminum bowl in a single gulp, Oleg knocked it over and sent chucks of dog food skidding across the floor. He made so much noise chasing after and scarfing up the pieces that Yardley had to step to the doorway in order to continue to eavesdrop.

"—nice. Yes. Good. You're a natural. Did you know Harmonie Kennels does a studmuffin calendar of dogs and their handlers?"

Oh hell no!

Yardley bolted through the doorway. "Georgie."

Georgie looked back to see her host's disapproving expression, but it didn't shut her down. "I was just telling Mr. McGarren he's perfect for Harmonie Kennels' next Hot Handlers and Cool K-9s calendar. Unless he's a total dough boy underneath that jacket." Georgie looked back at Kye, mischief in her gaze. "Are you a total dough boy? I need to know. Strictly for professional purposes."

Kye grinned as he glanced at Yardley. "How about a few audition shots?"

"Let's do it."

"Not here." Yardley's voice had gone all drill-sergeant-loud. She couldn't help it. She didn't want this man posing in her house. Certainly not half naked. Make that *abso-fuckin'-lutely* not! "You hated doing the calendar, Georgie. You said you'd never do it again."

Georgie ignored her. "Over by the Christmas tree. Lily, too. Oh yes, nice." He had shrugged off his parka to reveal a navy-blue Henley tucked into his board shorts. "You should know, Mr. McGarren, the calendar raised one hundred thousand dollars nationwide for training K-9s for law enforcement departments that can't afford them. That's why I'm thinking about doing the second one. I certainly hope you can qualify." She moved toward him, and then her nose twitched and she paused. "Oh."

It took Kye a second to register the reason for the funny look on the photographer's face. Then he remembered the dried stain on his shirtfront. He brushed it with his hand. "I, ah, held this baby on the flight while the mother took her six-year-old to the potty. He leaked."

"*Oooh*. That was so kind of you." Georgie turned toward Yardley, mouthing *Isn't he adorable?*

Yardley ground her teeth. He was something all right. None of it to her liking.

Georgie had moved on. "Let's get you out of the stinky shirt."

Kye didn't hesitate. He grabbed the back of his shirt at the neck and pulled.

Yardley didn't look away. She told herself that was because there was nothing special coming. She saw half-dressed men so often she had long ago stopped ogling the delights of well-toned abs and pecs, and other manly parts. But dammit. This was different.

Kye was a big man. He looked so much larger without that shirt. It was as if his chest swelled once released from the compression of his clothing. His pecs and abs, well, just every best part of his torso had expanded in a most amazing display.

Put it back on. Yardley wanted to look away but saw that he was watching for her reaction. Why did he care? And no, she wasn't going to display even a speck of interest. She folded her arms, cocked a hip to one side, and stared at him as if he were something broken that she needed to fix.

But he wasn't broken. He was pretty damn perfect.

"Nice forearms," she heard Georgie say from what seemed about a mile away. "Must be all that skiing. How about a foot braced on the hearth? No, don't cross your arms. Hold Lily loosely in one arm. Rest your other elbow, hand relaxed. That's better."

Forearms. Elbows? That's what Georgie was concentrating on when there were all those acres of hard-sculpted physique in between?

Yardley felt a decidedly unwelcome stirring down low between her legs. *As if!* But really, well, yeah. She wasn't lustproof. Only Kye McGarren–proof.

Completely at ease, Kye lifted Lily onto his bare shoulders. "When we're on SAR winter patrol she rides like this."

"While you're skiing?" Georgie was totally into her shots.

"Yeah. She's a great little balancer."

"You're so going to be Mr. December. Great gift to open under the tree, right, Yard?"

She knew Georgie was teasing her but she couldn't be a good sport about it. Not when Kye McGarren was the banana peel on which she was supposed to slip and fall.

She hooked her friend's elbow and pulled, ruining her next shot. "Can we talk?"

With a big sigh, Georgie lowered her camera. "I'll be right back."

Once in the kitchen Yardley turned on her friend, whispering angrily. "You can stop now. This isn't funny."

"Speak for yourself." Georgie chuckled. "Oh my God!

He's like made from the best parts of every hot dream I ever had."

"I can't believe you asked him to take his clothes off."

"I can't believe you're acting like you weren't thinking it was a good idea." Georgie glanced back toward the other room. "He's obscenely gorgeous. Shouldn't he come with a warning label or something?"

"You're drooling."

"And you're being unreasonable." Georgie lifted her camera, but this time Yardley's expression made her change her mind about taking a shot. "I've never seen you ruffled by a man."

"You're not seeing it now. He's just so, so . . ."

"Yes. He is." Georgie made a big production of wiping her mouth on her sleeve, but mostly she was smothering laughter.

"What about Brad? Is he better than Brad?"

"You really don't get it, do you? The guy in there is like a front-row seat at the hottest concert in town. It's fun, it's thrilling, he makes you sweat and feel faint. But it's not real because it's not personal. The feelings I have for the man I'll be in bed with tonight are real. Now I better get back in there and get some shots before my camera melts. Are you coming?"

Yardley rolled her eyes. "I've already seen everything he has to offer."

Georgie's jaw dropped. "How long has it been since you two . . . ?"

"More than a decade." Yardley put up her hand. "That's all I'm saying on that subject."

"Fine. Now, about that hunka-hunka burning Lava Love in the next room. I'm glad he's here. No, seriously. I don't like one bit that threat you opened last night. It's not nothing. You're in possible danger. The man in there doesn't look like he'd be scared of much. Having him about until your staff returns couldn't be a bad idea."

"You have no idea how bad that could be."

"Why? What are you afraid of? Oh. You're still into him, aren't you? Don't give me that look. I saw your face when he stripped."

"Okay, I'm not dead."

"No, you aren't. You're flushed and wiggling your left foot like you've got restless leg syndrome. You're feeling something. Do you even know what it is?"

"Anger, irritation, annoyance, exasperation, aggravation—should I go on?"

"You're scared. Kye McGarren scares you." Georgie smothered her laughter as she glanced again toward the doorway. "I wish I could stay and see how this plays out but I've got to go. I'm meeting Brad at the airport." She gave Yardley a long look. "Unless you need me."

"What, with that hunk of burning love in the next room? I'll manage."

Georgie grabbed Yardley and kissed her on both cheeks. "Love you. Happy New Year." She paused and gave her friend a serious look. "Please ask this man to stay until your staff gets back. There's a whole empty bunkhouse to put him in."

"I promise."

"Your fingers are crossed, aren't they?"

"That doesn't mean I don't appreciate your concern. Give Brad my love."

CHAPTER FIVE

Yardley waited until Georgie's car was heading down the drive before turning her attention to the man still standing shirtless in the living room. "I want you to leave. Now."

Kye hadn't forgotten what pissed-off looked like on Yard. He'd just forgotten how hot it was.

Her face was flushed, her legs braced in anticipation of trouble. Her breath came in little hard gasps that made her breasts tremble. Her expression alone should have had him diving for cover in expectation of a verbal grenade. But now that he was alone with her, all he could think was how damn fine she looked. And that the look in her black eyes was of a woman in jeopardy. Even if she didn't own it.

He made his living assessing and evaluating people in danger. What they said and what their eyes told him often weren't the same. Even if they didn't know it.

That wasn't only anger and uneasiness in her glare.

There was a heightened awareness of him. A feral female–male awareness. He saw it as her gaze traveled over his torso. He'd never been body-conscious. He'd grown up living on the beach in shorts and nothing else. But her gaze had his stomach muscles contracting, as if touched. His belly trembled. And his dick. Hell. He hoped his shorts were doing their job down there because it felt like he had a prizewinning hard-on in his pants.

Then he saw her eyes widen just before they jerked back up to his face. He didn't have to wonder why. Wardrobe malfunction.

"Don't you dare." The fire in her gaze clocked back to caution as she moved her fists off her hips in purely instinctive anticipation. Did she think he'd jump her? The idea shocked him.

"No worries." He lifted both hands in the universal sign of surrender. But, damn, she shouldn't blame a man for what he was thinking. Of course, he was accustomed to being able to control whether or not he revealed those thoughts.

Turning, he headed toward the smell of coffee brewing. She followed, her boots making angry sounds on the wood floor, and intercepted him before he could step over the dog gate.

"I asked you to get out. Now I'm telling you." Her expression doubled down on the anger. "I'm not interested in your dog's problems or you. Get out of my house, you no-good, turn-tail-and-run, worthless piece of shit."

Well, that left no uncertainty about her feelings for him. She still hated his guts.

When Kye didn't move, she moved in on him, turning her face up into his, chin thrust forward like a drill sergeant. It caused an adrenaline dump. Only for very different reasons. No non-commissioned officer in his experience ever had such luscious lips.

"Get. Out. Of. My. House." She poked his bare chest with a finger as she said each word. "Out!"

Kye blinked. Every time her finger touched him, he felt a corresponding jerk in his dick. Didn't she understand she was dealing with a man? One with a moral compass, but still a man who needed her to stay a respectful distance away. She was up in his face, crowding his breathing. Her chest was heaving. Her eyes were dilated and reckless. He saw a bead of perspiration form in that sweet cleft above her upper lip. It made him want to lick it off and keep on licking. To taste what she was offering.

Grab and hold. Oh yeah, he was in trouble.

His jaw locked with the effort to hold still. "Don't touch me again."

"Oh? Really?" Her dark eyes flashed, sending out sparks from the amber flecks he hadn't noticed until she was close enough to kiss. "Why? What are you going to do?"

She was poking him again, little jabs that his body reacted to like injections of testosterone. Her mouth was only inches from his, still forming words he no longer heard.

He snaked a hand behind her head and hauled her in until only an inch separated their lips. "You better stop that."

Stunned by how physical the confrontation had become, Yard stood still for three heartbeats. Then her hands came up and found his shoulders for leverage as she lifted her knee.

But he was quicker. His other hand moved quickly

behind to her cup her butt, hauling her hips in hard against his so that her knee jab struck halfway up his thigh, useless. Then he was locking them together. Chest-to-chest. Stomach-to-stomach. Groin-to-groin. It felt sexy as hell to stand like this with a tall woman. Through his board shorts his dick just naturally found the grove at the apex of her thighs. With shorter women, his dick invariably poked into less productive territory, like an abdomen. This time there was no room for her to maneuver without giving him more access. No room to escape his arousal, hot and hard and arching against her mons. But she moved anyway, unthinkingly rubbing her sex against his arousal as she tried to break free.

"Dammit, Yard."

Yardley stilled. He'd said her name in a rough whisper. It went through her like summer lightning, swift and piercing. No, she didn't want this. Alarmed, she raked her nails down from his shoulders onto his pecs, fingers curled to deliver pain. Only she couldn't. The feel of his firm warm skin and the contraction of the heavy muscles beneath was gloriously satisfying.

"My turn." He closed the gap, their lips meeting.

She gasped in surprise and he took full advantage. His tongue swept into the gap and touched hers. As he ran his tongue over hers, heat and desire hammered in his temples. Her mouth was hot and delicious. He'd wanted to do this since the moment he saw her.

On the other end of the kiss, Yardley fought not to lose control completely, though her grasp of his pecs altered. Her fingers gently curled on his chest in neutrality, she told herself. Not surrender. But it felt like surrender.

He kissed her like he was out to make an impression.

She didn't know if it was for his benefit or hers. Whatever. It was working.

His mouth seemed to melt every angry unhappy thought in her mind until her arms were sliding up his neck again, this time to hold on. Readying for what came next.

It didn't happen.

Kye groaned and suddenly he was free. Whether he had moved back when he released her or the other way around, all he could do was be grateful the chill air of the room was once again between them. His skin felt hot, as though burned by the sun. No, scorched from the inside by Yardley Summers's kiss.

He looked at her, an accusation in his expression. She was staring back at him like she'd never been kissed before. More likely she was reacting to the tsunami of feeling that had swamped his better nature. His dick was in charge of both his head and his heartbeat, and he knew she knew it.

Shut it down, McGarren.

He put up his hands, sending her a dark glance. "Now we both understood why we need to be careful around each other."

Careful. Yardley held the word in her mind as she stared at the raw scratches on his chest. Shame slammed into her. She had done that. Scratched him like a frightened child instead of using any of the many self-defense skills she'd learned and kept honed.

He'd warned her. She'd been reckless in her anger. She took full responsibility. And really, what did she expect after her provocation? If he hadn't fought fairly, she hadn't, either.

Kye swallowed, the effect of which revived the taste

of her in his mouth. He'd had too much, and not fuckin'
enough of her.

He took another step back, shaking his head when he
meant to nod. "It's okay. We both got a little caught up.
Won't happen again."

He looked around, seeking a toehold on the cliff of
good intentions crumbling out from under him. If it did,
Law would be on his tail for putting his hands on his
sister.

He spied Lily standing behind him, her tail wagging
but clearly in defensive mode as she gazed toward the
kitchen. Only then did he realize that Oleg, fully alert
judging by the ridge standing on his back, was growling, low and deep from behind the gate. How long had
the dog been doing that? Lust had made him deaf as well
as a dumbass.

Kye's action directed Yard's attention to the ready-for-
action growls of her Czech wolfdog. She gave him the
command for silence.

Oleg instantly fell silent. Yet his slanted gaze held
both humans in focus.

Yard turned back to Kye and folded her arms, waiting.
Ball in his court.

Kye had reached down and scooped Lily up, holding
her high against his chest to comfort her. He stroked and
whispered calmly to his partner. Which gave him an excuse not to look at Yard again. He was pretty certain
he'd had a plan when he arrived here an hour ago. Time
to calm things down until he could piece it back together.

He glanced up. "What do you know about conditional
reinforcers?"

"Why?" He watched her cross her arms over her very

nice rack. He knew he shouldn't be thinking about how moments before it'd been pressed nicely against him.

He dragged his gaze away. What was he saying? Something about reinforcers. Right.

"Lily works wilderness and urban SAR most of the year. This winter we tried our hand at SAR at a ski resort. We did avalanche prevention and guest rescue. I noticed behavior in her I need to have—modified."

He watched Yard's eyes narrow as he babbled. "You've got five seconds or I'm calling the law."

The law. Not Law. Kye thought fast. First imperative: Buy time.

"Okay. Let me just get dressed." Covering up would help. So would a cold shower.

Yardley's gaze flicked to the dog Kye lowered to the floor. Lily really was a pretty little thing, with a white blaze on her chest and the tops of her paws.

Smiling, she slapped a hand against her leg. "Here, girl."

Lily gave her a bored look then glanced away, as if Yardley hadn't spoken.

Yardley crouched down to make herself smaller and less intimidating, and used her friendliest doggy voice. "Come on, sweetheart. Come, Lily."

This time Lily refused to look at her. Yardley frowned, surprised that Lily was snubbing her. Dogs loved her. They came up to her unsolicited in parks, in grocery stores, on the street.

She glanced up at Kye, about to ask about his dog's attitude toward strangers. He was tucking his T-shirt into his pants. She did not stare. It was just impossible not to notice how his indrawn breath brought his six-pack into high relief behind the tight fabric. Or how his hand diving into the waistband of his board shorts was far more sexy than it had any right to be. Maybe that was because she'd just been all up-close-and-personal with what lay behind them.

She jerked her gaze away and stood up. Why was he still here after the way she'd behaved?

"McGarren." She waited until he looked up at her. "Why are you here?"

Instead of answering, he ran a hand through his hair. Distracted? Distressed? No. Determined. She recognized the dogged expression of a man who just wasn't going to back down, or explain himself. Had seen it enough times. On her brother's face.

"Law!" She didn't even need Kye's sudden alertness to confirm it. "You're here because of Law!" One wild guess to figure out the reason why Law had sent someone here. Law didn't trust her.

Fury pushed up through her every other emotion, and it was a crowded field. "Law put you up to this. Don't bother to lie. Tell him for me that I can take care of myself. Now get out of my house."

"Can't do that." He shook his head as he bent to offer some love to a very confused Lily, who had taken refuge behind her alpha's legs. "Like it or not, I'm here to keep you company for a few days."

"Like hell." She swung away and marched into her bedroom, slammed and locked the door.

She reached for her phone. Oh, right, it wasn't there.

Without thinking twice, she opened the door, walked up to Kye, and held out her hand. "Your phone. I need it."

"Why?"

"You'll get it back. Undamaged." When he'd handed it over she said, "Code?"

"Don't go trawling through my messages. And don't delete anything."

"I wouldn't dream of destroying your porno collection."

When he'd given the code to her she turned, went back into her bedroom, and locked her door.

Sure enough, Law's number was McGarren's most recent call. She punched the number, not waiting for the word *hello* to be spoken when someone picked up. "Call him off, Law. If you don't I'll never forgive you for this. Never!"

"Yardley?"

The woman's voice startled Yard for a second. "Jori? Put Law on."

"He's in physical therapy."

"What?" No one had said anything about therapy to her. Law had lost a leg in Afghanistan and wore a prosthesis. Yard felt the anger drain out of her. "What happened?"

"He's fine. A minor setback. I would have called but you know how your brother is. He never admits he's got any problems, ever."

"That's true." Even more reason she was glad Law had Jori in his life. She was good for him.

"Can I help? I know Law called someone to keep an eye on you. I don't know what all this is about, but if the guy isn't working out I can relay the message."

"No. It's okay." Yardley swore soundlessly for having to tell that lie. "Only Law should have warned me."

"Men, right? And yet we don't want to live without them."

Yardley didn't reply to that. Jori was the second woman in twenty-four hours whose voice had gone all soft with emotion when she talked about her man. Had hers done that when she'd mentioned David Gunnar to Georgie last night? She doubted it.

"Tell my brother I don't need a babysitter. Unless he's heard something about Dr. Gunnar that I should know."

"Don't know anything about that, Yard. I did overhear him say something about the FBI but he clammed up when I asked. Maybe the guy he sent can tell you."

Yardley slipped the phone into her pocket and glanced back at her closed door. Her biggest problem stood on the other side. How was she going to get rid of McGarren? No, first she needed to know what Law had told him about David. She'd bet it was some version of how she'd been kicked to the curb by a boyfriend and couldn't accept his silence for "see ya" and had called the FBI.

Yard chewed her lip. Was McGarren here to keep her from making a greater fool of herself? Or continuing her search?

Her mind went back to their kiss. She was sure it was just a show of force. That's all it could be. No matter how good it felt. The kiss had caught her unprepared. The sheer pleasure of it was both familiar and unique. Even he seemed a bit surprised by his own arousal. Well, that was his problem. She wouldn't be caught off guard again.

The phone in her pocket vibrated. She pulled it out to see a text from Law about her. "I don't think so." She stuck it back in her pocket, where she intended for it to stay. There'd been way too much conversation about her private life already. Now she needed some answers.

She walked into the living room, not sure what she was going to say. If she succeeded in uprooting McGarren, he would report that to Law, and Law wouldn't be happy. Yet if McGarren stayed, what would she do with him? Neither prospect had her jumping for joy. *If* he stayed, there needed to be ground rules.

Except it seemed the choice was already made. McGarren was gone.

She glanced around. Not in the kitchen. She doubted he would have gotten past Oleg, who was stretched out like a sheepskin rug before the doggy gate. And the door to the half bath was open. Surely he hadn't had the audacity to go upstairs to one of her guest bedrooms?

From the corner of her eye she caught a tail wag. As she turned her head Lily hopped up on the back of her sofa and gave her a series of high-pitched yips. A bronze arm reached up and swept the dog back down out of sight. Yardley waited a few seconds and then heard distinctly the sounds of soft, deep snoring. Kye had stretched out on her sofa and fallen asleep.

She backpedaled before she could change her mind. She was sweaty from her jog. And shivering from the cold seeping through her damp running clothing, though she hadn't realized it until now. She needed a shower. Then she'd decide what to do.

But first she ducked into the kitchen to grab that long-awaited cup of coffee.

As she took a sip, she glanced out back through the window above her sink. The sun had risen, promising a final nice day before rain rolled in.

Up on the ridge behind her property ran a narrow track, nothing like a road. It was sometimes used by utility trucks seeking to repair a line or cable or pipe. Most of the time, she wouldn't have noticed it. But the trees were January-bare. Up there, just opposite her window, a law enforcement cruiser was parked. Beside it stood an officer in uniform using a pair of binoculars. Unless she was mistaken, he was staring straight at her.

"What the hell?"

She put down her cup and went to the back door. By the time she opened it, the officer had climbed back into his vehicle and was moving away.

Even though the leaves were gone, the stockade of sapling tree trunks prevented her from identifying the emblem painted on the cruiser's passenger door. It didn't seem to be local.

CHAPTER SIX

Kye jerked awake as the front door closed softly. Three giant steps and he was at the door, face pressed to the single pane of glass in it. Yard was walking away, a leash in hand. Oleg was at the end of it. Even as he watched she veered off to the left toward the training fields.

With one ear straining for the sounds of a car engine coming to life, in case he was wrong about her intentions, he snatched his backpack from the floor. He pulled out a pair of jeans. After extracting his tactical boots and a thick pair of socks, he quickly pulled them on. No engine. She wasn't driving away. In the distance he heard her calling to the dog and his barks in answer. She must have let him off the leash.

He hadn't fallen completely asleep. He just hadn't alerted Yard to that fact when she'd come out of her room the first time. After the tense encounter that ended in the total surprise of that very passionate kiss, he'd thought they needed a break. He certainly did.

Of course, he was curious as hell about what the Battise siblings were saying, but he didn't want to risk being caught with his ear pressed to her bedroom door if she suddenly opened it. It was informative to hear her shouts wind down into mumbles. Whatever Law had said must have mollified her. He doubted even Law had enough authority with his sister to cower her. More like they'd settled for détente, no winners, no losers. At least she hadn't come back through the door to try to throw him out, again. A few minutes later, he'd heard the faint rush of the shower.

Kye rubbed a hand over his face. His peace of mind had lasted as long as it took for him to realize that Yard was naked on the other side of her bedroom door. All the pent-up lust that her kiss had ignited came roaring back to life. For ten solid minutes all he could think about was Yard, naked beneath a sluice of warm water. He had a very good imagination. It filled in her once coltish form with the ripeness of maturity. Curves and hollows he'd once explored with eagerness were augmented in his mind. Sweeter, more lush, more enticing. It was one of the longest, sweatiest ten minutes of his life. Pure torture that had Lily adjusting and readjusting herself on his lap. Finally Lily had abandoned his body for the more reliably smooth surface of the floor. All because of a woman he wasn't certain he even liked anymore. But when a man's dick was in charge, reason left the building.

Shaking his head at his insanity, he looked down at Lily, who was looking up at him with what seemed a detached, even disapproving expression. "Don't look at me like that. I stayed on this side of the door. I get points for that."

Ignoring him, Lily turned and walked over to the far side of the room. All the females in his life were giving him attitude.

After a careful examination of her surroundings, Lily stuck her head in to sniff at something on the floor of Oleg's empty cage.

"Yeah. You must be hungry." He dug in his backpack and pulled out a handful of dog food. "Lily. Catch."

Lily barked high and happy, leaping to catch piece after piece of dog food nuggets. Everything with Lily was a game, even eating.

"More later." Kye filled a pocket of his cargoes with the rest. He glanced toward the kitchen. Oleg, the reason he hadn't helped himself to coffee before, was of course out with his handler.

Smiling, he headed for the kitchen. If he hurried he could grab a coffee and a shower, and maybe something for breakfast. His stomach grumbled in agreement. And maybe he'd check in with Law himself.

He reached for his phone but his pocket was empty. Yard had it. He glanced at her bedroom door but decided against checking to see if she'd left his phone lying in the open. He had sisters. One thing a brother learned early was to never cross a woman's doorway without permission, even to retrieve his own gear.

Priorities. Coffee. Something to eat. Find Yard. Get phone.

The sun had climbed the eastern ridge of the mountains, flooding the property with light, by the time two of those priorities were accomplished. Remembering the January chill, he grabbed a hoodie from his pack, wrapped Lily's leash around his waist, and picked up his car keys. Just in case.

Ahead of his footsteps across the lawn, the grass glittered with diamond-bright crystals of frost. The sharp wind trying to invade every exposed area of his body, including his nostrils, annoyed him. He was damn tired of the cold. He was supposed to be where it was warm and sandy. The things he did in the name of friendship.

Once he entered the training area, Kye jogged his way toward the training structure where he could hear Yard giving voice commands. Lily kept pace, clearly enjoying the freedom. She'd tolerated the long plane ride and then two hours in the rental without a complaint. But being a toller, she needed lots of exercise to be happy. Otherwise, things got chewed or eaten, or occasionally disappeared altogether. Like his underwear. So far, nothing alarming had ever come out of her rear end. But he suspected it would, sooner or later.

Finally, Lily stopped short as they neared the buildings to sniff the frosty air.

Kye knew that Yardley had the Czech wolfdog with her. Belatedly, he wondered if Oleg was off the leash.

Before his thought ended the dog, lean, wolfish, and silver, shot out from behind the building. Oleg was moving full-out, straight at him.

Yelping in surprise, Lily turned and shot like a red-and-white rocket back toward her handler.

"Fuck." Kye grabbed Lily as she leaped up and twisted to angle his body so that she was protected. At the same time he braced for what he suspected would be at least one bad bite.

Yard appeared from behind the building. In relief he heard her voice, high and clear, giving orders.

"Oleg! *Fuj!*"

The wolfdog stumbled to a halt within a few feet of

Kye with head lowered and hair lifted along his spine. Unable to ignore his handler's command, he simply growled low in his throat as he watched his quarry. That's when Kye realized he was muzzled.

Yardley's voice broke the silence again. "Oleg, *ke mne!*"

The dog disengaged and rounded back toward her with bright barks and high yips.

Kye felt like a pork chop that had been dangled before the maw of a hungry wolf and, at the last second, snatched back.

Yard had the leash but Oleg wouldn't come the last few feet to be leashed. Instead, he came to a stop half a dozen feet away, turned his back on her, and stared off into the wooded area in the distance, always the outlier watching for trouble.

Yardley followed the wolfdog's intent gaze but didn't see anything unusual in the distance. Probably, the dog was still getting accustomed to his surroundings. The breed was very sensitive; a new environment could be overstimulating. Their attentiveness made them great guards in unfamiliar territory. Oleg had most likely heard a deer snapping twigs and breaking branches as it slipped unseen through the underbrush. "Oleg, *nech to.*"

The Czech wolfdog's erect ears twitched, the only indication he'd heard the command to leave alone whatever had his drawn attention. But he didn't move.

Satisfied that he wasn't about to run off, Yardley stalked toward Kye, her face pinched with anger. Without even another word from his handler, Oleg moved forward as she did, keeping his advance position in front of her like a VIP bodyguard.

"Are you a complete idiot? Bringing another dog out

here without warning me!" She was finally able to leash Oleg.

Kye put up a hand. "My bad. I didn't stop to think you could be working him off the leash."

"That just proves you weren't trained by *me*. And don't try to sneak up on me again. I might not be so quick to call him off next time."

"Copy that." He knew she didn't mean it. She wouldn't misuse a dog for her own ends. He didn't correct her, either, by pointing out that the dog was muzzled and so couldn't harm him, though he might still have been able to injure Lily with his paws. "What are you working on? I wouldn't mind playing decoy but I'd prefer to be suited up."

Mischief sparkled in her eyes. "You probably won't fit in our suit. But you can hide if you want. Let them work at finding you."

"Them?" Somehow Kye suspected that wasn't a free-lunch offer. She had something in mind. Still, he hadn't come up with any better way to spend time with her while working on getting her to open up. "Sure. What are your objectives?"

"Oleg needs companionship. Wolfdogs are hardwired for pack. He's beginning to show signs of separation anxiety. That almost-attack just now was the first time I've seen him work effectively."

"Lily and Oleg as road buddies? Sounds interesting." Kye didn't know much about wolfdogs, had never worked with the breed, but he was game. "You want me play the prey that brings them together?"

Yard stared at him for several seconds. Even when he was being obnoxious, he was damn attractive. And he knew it. That didn't mean he couldn't be useful.

Finally she gave a single jerk of her head in agreement. "Here's the key to the equipment room." She reached into her pocket, only to have a tennis ball pop free.

As the ball hit the ground, Lily leaped from Kye's arms and made a beeline for it.

Oleg, seeing his moment, swung around as Lily passed him and charged after her. Taken by surprise, Yardley lost her grip on the leash and the wolfdog was again free. Yard's shout of surprise echoed his as Kye's heart went into overdrive.

Lily snatched up the ball. In true toller fashion, she jerked her head back to toss it skyward, unaware of the menace barreling down on her.

Oleg hit her low, sweeping Lily's legs out from under her.

Lily yelped in surprise as she went tumbling over and over in the grass. The ball landed and bounced away.

Oleg was making a sharp turn. So did Lily, because the thing she lived for—a toy—was getting away. As she righted herself, Oleg made a sprint to reach the ball before her. He moved around to the other side so the ball was between them.

Lily paused several feet away, and Oleg, trembling with excitement, seemed unsure of what he was expected to do.

Kye had waited for his moment, not wanting to distract either dog, which might cause the big one to attack. "Lily—!"

"—Wait." Yard grabbed Kye's jacket sleeve. "I think they're playing."

Kye scowled at her. "He'll snap her in two."

"Muzzle, big guy."

As Kye watched, Lily bent down, bringing her head

to Oleg's level with her rear still in the air, tail down as if about to pounce on the ball.

The wolfdog matched Lily's pose, head down near paws, rear end high, tail wagging furiously. Not making eye contact, Oleg growled and jumped toward her. Lily backed up a few steps whining.

"Not yet." Kye felt Yard's fingers hard on his arm. He could break her grip easily, but he didn't. He didn't trust the wolfdog but he did trust Yard's judgment about him. That only moderately assured him that his toller wasn't going to be wolfdog dinner, muzzle or no.

Lily suddenly grabbed the ball as it lay within a foot of Oleg's nose then turned and sped away. Lily was fast but Oleg was like a gray flash of fur, smooth and accelerating with every bound. He was on her in no time, all snarls as he tried to nip her hind legs through the muzzle. It was rough-and-tumble, yet Kye noted that the wolfdog wasn't showing serious aggressive signs. Without the muzzle that might be a different story.

Yardley spoke. "Oleg, *ke mne!*"

This time the silver dog obeyed instantly. He loped over to her side and fell into heel position. He was breathing a little fast but didn't appear to be in distress as she attached his leash. Once again, his attention was directed toward the woods in the distance.

At the same time Lily ran to him, ball in mouth, and jumped up in the full confidence that Kye would catch her, which he did. When she was safe in her handler's embrace, she looked back over her shoulder and yipped at Oleg.

Kye grinned at her. "You were right."

She smiled back, easily this time. "I'm always right, about dogs."

Eye contact. It hit her with the impact of a star falling on her. Something in his gaze, as warm and powerful as a tropical tide, pulling her in despite her misgivings. Like his kiss, everything about Kye McGarren communicated the power of nearly irresistible persuasion. How could she feel like this when David was still a stinging memory of loss?

The sound of a car horn startled the quiet morning. Humans and dogs turned at the same time to see that a dark sedan had entered the gates. The car rolled to a stop about ten yards away from them. Two men exited, looking for all the world like an reenactment of *Men in Black*. Kye smirked. "Friends of yours?"

Yard shook her head, folded her arms, and cocked out a hip. She couldn't begin to guess what this was about. But she suspected that she wasn't going to be happy about it.

The younger of the two men approached while the other, a middle-aged man with a shaved head and brown complexion, remained near the sedan. They both looked deadly serious.

Yardley's heart stuttered. Bad news to be delivered by the subordinate?

CHAPTER SEVEN

The younger man, with crisp blondish hair and a slash for a mouth, paused out of range of the length of leash Yardley held. She couldn't be certain that behind the shield of his sunglasses he watched Oleg warily. But his voice held a trace of tension as he spoke. "Ms. Summers?"

She gathered up more of the leash to show she wasn't about to set her K-9 on him. "Who's asking?"

"I'm Agent Glaser. And this is Agent Jackson. FBI." He hitched a thumb over his shoulder before flipping open a badge. Yardley only saw a gold shield with an eagle on top before he flipped it closed and pocketed it. "We'd like to ask you a few questions."

"May I see your badge?" Yardley's heart skipped a beat as she felt Kye move in behind her. She really didn't want an audience for this. The less he knew about her life, the better.

As the agent reluctantly removed it for inspection Kye

leaned in over her shoulder to get a look. "That's DE.
What business could the Drug Enforcement Agency
have with Harmonie Kennels?"

Glaser glanced up sharply at Kye but directed his
words at Yardley. "Can we go somewhere more private
to talk, Ms. Summers?"

Yard shook her head, her emotions doing a one-eighty
at his words. Any story that began with *Can we go somewhere more private . . .* wasn't going to end well. If this
was bad news, she wasn't going to be treated like a civilian who needed to be coddled when told a hard truth.
The truth was, thanks to Law's butting in, Kye already
knew about David. No use trying to hide anything now.
"This is my property. This is as private as I get."

"Why don't you just tell Ms. Summers why you're
here, Agent." Kye's voice was calm, almost friendly. But
Yardley could tell by the way he moved in a little closer,
as if to offer her the support of his presence without actually touching her, that he was feeling anything but
friendly.

Glaser glanced again at Kye. "Who are you?"

"Kye McGarren."

"May I see some ID?"

"Not unless you have a warrant."

Yard pressed her lips together as the testosterone
cloud bloomed between the two men. She could look
after herself. Always had. "I have things to do. State your
business, Agent Glaser."

The agent gave her a small smile. "Can you tell me
the last time you saw or heard from Dr. David Gunnar?"

Yardley's heart jumped. Oleg begin to whine, breathing through his mouth as he stared up at her. Emotion
down the leash was working on him. Without realizing

she had tightened her grip, and Oleg could sense the pressure building inside her. She let the leash out, certain now that something bad had happened to David. Why didn't he just spit it out and put her out of her misery?

"Why are you asking?"

The agent shrugged. "You made inquiries into Dr. Gunnar's whereabouts a few weeks ago with the Department of Justice. I'd like to know why. How well do you know him?"

Yardley made her expression bland and jutted out a hip to force a relaxed pose she did not feel. "We're acquaintances."

Blondie smirked. "No more than that?"

Kye reached forward and laid a possessive hand on her waist, fingers closing hard on that feminine curve, effectively startling Yardley into silence. "She knows him. Asked and answered. A friend goes missing, the other friend tries to find out why. Isn't that right, sugar?"

Sugar? Yardley tried to keep the astonishment out of her voice. "That's right."

Agent Glaser's gaze flicked to Kye's hand then up his face. "Did you locate him, Ms. Summers?"

"Locate?" Yardley's pulse stuttered. "I was told by the FBI he'd left the country." Her gaze flicked beyond to the man by the car. "Has something happened? Do you know something more a-about him?" Damn. She didn't expect that beat of emotion.

A muscle jumped in Agent Glaser's cheek. "Have you seen or heard from Dr. Gunnar in the past few days, ma'am?"

"I think I just answered that question."

Beneath Kye's touch Yard was stiff with anger and,

knowing her, about to do or say something that wouldn't go down well. Kye slid his hand around to her front, spreading his fingers across her abs to draw her back against his body. "Go ahead, Yard. Tell them."

"No, Agent. I haven't heard a word."

"You're sure?"

Yardley brushed away Kye's touch and stepped forward. "Unless you're here to tell me exactly where Dr. Gunnar is or that something has happened to him, I'm not answering any more questions."

"We have no further information to share on Dr. Gunnar. If you do hear anything, we'd appreciate it if you'd be in touch." He handed her a card.

Yardley watched the two men reenter their car and drive away. Behind her she could hear Kye playing with Lily while Oleg sat at perfect attention at her feet.

Finally, she turned to Kye. He stopped playing with Lily and offered her a smile that really shouldn't do what it was doing to her insides, softening and melting her anxiety about David. So she heaped it all into her voice to push those feelings of thankfulness toward him away. "What do you think you were doing, provoking that agent?"

"Glaser? Force of habit." He returned to petting Lily. "My work brings us into occasional contact with the feds. When that happens, they often try to muscle their way into my business. They take but they don't share. I've become pretty territorial. Didn't want you to get pushed around."

Her dark brows drew together at his admission that he was trying to protect her. "What kind of business are you in, exactly?"

Kye glanced up at her tone and broke into laughter at

the look on her face. "Not whatever you're thinking." He pulled a card from his pocket and handed it to her.

Yard looked at it. "You own BARKS?"

"Heard of us, huh?"

Yardley gazed at the card again. Yeah, she'd heard of them. BARKS was a big fucking deal. Known world-wide for their skill and toughness. Why didn't she know about Kye's place in it? "You really own the business?"

"Yeah. Along with my partner, Oliver Kelly. He's an Aussie. Big strapping guy. Hairiest legs you ever saw. Knees like cannonballs. Loves the media. Me, not so much."

He stood up and squared off before her, folding his arms over his massive chest. "You really thought I was a ski bum? Had never amounted to anything?"

"No, of course not. You were great with dogs. It's just that—"

"You hoped I'd fail at everything I did because I failed you." There. He'd put it out there, the reason they were circling warily around each other twelve years after a past that should have been behind them. But wasn't.

"I need to find something. We'll do this later." She stared at him, daring him to say more.

He shrugged. "It'll keep."

She turned and walked away, Oleg trotting along meekly in obedience. Even a dog knew that when a woman was pissed, it was better to not make waves.

Kye stood a moment longer staring at the back of the woman he'd been sent to protect. She was still a pain in the neck. Her attire and parade-ground voice hadn't changed. But there was something in her posture, a slight rounding of her shoulders when she turned away, that made him pause. She was more than tired. She looked like the weight of the world was balanced on her shoulders. Was this the reason Law had asked him to come? To do some heavy lifting for his sister's sake?

She wasn't happy to see him. Hell, he wasn't happy to be here. Not when all he could think about was the kiss they'd shared. And that wasn't about to happen again. It wouldn't be smart. Or helpful. Or lead to anything. He couldn't allow that, not if his aching dick and balls turned blue with frustration. He wouldn't screw her and leave again. And since he couldn't stay, he wouldn't touch her again. For both their sakes.

But *damn*!

He thought for a moment about the litter of toller puppies he'd left in the care of Sheila Maxwell. Sheila wasn't his partner or anything like that. They worked together, had sex when the mood struck them both at the same time. The fact that that mood hadn't struck in months wasn't an issue between them. But now, looking at Yardley, he was thinking an evening in the company of a friendly woman would be a very good idea. Much better than the one he was wrestling with.

His dick twitched. Maybe he was only 60 percent dick these days. That was still a majority. Yet his little head no longer did the majority of his thinking. He was sent to do a job. Stick with Yard and keep her out of trouble. Piece of cake. Not.

He caught up with her just as she started the Jeep's engine. "Wait up."

She didn't, of course. She threw the Jeep in reverse and stepped on the gas, hard.

As gravel spewed from the back wheels, she braked and Kye saw his chance. With Lily in one hand, he yanked open the door of the moving vehicle with the other and jumped in, glad he was wearing combat boots because she cut him no slack as she swung the Jeep around.

"Where are we going?"

She didn't spare him a glance, but he caught the up-curve of her mouth. "I need to find my phone." The Jeep shot through the open gates and took a hard left onto the road.

A few minutes later they had parked on the side of the road and were on foot in the twiggy remains of underbrush.

"And you lost your phone in the brush how?" Kye hacked impatiently at the dry grass with a felled branch.

"I have a temper. Okay?"

"No argument there."

Lily, who'd been joyfully traipsing through the winter scrub while her doggy companion had been left in a crate in the Jeep, suddenly barked and leaped, pawing furiously at a patch of damp leaves until she could pluck something from the ground. Then she pranced over and nudged Kye's thigh.

Kye smiled. "Found your phone."

Yardley snatched and looked at it. Her expression drooped. "Battery's dead."

Kye handed Lily a few treats. "Want to tell me what's going on?"

"No." She pocketed the phone and headed back toward the Jeep.

Kye trooped after her. "Let me rephrase. Tell me what's going on before I throttle you."

Yard took a deep breath and turned around to face him. "I want to hire you."

"I'm already engaged, in a manner of speaking."

"No, you're doing Law a favor. I want to pay you so you owe your allegiance to me. That means you can't contact Law about me or with anything you learn about me."

Kye crossed his arms, feeling a trap opening beneath him. "What do I have to do?"

"I don't know yet." She turned and continued toward her Jeep.

"Hold up, Ms. Long, Leggy, and Inscrutable." He bent down to pick up Lily and slung her around his shoulders. "You need to tell me what's going on."

No." She hopped in her Jeep and turned on the ignition. She glanced at him. "You coming?"

"What do you suppose they were doing?" Agent Glaser lowered his Steiner MM30 8x30mm military binoculars, a memento from his years in the marines.

"Searching for something?" FBI agent Jackson couldn't help it. The younger man Glaser was so intense that he forgot sometimes to think in basic human terms.

"Looked like they recovered a cell phone."

Jackson nodded. "I'd purely love to know why she threw it away there, and then decided she needed it back."

"Something to do with Dr. Gunnar?"

"Everything to do with Dr. Gunnar, is my guess."

Witnesses fled the witness security program more frequently than the public knew. Over time that ache to "get back to real life" could overwhelm even the instinct for self-preservation. But they'd thought the doc was sturdier than that. If only because Dr. Gunnar had brought this case to the feds.

For more than two years a federal task force that

included the FDA's Criminal Investigations Unit, the DEA, and the World Health Organization had been investigating counterfeit prescription drugs entering the United States. Working overseas, Dr. Gunnar had put the pieces together for them, could name sources, drugs, and companies. Every one of those sources would like nothing better than to see the doc disappear. Without him, the case could collapse. Which is why they'd tucked him safely away. His doing a runner didn't make sense. Unless he was running *to* instead of *from* someone.

What they'd discovered by spying on the pair was that Yardley Summers probably knew more than she was saying. And that the McGarren fellow was more than he seemed.

"We'll keep watch, from a distance, for a few days. Or until Dr. Gunnar's been located."

CHAPTER EIGHT

Yardley and Kye drove back to the house in silence. But it wasn't empty of emotion. Yardley turned every which way the conversation she'd had with the federal agent, looking for unspoken clues in his manner, his tone, his refusal to tell her much.

What she did know: The FBI and the DEA were looking for David Gunnar. Nothing else explained their visit. And they thought she might be his contact.

Her heartbeat quickened as she pulled into the driveway. She had only one mission in mind, to plug in her phone and find out if David Gunnar had been in touch.

There was a reason David had stopped texting. A reason with federal implications. Though it should have frightened her, the thought very selfishly made her feel better. She hadn't been ghosted. *Something big had kept him from her.*

She glanced sideways at Kye, feeling guilty for no reason she could put a finger on. One quick kiss didn't negate a relationship of more than a year's standing. She wasn't a teenager, about to blow things out of proportion. So what if it felt nice? But Kye couldn't be around when she read David's messages, if he'd sent anything.

David needs me. She'd stopped hoping just when he needed her to most believe in him. Screw what anyone else thought!

She stepped hard on the brake. "Make yourself scarce for a while. I need some privacy." She didn't wait for Kye to agree but jumped out, grabbed Oleg's leash, and headed for the house.

"Feed Lily?"

She paused on the porch and turned. Kye released Lily, who shot straight toward Yardley. "Her food's in my backpack. She needs water, too."

Yardley nodded and opened her door, letting both animals through. She did not need to feel bad about leaving Kye in the cold on the driveway. But she did. Damn. He was getting to her without even trying.

She went like a tornado through the drawers of her kitchen utility drawer, impatience turning to giddiness when she found the white charger cord at the back.

Oleg and Lily had followed her into the kitchen. Oleg still wore a muzzle but he didn't seem overly concerned about the fact that Lily was wandering freely through his territory. He seemed to think he could still get at whatever was producing those wonderful smells in the garbage.

"*Pfft!*" Both dogs stopped nosing the can to look up at her. "Sorry, guys. You'll have to wait a second. I'm busy here."

She reached over and stuck the plug into the socket, then attached her phone. Nothing. She groaned in frustration. It was going to take at least a few minutes before the phone would be charged enough to be active.

Fine. She had other business to take care of.

She refreshed the water of both dogs and then carefully removed Oleg's muzzle. "Play nice or it's back in the crate."

The two dogs eyed each other in sidelong glances but made no provocative moves as they lapped thirstily at their individual bowls.

Satisfied for the moment that there'd be no doggy Armageddon in her kitchen, she headed back into the living room, grabbing up Kye's gear as she went. The last thing she wanted to do was explain to him what was going on. When she had collected it all, she grabbed a piece of paper from her printer tray and scrawled across it with a marker.

You can stay at bunkhouse. It's open. Key to frig is in the Ladies in the spark plug dispenser.

Grabbing up everything, she headed for the front door. When she looked for Kye, she discovered he was closing the main gates, probably to keep any more unannounced callers from simply driving in. He was protecting her. The knowledge felt strangely comforting, and disconcerting. She wasn't accustomed to anyone taking care of her. As she watched, his tall, long-legged, hard-shouldered silhouette turned to stroll back up her long drive. The sight was striking. He was striking.

"Damn." Every time she glanced at him she felt it all again. The sudden heat as their lips met earlier. The heavy assault of heat, tongue, and expertly wielded pressure that was his mouth. Her fingers tingled as if remembering the hard heat of his bare chest.

So McGarren could kiss. So what? She'd known that

twelve years ago. Maybe he was better at it now. That didn't mean anything.

She blinked, feeling hot and shivery, but it only made her work more quickly. She needed Kye out of the way while she got in touch with David. Only then would she know what to do next. She placed his things in one of the handmade rockers that lined the porch, attached her note, then went back inside and double-locked the door.

She went into her kitchen and checked the phone: still not enough power to turn it on. She poured the last of the hours-old coffee into her mug and stuck it in the microwave. But every cell of her body seemed to be in overdrive. Strangely, it wasn't about David, but Kye.

She pulled the fatigue cap from her head and flicked her ponytail over her shoulder. It wasn't like her to get caught up in sexual sensation. She wasn't one of those women who could while away hours recalling her lover's every look, every sigh. But the sensations kept on coming, overwhelming her desire to think of anything else. This time it was the pressure of Kye's hips locked into hers, her height making the fit perfect as her lower belly absorbed the rigid length of his arousal.

Desire hit her like a German shepherd running flat-out. Only there was no protective bite suit around her emotions. For a moment she stood in her kitchen, not moving, but imagining everything. Her arms moving up to encircle Kye's neck. Her fingers sliding into the silky short hair at his nape. She'd been a few heartbeats from surrendering her anger to the sensations of the moment.

Yardley firmed her mouth against a sigh. She wasn't one of those women who had to have a man. But Mc-

Garren had made her want—bad—in just a kiss. It had been an eye-opener for him, too.

She had seen how he'd looked at her after they separated. That simple surprise had quickly turned into a knowing gaze she couldn't argue with. She had responded. His heavy-lidded eyes and lazy smile said *Let me do you* with such confidence.

But then he'd backed up, averting his gaze and saying something about the need to be careful around each other.

She glanced up uncomfortably when she heard McGarren's footsteps on her porch. Why did that irritate her? Why did everything about him make her want to convert thoughts into actions, actions that brought her into physical contact with him? It struck her that maybe it wasn't only lust, but guilt fueling her contrary feelings toward McGarren.

He hadn't pushed himself on her. In fact, she'd provoked him beyond reasonable need. And in the end, he'd done the honorable thing by backing off without being asked. She had been wrong. She was avoiding him because she didn't want to face those facts.

Not one to hide from a tough truth, Yardley took a breath and marched over to unlock the door and face Kye.

She stepped out just as he slung the backpack over his shoulder. He paused, several feet away, but he didn't speak. His expression was closed off. If he was angry, he was handling it. If he was thinking hard thoughts about her, they didn't show through the dark depths of the candid gaze holding hers. The only thing about him that betrayed any emotion was the tautness of the bronze skin riding his cheekbones. And the tight grip of the hand holding his backpack on his shoulder. He was waiting. Nothing more, nothing less.

She understood. He didn't need to say anything. Her conscience was doing his job for him. It told her she had behaved badly, leaving him outside. She was wrong. No excuses.

She swallowed a fair amount of crow before she spoke. "Can I talk to you?"

"Sure." He folded his arms across his chest and stood back on his legs.

Lily, who'd coming running at the sound of her handler's voice, shot through the door and launched herself at him, yipping in a delirious frenzy to see him. As if she, too, felt she had been mistreated.

Yardley's gaze flitted away from the toller, feeling even more rotten. When a dog thought you were wrong, you were wrong! "We need to clear the air."

He studied her for a second. "Shoot."

Her gaze flicked back to him, emotion making her eyes feel hot. "About earlier. I don't want you to get— have the wrong impression."

"Which would be?" A slight curve of amusement appeared in his left cheek.

"That I—that we." She looked away briefly, seeking her inner bitch. When she located it, she looked up again. "It's been a shitty couple of months. I've been feeling a little sorry for myself today. You happened to be in the way."

"Of?" Damn him. He was going to make her say it.

"Of my temper. My anger-management skills are rusty. You caught me at a low point."

"Just curious. Was the low point when you poked me or kissed me, or left me out in the cold just now?"

She wondered if he was aware that he was rubbing his chest with a hand. Mesmerized by that motion, she could almost feel again the dense heat of his skin under her own fingers. Dear Lord! Why had she ever gotten so close to him? Was her conscience going to punish her with every distracting detail until she could no longer even glance at him without the heat of embarrassment? No, not embarrassment. This scalding heat was desire. Every sexy detail of the man was a flashpoint of hunger for something out of reach.

What about David?

She stiffened, remembering the phone waiting for her inside. She backed up a step. "I owe you an apology. I'm not very good at them."

The sensual curve of his smile arched into being. "At least you're honest. A real apology would have been better. But I'll take it, since we both know what that was really about."

What was it really about? She wished she knew.

She looked away. "I guess you think I'm a bitch."

He caught the curve of her shoulder in his palm as she tried to turn away and rotated her back to face him. His expression was no longer neutral. It was equal parts lust and amazement.

"I would never call you a bitch, or any other ugly word. Complicated. Suspicious. Gorgeous. Distrustful. Sexy as hell with a mouth made for sin. You're all those things."

She turned away, not wanting him to be nice because she made her feel like the earth was shifting beneath her feet and that, maybe, she should grab on to him to steady herself. Yeah, that sounded like a fine idea. And a scary one.

She really couldn't handle that right now.

But he wasn't ready to let her go, and slid between her and the door in a move a man his size shouldn't have been able to make so fluidly.

"Law sent me to find out what you think happened to a guy you care about. I had my doubts. But now you've got the feds watching you. Something big is going on. I'm not going anywhere until I know you're safe."

"Promise?" Damn, the question slipped out of her.

He looked at her a long time, giving away nothing. "You want honesty, Yard? I don't know what's going on between us. Hell, yes I do. But you don't need to worry. I didn't come here to mess with your life. Nothing's going to happen you don't want to happen."

Something struggled inside her, something old she'd buried so deep she'd forgotten it was there. "What if?"

He shook his head. "This isn't going down like that. You need to take care of some old business. I need to wrap my head around some things, too. We tried living on emotion once before. It nearly ruined both of us." He was backing away as he spoke, as if their bodies shouldn't occupy nearby spaces.

She felt it, too, the dangerous undertow stronger than reason. She dug her nails into her palms, afraid to say anything more. Because she knew where they'd end up.

He moved away first, toward the bunkhouse, but then swung back with the note held high in his hand. "What the hell is a spark plug dispenser doing in the Ladies?"

"It's what the trainers call the tampon dispenser."

Kye shook his head before sending another serious assessing glance her way. She felt him weighing and cataloging everything about her, as if she were a map he was only going to get one chance to memorize. "Are you okay?"

"As always."

He stared a little longer, then turned away.

Yardley stared after him. He moved with an easy loose-hipped stride that was both liquid-smooth and ultra-masculine. It felt like a mistake, letting him go. But what else could she do?

She rushed back into the house and into the kitchen and snatched up her phone. It took what seemed forever to power on. And then she was staring at the main screen.

NO MESSAGES.

She blinked. Pushed the MESSAGE button again. Blank.

A chill splashed through her. A space hollowed out in her middle. The air suddenly seemed too thin.

She'd been so sure, so positively certain she would be the person David contacted when he got the chance.

She started typing a message on her phone but then paused. Just because she and the FBI thought she would be David's primary contact didn't mean that was true. Whatever he was into had nothing directly to do with her. The last she'd heard, he was overseas. Her mistake to think he'd turned to her in his time of need?

She put the phone down. Only time would tell.

CHAPTER NINE

An hour after she had plunked herself down before her computer to pay some bills and calculate expected income for the coming year, Yardley heard the sound of Kye's SUV come to life. She went to the window and wondered why he was driving away without a word. When he had swung the vehicle around in an arc, she could see that Lily was in her crate in the backseat.

She sprinted for the door but by the time she got it open, the SUV had moved through the gates—when had he reopened them?—and onto the road. Her stomach lurched. He'd said he'd needed time to think. But he'd also promised he wouldn't leave her. Where was he going?

She gazed up at the late-afternoon sky, trying hard not to feel *any* way about what had just occurred, but failing miserably. He had probably had time to realize she wasn't treating him very well. Maybe he'd decided he'd had enough and just left. But that didn't seem like Kye.

He was the most direct and honest person she'd ever known. He'd have marched in here and said *Screw you* to her face before he left.

Her gaze refocused. Thick gray clouds with faint purplish undersides rimmed the northern horizon. The turn in the weather due by nightfall was on its way in.

Yardley moved back into the house. Oleg was curled up inside his crate dozing, even though the door stood open. No music, no TV, no other sounds. Her life was back to normal. She was alone. She felt . . . empty.

The day was quickly getting away from her. Not that it mattered. As New Year's Days went, this one wasn't worth holding on to. In fact, the sight of the spreadsheet she'd been sitting in front of made her shake her head. She ran an empire, a small one. But she ran it all alone, which meant every decision was hers, from what feed to buy to which breeder to buy from, how best to feed and house their handlers, and what cleaning products were safe. Exhausting. Her life nibbled away at by a thousand tiny pecks.

She turned from her computer. She didn't feel like being productive anymore. She counted off the reasons. They were good reasons, too. Too much champagne the night before. Too many unpleasant surprises, starting with the obscene Christmas card.

The raw edginess of earlier in the day had given way to a dragging tiredness that felt like being harnessed to a tractor tire. But absolutely none of that had anything directly to do with the man who'd driven away.

And yet, he was all she could think about. When, if, Kye came back, she'd be nicer, more available. He said they needed to talk. They'd talk.

She rubbed her forehead, wondering why even eating

felt like too much of a burden. What she wanted most at the moment was for this lousy holiday season to be over with. Once she was back to work, surrounded by the men and woman who looked to her for every major decision, she wouldn't have time to think about anything else. She excelled at solving others' problems. She just stank at handling her own.

She wandered into her bedroom and slipped into bed without really thinking about it. She'd take a nap. Just a nap.

Oleg followed her in and curled up by the door, joining his handler in sleep.

Wind shoved the house, hard. The scraping sounds of things being rearranged beyond the walls of the house woke her as the room filled briefly with brilliant jagged light.

Yardley sat up, completely disoriented by the dimness. She'd only meant to sleep half an hour. The locomotive sounds of wind traveling in a hard straight-line *whoosh* rattled the windows of the house a second time. But that wasn't the sound that riveted her. It was the crying shriek of something wooden being pried loose.

She bolted to her feet, fumbling for the light switch of her bedside lamp. The glare was harsh, like being caught in headlights. Blinking against it, she saw that Oleg was already at the open door, his gaze fixed on something beyond.

A third burst of wind struck so hard, Yardley seemed to feel the assault through the walls. The sounds of banging joined the shrieking metal and crying wood. It sent Oleg darting into the living room barking furiously.

Heart lurching with the unexpected injection of

adrenaline, Yardley reached for the flashlight she kept by the bed and followed the wolfdog.

As she entered the living room a lightning burst so blue-white it outshone the yellowish interior light stabbed her eyes. In the crack of thunder that followed, she recognized the source of the banging. It was the loose screen on a living room front window. She'd been meaning to fix it, along with half a dozen other things, for weeks.

Propelled by the next gust, the edge of the frame struck the glass sharply, moving that repair job to the top of her To-Do list.

As the crackle-slam of thunder rolled through the house, she rushed back into her bedroom. She pushed her feet into her boots, not bothering to tie them, and scooped up a jacket from a chair. As she hurried back through the rooms to the kitchen, she pushed her arms into the sleeves and zipped up. The temperature had dropped while she was asleep. The house felt cooler, and more empty than before. Yardley opened a drawer and grabbed a hammer and a screwdriver, then headed toward the front door.

Oleg crouched down with gaze fixed on the second of the three windows that fronted the porch. As she reached for the locks, he charged forward, trying to beat her out of the door.

Yardley shook her head. "Oleg. *Zustan!*" The K-9 froze and swiveled his head her way. He didn't look the least bit happy about the command to stay. His gray fur twitched with nervous energy, as if he thought he could solve the problem if allowed out. "Stand down, guy. This is a job for opposable thumbs."

A few thick cold raindrops thudded on the porch planking as she opened the door. Once outside, she saw the screen in the light of the porch bulb. Tethered by one hinge, it bounced and banged against the glass like an angry kite trying to free itself from a tree. Easy enough to fix. She shut the door behind herself.

Tucking her flashlight away, she grabbed the screen's frame in one hand and reached into her pocket for the flathead screwdriver to pry the hinge loose. No time for niceties like trying to unscrew it. Despite the efforts of the wind to thwart her, she pried the screw out of the wood without much damage that she could tell. Smiling in triumph, she turned toward the front door.

A man stood beneath the porch light. In the seconds it took for his identity to register, he spoke.

"I've been watching and waiting for you all day. First that fellow with a dog showed up. Then the feds. But they're all gone."

Officer Vance Stokes, dressed as a civilian, had mounted the porch steps and stood a few feet away, just out of the rain. "Of course, I never thought it would be this easy to separate you from your dog. But then the wind came up and the screen started banging. And here we are. All alone."

Too late she realized that Oleg had been far too agitated over the sounds of mere inanimate objects in a storm. He'd known or suspected someone else was out here in the gloom of the winter evening. An ugly sensation moved through her stomach as fat drops of rain struck her face. Still, this was her property. "Officer Stokes. Why are you here?"

"Did you get my holiday card?"

She didn't answer, thinking now for the first time since she'd opened it of the red envelope with the obscene Photoshopped picture.

"Guess I forgot to sign my name."

Yardley clamped down on the first insulting words that came to mind. No need to antagonize a man who was already angry. It didn't show on his face. He was a cop. His feelings wouldn't show until he was ready for them to.

"What do you want?"

"You sound more receptive to my requests today. Good to know." Lightning flickered around them, throwing sharp angles of contrasting light and shadow over his features as if he were a character in a horror movie. Only this was very real. "I need you to write my K-9 sergeant and apologize for not giving me a dog."

Yardley shook her head, holding the screen in both hands like a shield. "Our decisions are final. You show no aptitude for working a dog."

Stokes canted his head to one side. "You're not listening. I'm not asking, I'm telling you how it's going to be. I need this position. I'm not working vice and I'm sure as hell not going back to patrol. So you just write the letter and give me a dog and we're even."

He had taken a few steps toward her when the curtains in the window beside her collapsed from the inside and Oleg appeared in the window, lips drawn back from his feet as he furiously tried to scratch his way through the glass.

Stokes banged the glass with a fist and laughed as Oleg's fury redoubled. "How you doing, fella? That's right. Me and your bitch handler are gonna have some good times together."

Yardley's left foot began to jiggle. This wasn't the attitude of a sane man. It was way too reckless for an officer on the job. Even bad cops knew they could push

:ir outlaw tendencies only so far. The appearance of
:spectability was essential.

"Your department's let you go."

Stokes's attention snapped back to her. "That's why I
need the letter. I need my job and my position as a K-9
officer back."

She couldn't get him either of those things, even if she
wanted to. But she knew better than to further anger him.
"You're not the only officer who's been turned down by
the kennel." *Keep it neutral*, she thought. *Don't acknowledge his anger with your own.* "There's at least one person a year who doesn't—isn't compatible with our
program."

"Bullshit." His neutral expression slipped. Anger
glinted in reflected flashes of lightning. "I watched you.
You get your jollies out of putting grown men through
their paces, making them watch you. Eager to follow
you around like lapdogs in case you give one of them a
chance to cover you."

Yardley stopped listening. She couldn't afford to take
the trip he was about to give her into the inner workings
of his mind. She got it. He was going to attack her. It was
a struggle she needed to win. That's all she needed to
know.

She was out of practice. Hadn't taken a self-defense
course in a while. She wasn't by nature a fighter. Even
as a child she was always struck before she hit back. But
she always hit back harder, longer, stronger until her opponent cried for mercy. Reservation life wasn't for the
faint of heart.

She didn't realize she was backing up until she noticed he was coming toward her. "—think you're hot

shit. What you need is for a man to show you w.
charge. What you need is a good fucking over."

She hesitated too long. His hand shot out and grabb
her wrist just as she was about to swing the two-by-four-
foot screen at him. She cried out as he twisted her wrist
painfully and her fingers lost their grip. Her legs hit the
banister just below butt level. He tried to jerk her forward
but she used the screwdriver in her free hand and stabbed
at his wrist holding her hostage. He cried out, freeing
her. And then she was falling, off the edge of the porch.

The sky opened up in that moment. As she hit the
ground painfully, weight on one shoulder while the
bricks of the flower bed border dug into her back and
scraped one elbow, rain like a fire hose sprayed down on
her. Scrabbling like a turtle, she tried to right herself.

Stokes got there before she gained her feet.

He didn't say a word, just grabbed her from behind
and flipped her onto her back. And then he dropped his
full weight on her as she sprawled in the grass.

Yardley worked with strong muscular animals, still
donned a bite suit on occasion, and knew how to leverage the bite of ninety-plus pounds of canine fury to stay
on her feet. But she hadn't been in a real fight since she
could vote. Now she was in the fight of her life.

He was tugging at her cargoes. He was bent on rape.
That. Was. Not. Going. To. Happen.

She was so angry, so angry. She reached into her
pocket, looking for the hammer she'd brought outside.
She found it.

She was remembering things now. Go for the soft
parts. Neck, crotch, eyes. Painful and messy but effec-
tive.

...es had forgotten about her as an adversary. He ...in full rape mode. His mouth was all over her, ...neck, a breast he'd freed. She was drowning from .ne rain pouring into her nostrils as she lay pinned to the ground. She raised the hammer very slowly, twisting it so that the claws would strike. Something soft. Something vulnerable. More vulnerable than she was.

She swung but didn't connect. He was flying backward. Propelled by what seemed to be superhuman forces—a mini tornado? Then she heard voices, two men shouting obscenities as they struggled. Freed, she levered forward into a sitting position. That's when she saw two men backlit by a vehicle's brights. Kye McGarren had Vance Stokes in a head lock on his knees.

It was surreal, so surprising, she shouted the first thing that came to mind. "What are you doing here?"

Kye didn't bother to answer as he rose and hauled the man to his feet.

"Do you know who the fuck you're dealing with? I'm the goddamn police!" Vance jerked and twisted, trying to find an advantage, but Kye had him locked in with an elbow about his neck and his arm twisted up behind his back.

"What you are is about half a second away from a dislocated shoulder. I can feel your rotator cuff shredding under the pressure. Your call."

"Let me go!"

Kye gave him a push that forced Stokes down hard onto the gravel on his hands and knees.

Yardley was on him in an instant, kicking and punching and lifting the hammer to strike.

"Whoa, Yard." Kye grabbed her from behind, one hand gripping the hammer to stop its descent as he lifted her off the man. He pulled her back in tight against his chest, one arm clamped across her torso to hold both her arms to her sides. In the driving rain, no easy task. "You're okay. You're okay, Yard."

"You bastard!" It was a desperate cry torn from the back of her throat.

Over the roar of rain and rumble of thunder Kye kept talking low, directly into her ear. "Breathe, baby. Come on, get a grip. I don't want you hauled into court behind this. He's not worth it."

Finally she stilled and he let her go. She swung around on him, her eyes wild, her hair streaming water, fury in every line of her. "I had that."

He grinned at her. "You did. You sure as hell kicked his ass. Now call the police."

CHAPTER TEN

"You say Ms. Summers was on the ground when you arrived." Sheriff Wiley looked at his notepad. "Where, exactly, was the alleged perpetrator?"

"On top of Ms. Summers. I can draw you a picture." Kye's tone was arctic as he watched Yardley, who sat a few yards away talking with a female EMT.

"I know it's irksome to have to keep repeating things. Ms. Summers has a lot of respect in this community. Her story isn't in dispute. But we need to make certain we haven't overlooked anything that could allow the suspect to beat the charges. Stokes is pretty beat up." He smirked. "You take a few swings? Just for fun?"

Kye's gust of laughter was more of a snort. "Ms. Summers was giving as good as she got when I got there."

The sheriff's eyes widened. "Everything they say about her being hard-core is true, I guess. Still, it's too bad he caught her without her dogs."

Both men glanced toward the front windows. The

drapes and blinds were in shambles on the floor. Long Cujo-type scratches marred the glass. Deep claw marks in the wooden window frame looked like a buzz saw had been at work. On either side of the front door, huge pieces of plaster had been gouged out down to the studs. Oleg had tried his best to come to Yardley's assistance. The dog was now kenneled in a back room, to protect the enforcers of the law.

The sheriff grunted. "Maybe Stokes is lucky you came along when you did."

Kye didn't reply. His heart had just stopped slamming in his chest.

At first, he hadn't been able to accept what he was see-ing in his brights as he came up the drive. Rain was sheeting down his windshield so fast the wipers were al-most useless. But there, in the twin cones of his head-lights, were two figures wrestling in the mud. A flash of lightning confirmed that the figure on the bottom was Yard.

Despite what movie-choreographed brawls portrayed, being on the bottom in a fight was a position only the most highly skilled fighters ever reversed. She'd needed help. Or a weapon.

His mind did a quick flashback to the hammer she'd raised just as he'd reached them. She might have made that first strike count. It didn't bear thinking about what Stokes might have done to her if she'd missed, or only slightly injured him. And he hadn't been there for backup.

"You haven't said what brought you out here today."

Kye looked back, surprised that the sheriff was still talking to him. "I'm visiting. As a friend of the family," he added as the man's gaze turned speculative. "I trained with her father, Bronson Battise. Her brother Lauray Battise and I served together in Afghanistan. K-9 military police." He pulled out his business card for the second time that day. "In case you need me to make a formal statement or anything."

Sheriff Wiley nodded. "We're just about done here."

Yardley straightened from her slump when she noticed Sheriff Wiley and Kye coming toward her. Kye had hardly taken his eyes off her. He came toward her now like some vengeful totem, his face a mask of controlled anger as he stared down at her.

She didn't need his tight expression to tell her she looked like hell. Beneath the swaddling of an EMT Mylar blanket, she was soaked to the bone. There was a muddy puddle around her shoes of water that had dripped from her clothing and boots. She could feel bruises beginning to set in different parts of her body. Somewhere in the struggle she'd bitten her tongue.

The sheriff spoke first. "We got your attacker locked up tight, Ms. Summers. You can rest easy on that. With the holiday weekend, he won't be able to post bail until Monday morning." He glanced at the EMT who nodded before saying, "We're going to send you to the emergency room to be checked out. And then we're done for tonight."

Yardley shook her head. "I don't need medical attention."

"It's not really an option, Ms. Summers. We need a medical opinion, and photos, of your injuries for our report. Plus DNA evidence from your clothing and under your fingernails. You don't want us to overlook any detail that might set him free."

Yardley set her mouth but nodded. She'd been debating whether or not to mention it. But the thought that Stokes might weasel out of the charges, because she had not actually been raped, made her decide.

She pulled the red envelope out from under her blanket. "This came last night. Left on the doorstep. I didn't think it was important. But now . . ."

Sheriff Wiley slipped the picture out then looked back at Yardley, his expression carefully blank. "You should have called me right after you opened it."

"I thought it was just a prank."

"Let me see that." Kye leaned in as the sheriff turned it his way. The look on his face said everything the lawman's hadn't. "Son of a bitch!"

"Easy, son." Sheriff Wiley continued to watch Yardley, his face still void of expression. "This kind of thing happen before, Ms. Summers?"

"No. Oh, I get angry letters, once a year or so. All businesses do. But nothing—nothing like that." A shiver she couldn't repress quaked through her. She shot a hard glance at Kye, daring him to make any kind of comforting or protective move.

She'd lied to herself about the ugliness of the picture because she didn't want to think anyone could hate her that much. But she saw the fallacy of her thinking on Kye's face. She followed his gaze and saw that her blanket had slipped so that her torn shirt showed. There were finger bruises on her upper breast. She hiked the blanket up, its surface making a metallic rustle.

The sheriff handed the envelope off to a deputy, who carefully bagged it. "What makes you think Stokes had something to do with that piece of shit? Excuse my language."

She told him about an incident two weeks earlier

when Stokes had set a dog on another handler. "He said his department had let him go after they got my report. He wanted me to reinstate him in our program so he could get his job back. I refused."

The sheriff and Kye exchanged looks. "I'm going to follow up on that. Police officers don't usually get fired unless there's a well-documented pattern of misconduct."

He turned to Kye. "You staying here tonight?"

"Yes." Yardley glanced up at Kye in surprise. He didn't give her a chance to argue. "I'll feed the dogs and lock up. Then I'll be along to pick you up."

Yardley nodded and stood up. She was okay until she looked into his face. Grim and tense and gray beneath his bronze skin, he looked at her with such protective tenderness that she had to work at not responding to it. No, better to stay away from his big solid strength. She was still shook up and scared to discover how vulnerable she was. She couldn't afford to want the things his expression offered. It was sentiment, the feeling one would have for any vulnerable creature.

Count on no one. Need is weakness.

She turned to the EMT. "Let's do this."

Kye slanted a glance at Yardley. In the light from the dashboard he could only see her in profile. She was solemn and much too still for his liking. She'd stopped talking the second they'd exited the hospital. Her lip was swollen so it probably hurt to talk. The bandage above her eye covered the glued-together cut above her brow. Only her hand moved, stroking Lily, who uncharacteristically lay quietly in a lap that wasn't his.

The emergency room was satisfied that all her injuries were superficial. She'd be sore and bruised for a while. Nothing more.

Gut churning in lingering anger for her sake, Kye turned his attention back to the road. The storminess was nothing more than flashes on the southern horizon. But the rain had grown pebbly with ice crystals. Driving had turned treacherous, requiring nearly all his attention. The part that wasn't driving was reassessing the day.

In the little more than twelve hours since his arrival, he'd encountered the FBI, the DEA, and been witness to a felony assault that brought out half the county's sheriff's department. It hadn't occurred to him that Law's instinct was right. That there was real trouble brewing in Yardley's life. The kind in which people could get hurt.

He needed to get up to speed. Find his phone. Check in with Law. He needed intel. Though heaven knew he couldn't count on anything more from Yardley tonight.

His last clear view of her face was of a woman moving from anger to shock. Her eyes were unfocused by exhaustion and pain. Like a soldier sometimes did in a tough situation, she'd gone to ground, silent within her own thoughts. With only her thoughts keeping her company, he could feel her veering into dark territory.

Get her home. Get her cleaned up. Get her fed. Get her to bed. In the morning, get her to talk.

Setting his priorities helped.

After sitting like a statue on the drive back, she reacted quickly upon their arrival. Before he could even put the SUV in park she pushed Lily from her lap and was out of the vehicle.

He and Lily followed, catching up before she could open her front door. He snagged her arm. "Hang on,

Yard." She shot him a wary glance. "You should have told me you'd been threatened."

She swung back to him, her eyes like liquid onyx in the porch light. "It had nothing to do with you."

"You're my business right now, Yard. I wouldn't have left you alone for a second if I'd thought there was the slightest chance of you being in danger."

Her forehead furrowed. "Why?"

"Because." He wished he had better.

She studied his face. He knew she was seeing everything he felt, hurt and worry and an inexplicable attraction, and it was all for her. "Why did you leave earlier without a good-bye?"

"I didn't leave you. I went to find us something to eat." He rubbed his hands together, cold because she was wearing his SAR jacket. "It's New Year's Day. Nothing, and I mean nothing, is open in this valley. I had to drive almost to Richmond to find a place where I could get a hot meal. I was bringing back dinner for us, but we got distracted."

The softening in her expression surprised him. He stared at her, trying to hold back what he felt. Resisting the urge to touch. But something tender moved through his voice. "I wish the fuck I knew what was going on between us."

She stayed perfectly still, as if she didn't understand. Or because she did.

He reached out and touched her face as tenderly as he could, fingertips barely resting along her jawline. "I owe you an apology for this morning. I should never have put my hands on you. I'm sorry."

She looked perplexed for a moment, but she hadn't backed out of his touch. "The kiss?"

"Okay. Yeah."

Is that how she remembered their physical confrontation? Not the fact that he, much like Stokes, had forced her to deal with the fact that he was bigger and stronger than she was? No, that wasn't honest. He hadn't been doing that. He'd taken the opportunity to give in to the urge to touch her because he couldn't help himself. It was there now. His gaze locked on her mouth but he dropped his hand before he could finish the impulse to pull her close.

That urge had been hammering away at him ever since he saw her walking up the drive this morning. He'd heard some scientist say recently on a show about intergalactic travel that time and distance were elastic in the universe. Changeable by circumstances. Time and distance had collapsed when he saw Yardley this morning. The years in between had been sucked into a black hole of emotions that had not dimmed and winked out, hadn't even aged. As fucked up an idea as it seemed, he still felt—everything—for Yardley Summers.

He'd come here to serve Law's request and protect Yard. But once he saw her, he was never far from the uncomfortable truth that there was a third imperative to his unspoken charge. Touch. He wanted to serve, protect, and touch her.

But wanting wasn't having. Thinking wasn't acting. He wasn't going to act on that third imperative. Then she'd touched him first.

He could still feel the irritation of her poking him with her finger. Only it didn't provoke anger from him. He'd gone hard as rock under that prodding touch. With her face only inches from his, the sensual warmth of her breath feathering across his face while the dark gleam of her angry stare dared him to act, he'd reacted to the only command getting through to his blood-starved brain. *Grab her. Hold her. Take her.*

He'd grabbed. He'd held her. He'd kissed her.

A good guy wouldn't have taken advantage. Wouldn't have pulled her in and kissed her thoroughly with lips and tongue while giving her a full-body massage. A good guy would have had more control. Yeah. His apology had been all about the kiss.

It took him a few seconds to think those thoughts. At the end of them he realized he wasn't the only one evaluating their silence.

Yard was looking at him with eyes wider than before. Her lips had parted softly, as if she needed more oxygen than she was getting. He'd swear she was leaning toward him, her chin raised a fraction. Was she reading him, feeling the surge of impulses he plainly wanted to bury but couldn't completely master? Was her quickened breath an indication that she was not averse to the carnal thoughts running through his head?

"Dammit, Yard. Stop staring at me."

She blinked and looked down, but there was a curious smile on the uplift of her mouth.

He reached past her, registering but ignoring the brush of his arm across her breasts. She didn't move away. In fact, it felt like she moved deliberately against him, her warm moist breath expelled practically into his ear. His dick jerked, angling like the needle on a Geiger counter toward the source of the near-radioactive lust surging through him. Hell. Gritting his teeth, pretending he didn't register the lush mounts pressed against his arm or the sweet breath tickling his ear, he opened her door. "Inside. Now. You're shivering."

* * *

Oleg greeted Yardley with excited yips and jumps of greeting. She bent down to accept his doggy affections, glad that Kye had left him free to protect her home. Even if Stokes was safely behind bars in the county jail, she knew she wasn't going to feel safe again in her house for a very long time.

She suspected all that chewed paper strewn across the floor had been once been a roll of kitchen towels. But Oleg hadn't damaged anything else within her view. Or continued to tear up her house. She'd seen the damage he could do. He'd tried to take down a wall to get to her, to protect her. The crisis had bonded them. She and Oleg were a K-9 team. She'd never doubt him again.

It took her a few more seconds to realize that, beside the chewed towels, the living room was clean. Without asking, she knew Kye had picked up the shattered blinds and removed them. The chunks of plaster had been swept up and the drapes had been rehung, even if they did droop unevenly from a bent rod. He must have done it before following to the hospital. His efforts touched her more than she would have expected.

She turned back and noticed he hadn't come in behind her. She went out to the porch and saw a dark form moving away. He was carrying Lily on his shoulders toward the bunkhouse.

"Wait!"

He turned around. If surprise had a posture, his was it.

"You said you brought food. Did you eat?" Not waiting to see if her indirect invitation would be accepted, she turned and went back in.

A few minutes later Kye entered and lowered the crate he carried with Lily onto the floor. He was smiling at her with more gratitude than she expected, or deserved. She didn't want to be alone just yet. Anyone, she told herself, would have been welcome.

She ignored the little voice whispering *Liar.* Kye had been there tonight. It meant everything.

He came in quickly and lifted a pair of leashes off their pegs by the door. "I'll walk the dogs while you hop in the shower. Then I'll heat up dinner."

He didn't wait for her to respond but began leashing Oleg and then Lily. When he was done he opened the door. "Let's go, Lily. Oleg. *Jdi ven.*"

"Hold on." Yardley swung his coat from her shoulders and held it out.

He smiled at her with more tenderness than her offer required. "Thank you."

Yardley stripped and stepped into the shower without even peeking at herself in the mirror. Afraid to register how bad she must look. The hot water stung her skin in a dozen places—her left cheek, one shoulder, her left breast, her knees—but she didn't care. She would have stood uncomplaining under water twice as hot if it would erase Stokes's touch.

She wasn't badly hurt, she reminded herself. She wasn't raped. She wasn't any of the many awful things that might have been. She was only roughed up.

But the longer she stood scrubbing at her body, the angrier she became. By the time she stepped out to towel herself off, she was more torqued up than she could ever remember being. Flame-red furious. No longer at Stokes. At herself.

CHAPTER ELEVEN

Kye looked up from stirring a pot when he heard a door slam. A moment later Yard appeared in the kitchen doorway. Her damp hair was twisted up in a topknot with one take-out chopstick pushed through to anchor it. She was dressed as he'd never seen her, in leggings of some soft pastel sweater material and a matching oversized top that slipped off one shoulder and still managed to cling to her braless breasts, outlining their fullness. His eyes hung there for a second too long. He knew it. Because when they rose to her face she looked ready for a fight.

He glanced back at the pan he stood over. "I hope you like beef tips with onions and bell pepper. Or smothered chicken. I'm heating both up."

"I tried to kill a man."

Ah. He didn't look up as her voice echoed through the kitchen. "You wouldn't have killed him. Maimed him, maybe. You want mashed potatoes with this?"

She came up beside him, forcing him to glance over at her. A few tendrils of hair had escaped. The long ribbons of her damp hair were leaving wet streaks on her top. One drip formed a wet line down her breast so that her nipple showed like a dark smudge beneath the fabric.

Swallowing carefully, he looked back up into the furious expression of the beautiful woman before him. "Beef or chicken?"

She moved away from him, using her hands to punctuate her thoughts as she moved around. "At first I didn't think Stokes would really try to hurt me. But then he did. He had me on my back. The rain was running into my nose. I couldn't breathe." Her hands had formed fists held at shoulder height, as if she might need at any second to protect herself.

"You're a warrior." Kye spoke in a casual tone as he filled one of the plates he'd brought to the stove. "Win or lose, a warrior goes down fighting. If you're alive you're surviving. That's what they teach you in the service."

She stared at him, as if trying to absorb his words despite the turbulence he could see swirling inside her like an offshore hurricane. "I would have killed him, Kye. I wanted to." Saying the words seemed to intimidate her, but she continued. "One second I was scared. I knew he was going to hurt me if I don't stop him. I was screaming. Oleg was going mad, hurling himself at the windows because he couldn't get to me. All at once this crazy mad anger just boiled up out of me. All I could think was *I mustn't lose this fight. Whatever it takes.* Then the hammer was in my hand. And I would have done anything, anything to win."

He put down the plate and approached her slowly. "Yard. That bastard deserved anything he got."

"No." She shook her head, fists flying open as if to hold him off. "I train my K-9 teams to be the best. That means being in control of a situation. But I wasn't ready. He came at me before I could think. I should have been ready. I train my K-9s every day to be certain they are ready. I shouldn't have let him get the better of me."

He took her gently by the shoulders and ducked his head to make her glance up. "Now listen to me. You were about to—" His heart shifted into overdrive at the thought of what might have happened if he hadn't arrived, but he didn't let it show. "You were fighting for your life. You were doing what you had to do to protect yourself."

She looked past him suddenly toward Oleg, who stood silently watching them from the doorway. "Oleg knew Stokes was out there. He was trying to get to the door before I went out. I thought it was just the storm upsetting him. That's why I wouldn't let him out with me. I should have trusted him. He knew something was wrong. I made a rookie mistake."

"You made a decision based on the best information you had."

He steered her toward the place where he had put the plate down and pushed her into the chair. Then he bent down on a knee in front of her. "I saw you fighting Stokes. And I believe you when you said you had it. Maybe I should have waited for you to prove it. Then Stokes would have to explain in court how he got beat by a girl."

He watched her try to smile at his small joke. But it was as faulty as a shorted lightbulb. She twisted her arms together under her breasts. He had to use every ounce of control not to look down. "It's over now, Yard."

"It doesn't feel over." Her expression was rigid, as if the pressure of holding back her emotions had tightened every muscle in her face. "I'm still so angry. Like I want to explode. And I don't know why."

Kye nodded, in sync at last. This wasn't about Stokes, exactly. Being vulnerable frightened her more than being attacked. He supposed that made sense. For a person who thought she had to fight every battle alone. "What do you want, Yard?"

She glanced as one of his hands curved tightly on her shoulder. She saw that the knuckles were slightly scraped. He'd fought Stokes, too, until she'd been able to release Oleg.

One sight of the wolfdog baring two rows of gleaming teeth had been enough to bring Stokes under control.

He'd actually whimpered and groveled in the mud as Kye secured him. "Don't let him bite me. Okay? Please don't let her sic that dog on me." Stokes, the man who'd set one of her K-9s on a fellow officer, was terrified of being bitten.

Yardley whipped tendrils of hair back from her face with her hand, bewildered by her own memories. "Stokes was a coward. I was fighting a coward."

"Bullies often are cowards when they find themselves the victim. Let it go, Yard."

"I can't." She stared at him, her dark eyes gleaming with angry tears she would never shed. "I want the anger to stop. But it's stuck here." She thumped her chest with a fist. "Maybe I should get stupid drunk and pass out."

"I don't think that's what you need." Kye's voice sounded strange even in his own ears. That was because her thump had caused her breasts to jiggle very provocatively behind her shirt.

His tone brought her head up. "What do you think I need?"

His smile was slow and deliberate. "Something physical, something that will make you sweat and your heart pound and—"

She stiffened. "Now look—!"

"Hold on. I've got an idea." He pushed her plate toward her. "Stay here and eat. I'll lock the door behind me. I won't be long."

He stood and headed out into the night.

By the time she finished half her chicken—rage wasn't an appetite suppressor, she discovered—the front door was being opened. Oleg, who'd been lounging at Yardley's feet, stood up and walked calmly to the kitchen door. Yardley followed.

Kye was back, a dusting of snow in his hair and on his shoulders. His duffel bag was slung over one shoulder, and he carried a set of big stuffed boxing pads in one hand and a pair of boxing gloves in the other. It was gear from the bunkroom gym. After hours the handlers often felt the need to blow off steam.

Grinning from ear to ear, he held up the gloves to her. "Let's get physical, Ms. Summers."

Yardley frowned. "You can't be serious?"

"Damn straight, I'm serious." He dropped his backpack on a chair and motioned her forward with an impatient hand. "You're angry. You were ready to go the distance. I get it. Sometimes, when the fight's over too quickly, even a professional fighter can be left high and dry with all this leftover energy he can't shake. You need physical release. Come on, take your sweater off. Get comfortable."

"I—uh, I don't have on anything—"

"Oh." He frowned for a second then tossed her the gloves. He rumbled through his backpack and came up with a sleeveless muscle shirt. "Put this on."

Reluctantly Yardley took it with her into her room to change. It was much too big, the armholes bagging away to expose inches of her torso. She thought about putting on a sports bra, but there were bruises she didn't want to irritate. She gathered the shirt bottom, twisted, and tied it in a knot at waist level. This time she couldn't avoid her image in the mirror: slightly swollen eyes with an angry dark-red bruise riding her cheek. She turned from side to side until she was satisfied that she was minimally decent.

Even so, she saw the interested look Kye gave her when she returned to the living room, though he didn't say a word. She also noticed that Oleg had joined Lily in being kenneled, separately.

Kye slipped the gloves on her and secured them tightly then stepped back and picked up the punch mitts. "Okay, you know the drill. Aim for the middle. Mark an X in your mind and throw the punch toward that X. Smash it!"

Yardley shook her head. "I feel foolish doing this here."

"Come on. It's just you and me. And we both know you don't give a damn about what I think. Step forward and put your weight into the punch. Jab like you mean it."

She took a stance, knees slightly bent, gloves up, then sized up her target and threw a punch.

"That's right. Again. Yeah! Again, Yard." He chuckled as he watched her. "This isn't the first time you've had the gloves on."

She shrugged, bobbing and weaving a little as she gained confidence. "I took a kickboxing course years ago. Ex-marine instructor said I punched like a girl. So I trained until I could prove him wrong."

"Why does that not surprise me?"

She smiled, remembering what she'd once liked best about him. His humor. His laughter contained irresistible infectious joy.

"Come on, now. Back to work, Ms. Summers. Give me a few more jabs. Hard! Harder! Cream puff! Girl, put your back into it! You're fighting yourself. You're fighting your fear. Change it up. Roundhouse kick. Make the mitt the face of that asshole who tried to get a leg over on you. There! There you go! Again. Again!"

Kye was smiling but his tone was tough, barking orders in rapid rhythm over the next few minutes.

"Do it. The left! The right! Good combination! Again. Yes! Again. That's a beaut!"

They sparred until Yardley waved him off and collapsed on a chair, legs rubbery with sweat slicking every inch of her body. Her hair had come undone, cascading over her shoulders and into her eyes. Yet she no longer felt stiff or achy. Or wound too tight.

"Feel better?" He reached out to undo one of her gloves.

She nodded, her breath coming in quick gasps. "I feel—" She laughed. "Relieved."

He nodded and smiled. "Anytime you need to let off steam, you come see me and we'll go a few rounds. Anytime."

Something changed between his other words and the last one. *Anytime.* Like he was there for her. Ready and willing to help. With anything. Anytime.

For a moment, while his gaze moved over her, taking in every aspect of her, she felt the warm flush of another kind of heat. Hot. Explosive, expanding her lungs and melting everything below her belly button.

She knew her face must be maroon from her exertions. Sweat dripped from the end of her nose. No need to think she looked the least bit attractive anymore. Yet she didn't think he was seeing any of that.

His eyes were now hooded. The gold in the hazel glittered beneath his lashes, amped up by their exertions. That golden gaze dipped to follow the track of a sweat droplet skiing down her sternum into the cleft between her breasts. Her nipples were stiff. Now that she thought about it, she could feel them achingly tight and sensitive from the abrasion of the shirt she wore, his shirt. And he was looking his fill. She could feel the heat. His chest was rising and falling a little fast. His smell became a bit sharper. Every female instinct within her came alert. It wasn't fear of the predator this time. It was the instinct of sighting a potential mate.

But he didn't make a move. Instead he let his lids droop, his gorgeous mouth going downright grim as he worked the fastener of her last glove. When he had slipped them both off he got up and walked into her bedroom. He came back with two towels and tossed her one.

He disappeared into the kitchen and reappeared with a glass of water. "Drink it slow."

He moved back a few steps, leaned his shoulders

against a wall, and crossed his arms. She drank half the glass before he spoke again. "You should keep up your boxing practice. With the proper coaching, you could do some damage. Of course you'll have to keep getting your wardrobe from the house of McGarren." His gaze slid from her face down to the soaking-wet shirt plastered to her body. "What you do for an undershirt is just short of illegal, Ms. Summers."

His slow seductive grin made her toes curl inside her shoes. The heat in her middle slid lower down. He was flirting. This was crazy. She wasn't ready. "I need to go to bed."

"Yes." He said the word slowly, keeping eye contact as he moved away from the wall toward her. "I suppose you do."

She stood up, the action bringing them closer together. "Thank you."

The humor had left his face, replaced by an intensity she recognized. "Anytime."

She looked away, unwilling to encourage what she was beginning to think she wanted very much. "I mean it. You let me be angry. You didn't try to deflect it, or tell me the anger was useless, or unneccssary and un-productive."

"I figured you could work that out for yourself."

"I—did." She stopped to listen to her heart, which beat hard but steadily. "The fear's gone."

She was feeling brave and fearless. And he was suddenly much closer and much more available than she'd expected. It was there in his expression. His breath was coming a little fast between his lips. Lips more lush than should be legal on a man. He was sweating, too. After

all, he'd been on the receiving end of her very physical
workout. But sweat didn't drip off his nose or run in riv-
ulets down his back. No, he—glowed.

She hadn't allowed herself to feel the rush of gratitude that had overtaken her when Kye appeared over
Stokes's shoulder. Now it came back with heightened
awareness that he had probably saved her life. Even in
her extreme distress, she'd registered that he'd looked a
whole lot like her own personal avenging angel. Protector. Rescuer. The Good Guy.

She raised a hand to his chest, palm spreading over
the heated surface of his shirt. For just a moment she
longed to lean her head against that solid wall. As if she
could hide her face in the warmth of the man smelling
faintly of sweat, and desire. And be safe.

Lust, pure and simple as a struck match, caught fire
inside her chest. The instinct to survive was still raw
and bright and needy inside her. He could meet that need
and soothe it. She saw that as his eyes widened and
darkened looking into hers.

She heard a raw sound coming from her throat, his
name. And then her arms were sliding around his neck,
and she was reaching with her mouth for his. She found it.

Warm firm lips met hers. But he didn't touch. This
time he hesitated, but she didn't. She licked at the seam
of his closed mouth until she heard him moan. His arms
came up. One found her shoulders, the other sliding
down her back until a hand gripped her ass and pulled
her close. She was tall enough to fit perfectly against
him. His arousal pressed thick and hard against her sex.

The hot caress of his tongue sent shivers of pleasure
through her. Little fireworks went off behind her dropped

lids. She strained against him, not wanting to break the kiss to tell him what she wanted.

"Yard?" He'd lifted his head. When she opened her eyes he was staring at her. "Damn. This really isn't the best idea. After tonight." The want was plain in his taut features, but something else shown through in his gaze. Regret. "Rain check?"

She stared at him. Trying to hear sense over the thunder of her heart. *After tonight?*

She must have said the words aloud. He nodded and backed off, the moment avoided. "Good night, Yard."

She glanced at his retreating back. He picked up his backpack.

"There's no need for you to leave. The beds upstairs are made up. You can sleep here."

He watched her for a moment then nodded slowly.

She wasn't sure if she'd just made the best decision of the day, or the worst.

It was two thirty-seven a.m. Sleep had long ago gone from being elusive to becoming the Impossible Dream. The silence magnified everything in the dark house. Kye could hear each time Oleg shifted in his sleep inside a downstairs crate. He'd listened to the clock down the hall ticking until he had to get up and unplug it. He would swear he could hear the snow falling. He was absolutely certain he could hear Yard breathing directly below him.

God, she tasted and felt good. He'd almost muffled the voice in his head telling him he was taking advantage. Yet he'd spent the past four years dealing with vulnerable people, some of whom had survived horrible ordeals. You learned to pull back from sometimes spectacular

offers of generosity, even if the victim didn't understand.

Tonight that self-control was costing him. Costing
him more than peace of mind. It was taking him back
to a time when he'd failed her.

He'd been military, sent to Harmonie Kennels for
two weeks with his K-9 unit for rappelling practice from
rooftops and helicopters with their dogs. He'd heard all
the stories about Yardley Summers, seen her from a
respectful distance. Every man knew the boss's daughter
was off limits. They made jokes about her, calling her
the Citadel. He'd never even spoken to her. Until the
day he'd stumbled across her alone cleaning out the
kennels.

She was on the phone. She was talking with her father,
a one-sided conversation that had her in tears. He hesitated, unsure how to back away without being seen.

Then she'd looked up, trapping him with an angry and
defiant stare as she wiped hard at the tears staining her
face. "What are you doing here, McGarren?"

He was stunned that she knew his name. And grateful. Feeling like the top of his head was floating away,
he'd smiled at her. "Who do you want me to kill?"

She blinked. "What?"

He pointed to her phone. "Way I figure it, anyone who
makes someone as special as you cry needs murdering."

He wasn't sure why he'd said such an outrageous
thing. He knew he was talking about her father.

She looked at him in surprise. "You'd take on Bronson Battise?"

"For you? Hell, yeah." It was supposed to be an empty
boast. All the handlers admired Battise's K-9 training
techniques. Some noticed how he treated his daughter.

Like less a member of the family than a hired hand. Not his business

Until Yardley laughed, a sound so sexy that it nearly brought him to his knees. Then she'd looked at him with those shining black eyes and he'd heard trumpets sound and swords clash. One glance had him thinking he could slay her dragons and share a happily-ever-after. It was like a goddamn Disney movie playing in his head.

They began meeting in secret. No one could know. By the end of his two weeks he'd known this was love, the real thing. They were going to be together forever.

But he'd underestimated her father.

He'd never forget Battise's words to him. *Youngsters like you are good for sport. But if you think you're going to get a piece of Harmonie Kennels by shagging my illegitimate daughter then you got shit for brains, son. Bang her all you want. She gets nothing.*

As if a man needed any enticement beyond Yardley herself.

But Battise had gone one better. *Now get the fuck off my property before I tell your sergeant you aren't fit to handle one of my K-9s. Your dick or your job. What's more important to you?*

Kye blew out a breath, feeling the heat of that long-ago embarrassment race across his skin. He couldn't save Yardley. He barely saved his job. The army didn't let you go. It dishonorably discharged your ass. He left with his unit, without even a good-bye.

Now the damn trumpets were back. Blaring louder than a phalanx of Roman legionnaires announcing their entrance onto the field of battle. Behind it all pounded the drumbeat of desire. He still wanted to be Yard's hero.

He'd learned something tonight. Not all wars are

fought against an enemy. Not all battles take place in combat zones. Sometimes the fight is within, heart against mind against emotions. Three entities roiling and writhing to take control. To be victorious, the three had to turn from enemies into allies.

Yardley could and did fight for everything else in her life: her dogs, her business, her brother. But she didn't seem to have the first clue about how to protect herself from herself.

She'd kissed him tonight, just like she had the first time twelve years ago, with everything she had. Everything. And he'd wanted more. He still did.

He heard a door open downstairs. He was suddenly so alert he knew he could have heard a dog's whistle.

He heard whispered footsteps crossing the room below and stopped breathing. He couldn't hope for anything.

Footfalls on the stairs almost stopped his heart.

When Yardley's shadow appeared in the open doorway Lily sat up but she didn't move from her place on the floor.

Yardley didn't say a word, merely lifted the covers and slid down next to him. Surprise held him still. She settled in and lay flat on her back, not touching him anywhere.

"The generator's out. I was cold."

Kye didn't answer. It really wasn't important why she was here beside him. Now he had a whole lot of new decisions to make. Or just one.

He slowly moved his hand across the sheet until his little finger met hers. When she didn't jerk away, he hooked his over hers, curled and held on. "In the morning."

He felt her relax.

He wanted her in the worst way. Wanted her so badly it hurt to breathe. But he'd seen her bruises. The last thing she needed to know after Stokes's assault was that the man she trusted enough to climb into bed with for a sense of safety and comfort was lusting after her like a dog.

She needed to know there was refuge here. In the dark. In this bed. With him beside her.

He took a deep breath. Maybe it wasn't going to be so hard to sleep after all.

CHAPTER TWELVE

Kye woke to Yard swearing like a drill sergeant. He sat up, muscles tightening for combat even before his eyes were open.

She was sitting beside him on the bed in the half-light of dawn.

"You're shaking like a leaf."

She shrugged off his touch on her shoulder. "Bad memories."

"Of last night?"

She gave her head the barest shake. "Something that happened before."

Kye's whole body tensed. "What happened before?"

"Nothing."

"Try again."

She was silent so long he thought she wouldn't answer. "The week after you left rumor got around Harmonie Kennels that I was putting out."

Kye swore under his breath. "I don't expect you to be-lieve me. But I didn't tell anyone about us. Not even Law."

"Whatever." Her voice was flat. "Some guy caught me hosing down the cages while training was going on. He—" She bit her broken lip hard, causing it to bleed freely. She didn't seem to notice. "Bronson came in. Beat the guy half to death before some of the staff heard me screaming and came to pull him off."

"At least he behaved like a father that time."

She turned only her head to look at him, her eyes so dark with remembered pain it was hard to hold her gaze. "Bronson blamed me. He said it was my fault he had to half kill a decent man as an example so other handlers wouldn't let themselves be seduced by me. It was bad for business."

Bad for business. The words made Kye want to hit something but he didn't dare scare her confession away. "And?"

"My father said he'd known about us but that he'd let it go as a onetime fuck." She swallowed. "However, if I wanted to be a slut like my mother, I'd have to do that somewhere else."

Kye thought quickly through what she had told him, trying to keep his anger out of his calculations. But doing that felt like sitting on a rumbling volcano.

Fact one: Word had gotten out that he and Yard had been together. He supposed someone besides Bronson must have seen them. Young lovers were often reckless when they thought they were being discreet. Had the way he looked at her given them away?

Fact two: Shortly after he'd left, a guy had tried to rape Yard.

Shit. Little eruptions of anger broke through his defenses, making his heart pound.

Fact three: Bronson had beat the assailant to a bloody pulp—not to avenge his daughter, but to protect his business.

Kye's fists curled down tight, abraded knuckles itching to hit something, hard. "Why did you stay with Battise?"

"I had nowhere else to go. I'd enlisted in the army at eighteen because it was the best option to get away from the reservation."

"You went to war?"

"It was easier in some ways than reservation life." She shot him a dark look that dared him to ask her about that. "As my first tour of duty was coming to a close, I was suddenly out on my ass with discharge papers when everyone else was being stop-lossed with extensions. Once stateside, I learned Bronson had pulled some strings with the military, saying I was more valuable at Harmonie Kennels to help train military dogs."

Kye whistled. "I knew he had pull. But to get you out of the army in wartime?"

She shrugged. "Bronson always got what he wanted. He promised to pay my college tuition for the fall semester if I'd work for him. So I agreed. But after the incident he took back that promise. He said I had to work for free. The bills for the guy he had to beat up were coming out of my wages."

"Jesus, Yardley. No wonder you hate me."

"No. What happened was my fault. I was weak. I was an illegitimate reservation girl with a lot to prove. But I stumbled when my goal was within reach."

"That sounds like something you were told. Not

something you believe." Kye swallowed the rest of his words. Every time he thought he couldn't dislike Bronson Battise more, she said something that made that a lie.

He'd heard the PR spin before he ever met Bronson or his daughter. It was part of his bio. Everyone said how magnanimous Battise was to take in troubled teens from reservation lands and teach them a trade. It made a touching story. Except that in the instances of Law and Yardley, they were his kids, abandoned years before.

He glanced back at Yard. She was staring at him with those eyes that seemed as large as the ones in velvet paintings of trembly-lipped children and animals popular when he was little. He wanted to hold her and take her pain away.

But she didn't need his pity. She was a fighter. She'd had to be.

"I don't know how your father found out about us. He confronted me the day my unit was leaving. Told me to keep the hell away from you. If I ever contacted you again, he'd see to it I was tossed out of my K-9 unit." He'd go to his grave keeping silent about the part where Bronson said his daughter didn't matter and wouldn't inherit jack shit from him. But he owed her this truth.

"I was young and stupid. And a coward. I didn't know what else to do. So I left. I know it's too little too late but still I owe you an apology. I'm sorry."

She shrugged. "At least you're honest."

The silence stretched out again.

"Why did you come here?"

She'd asked that question many different ways in the past twenty-something hours. Here it was again.

"It was a chance to see you again." It was that simple

and that true. And he didn't know what to do with that. "I don't want anything from you. Not even an acceptance of my apology. It's just that it's always seemed like there was something unfinished between us."

She turned her head again, canting it to one side. At first she simply stared; then her gaze became something more. Something turning up the heat in the dark depths of her eyes. Something thickening the tiny pulse that beat in the sweet hollow of her throat. Something climbing her cheeks like wild roses. He saw her lick her broken lip, the husky words forming there before she spoke. "I want something from you. May I?"

He smiled, not quite sure yet but going there anyway. He leaned back onto his pillow and folded his arms behind his head. "Help yourself."

She reached for the bedding and threw it back. He watched her eyes widen at what she'd revealed.

He slept naked. Of course, he hadn't been expecting company. Too late now to play coy. Free of the bedding his cock sprang up, thick-veined and heavy. It lengthened and bloomed under her gaze until it arched high off his thigh, trembling with each pulse of his heartbeat.

She didn't hesitate. She scooted out of her pajama bottoms, leaving her top on, and then threw a bare leg across his. He caught a glimpse of a Cherry Coke shadow between her thighs and then she was settling her weight on his legs just behind his swollen cock.

She took him, using both her hands, and squeezed firmly. "I want everything you've got." She tugged, pulled at the root of him until he gasped. "Can you give everything?"

"All yours." His voice was a husk of a whisper. He'd long ago given up trying to understand the workings of a woman's mind. After the business with Stokes, and then her confession only moments before about how her father had treated her after he left her all those years ago, he'd have thought she'd want his balls on a platter. Instead, incredibly, her smooth warm fingers were cupping them, massaging his dick in mind-blowing ways that felt too damn good to analyze.

His lids dropped down until his eyes were mere slits as he watched her work him with the concentration of a man in mortal danger. He could feel himself growing and thickening with each stroke until she had coaxed him to near bursting.

"Yard." He heard the plea in his voice and wondered if he were dreaming.

"*Shhh.*" She leaned forward and placed a finger over his lips. Her hair, free from the usual knot, slid down over her shoulders and tickled his arms. And then she kissed his chest. Quick little butterfly kisses that barely registered had the power to expand his lungs with the need to keep breathing so he could experience every second.

She licked his small flat nipple, her tongue making little wet circles around the center. He wanted to touch her back. To hold and stroke and taste. But he didn't. Not even when her tongue licked across the arch of his ribs. And then his other nipple. Her hands had not left his cock. She was working the shaft with both hands, pumping him as she slid her tongue down his chest. It left a wet trail that quickly chilled in the cold room. Yet the shivery feeling running over his skin only made him hotter, and stiffer. Her tongue trailed liquid sex as it dipped into his belly button and circled, slowly, twice.

He lost the battle to keep silent. A groan vibrated deep

in his throat. He moved an arm to throw it over his eyes so that he could feel. Just feel. Everything.

He felt her shift backward, her bare ass sliding down his thighs. He braced in anticipation. Knowing, hoping, what came next.

When she touched her tongue to the tip of his cock it jerked involuntarily. And then her lips, warm and wet, were sliding over it, expanding to accommodate the smooth knob.

She licked him, tracing the length of underside with her tongue as she sucked him in. He levered up in the bed, unable to remain still any longer.

"No." She raised up and put a hand on his chest.

He stared at her with hot eyes. She still wore a slouchy top, covering every inch of her from neck to fingertips to thighs. How easy it would be to grab her arm and pull her forward and snatch off that offending garment. Then flip her over so that the wonderful warm womanly length of her would be skin-to-skin under him. But it wasn't going to be like that. To his astonishment, he went back onto the bed when she gave him a little push.

He'd never understood the supposed pleasure in a man giving up control. With Yard, it was an aphrodisiac. They weren't kids just learning their own sexual natures. They were partners in pleasure. Her play. Her moment. His to accept. Hot damn.

She rose up on her knees and inched forward until a knee was aligned on either side of his hips. Still holding his cock in one hand, she lifted the hem of her top to reveal her sex. He stared at the apex of her thighs. His hands clenched. He could look but not touch. Oh, but if looks could thrill.

From somewhere—as if it mattered—she had produced a condom and was smoothing it down over him with the firm potent touch of her hands. He was grateful because he was beyond caring about such considerations. But that was Yardley, always prepared, whatever the situation.

She squeezed his cock, directed it to the right angle, and began making little circles with her hips. Each undulation brushing his tip with her sex. Each rotation producing a little more friction. Parting her lower lips. He could feel the heat. The wet warmth of her spread over him like honey. It was the most erotic dance he'd ever seen. More sensual than a lap dance. Slower than a bump and grind. It was all he could do not to arch his hips and claim her.

But this was her party.

She sank down on him very, *very* slowly. An inch at a time. After each inch she paused, closed her eyes, and breathed slowly, as if encompassing him was a pleasure to be savored, recorded with her senses. The walls of her sex fluttered, expanded, caressed. He'd never felt more potent, or important, or appreciated.

When she had slid that final inch onto him his rougher sigh echoed hers. She was near to bursting with him. He filled every space within her so tightly that just breathing made little contractions erupt around him. And then she began to move.

She rose up, her hands pressed to his chest, and again circled her hips before dropping down so that he sank deep within the wet silk of her core.

He tried to be patient. But first one hand and then the other moved to find the shape of her waist. To hold her, rock her, help direct the exquisite torture of her lovemaking. Yet she set the pace. This wasn't for amateurs.

Twenty-one wouldn't have made it last. Thirty-six gave him just enough control to dangle on the edge of sexual oblivion, for her pleasure.

He began to sweat. His chest became slick with the exertion of holding back. Her hands moved and firmed on the curve of his biceps, fingers digging in on hard muscle as she began to ride him harder, quicker, with an urgency he had no trouble matching.

Little gusts of pleasure pulsed through her parted lips as she moved, riding rough sweet desire.

She suddenly changed rhythms, went into a frenzied pumping action. His hands clenched her hips so that he could match her thrust for thrust. He heard her hiss in pain, remembered the bruises, and let her go.

She looked down at him, frowning. "Don't stop."

That was all the invitation he needed.

Climax. Such a pitiful word for the explosion of body, mind, and emotions that erupted between them. She was breathing harshly, a woman on the verge, and he was gasping at the freight train rumbling straight through his cock.

There was nothing staged or controlled about Yardley's orgasm. She rode him like an expert rodeo bull rider, hanging on for dear life yet still driving him on until she'd wrung every drop from him.

He came so violently it bordered on pain and then drove right through it.

She collapsed across him, sweaty hair veiling his face, clinging to his lips, her heart pounding against his ribs. Bodies glued together. Her mouth open and pressed into the side of his neck.

Kye swallowed, trying to slow his heart but too damn

impressed by what had just happened to care if she'd given him a heart attack.

They hadn't even kissed.

He hadn't gotten to undress her.

Hadn't really gotten to touch or hold or taste her.

Now he knew those puny things didn't count.

This was ecstasy. He'd only visited in the neighborhood before.

Yardley Summers was the Sweet Spot.

CHAPTER THIRTEEN

Yardley woke up smiling. She couldn't remember why until she turned her head. Inches away, Kye lay facing her. His eyes were closed, long dark lashes lying like fringe against his upper cheeks. She almost reached out and ran a finger down the blunt wedge of his nose but hesitated, in case she woke him.

It was hard to take him all in when his eyes were open. His friendly but oh-so-direct gaze took in more than she wanted him to see. But now she could look her fill.

Her gaze shifted to his mouth. His wide, full lips might have made a lesser man seem vulnerable. But there was nothing vulnerable about this mouth. It conquered and possessed and demanded surrender in its kiss. The hard square jaw was like the man. Bold, imposing, uncompromising, 100 percent masculine. And yet he could be goofy. That *aloha* smile of his was 90 percent kid at play. She felt an unaccustomed fondness for his face. It was a funny feeling that made her stomach flutter. It had nothing to do with the parts that made up a pretty spectacular specimen of human male.

He had been more than she remembered. The young man all eager and sweaty was not the consummate adult in full possession of his powers. Which he'd demonstrated by giving control to her. What was he like when he was in charge? It made her hot just thinking about it.

She lifted a finger toward his nose, a smile blossoming on her mouth. Maybe she should test her curiosity.

She heard it across the house. The soft *ping* of a text message being delivered to her phone. The sound went through her like an electric current. She bolted from his bed, shock and disbelief powering her.

He opened an eye. "Where are you going?"

She looked back, frowning at the intrusion into her amazement. "Bathroom."

She took the stairs two at a time. She was wrong. Probably wrong. It must be Kye's phone.

But the phone plugged into her bathroom socket was glowing. She could see it from the doorway of her bedroom.

She approached it as if it were a bomb. She picked it up as if it might burn her. There was a message. The first on this phone in more than three months. From an unknown number.

She opened the text message. It was a link to YouTube.

Holding her breath, she touched the link and suddenly the voice of Nat King Cole filled her ears. It was an old recording of a song she'd never heard before. But the lyrics were clear. "Do Nothing Till You Hear from Me."

David.

She jabbed a return text into the phone, her hands shaking so badly that even autocorrect couldn't make sense of it.

"Damn." She cleared it and started again, making herself type slowly, her thumbs taking turns. It was simple. *David? Are you okay?*

She hit the SEND button and waited, staring so hard at the screen it began to blur.

It was David. It had to be him. *Do nothing until you hear from me?* What did it mean? Was he going to contact her again? Could he not just call her? Or text her? Was he in trouble? Oh God, she'd given up—

"That's a pretty sight."

Yardley jumped so hard she fumbled the phone and it fell into the sink. In the mirror she could see Kye standing in the bathroom doorway. He was naked. But the grin on his face said he was more interested in her state of undress. She could feel the winter air against her bare butt, only partially covered by her top. But she couldn't get caught up in the anticipation on his face. Not now.

She half turned to him. "I heard my phone. Business."

"On Sunday morning?"

"Dogs are like children. They don't take things like weekends and holidays into consideration when having a crisis. Can I have a sec?"

"Sure." He rubbed his chest lazily. "I can use some coffee. I'll put the pot on."

"Aren't you cold?" She couldn't help it. She was suddenly freezing while he was standing there like it was at least eighty-five degrees in the shade.

His grin answered before he did. "I was, a bit, until I saw you."

She didn't have to ask what he meant. The source of

the heat between them had him rising to the occasion. Except there weren't going to be any more occasions for them.

She couldn't find the words to object as he came toward her. He looked so happy, like a kid who'd discovered the brand-new bike he'd gotten for Christmas was still there the next morning when he opened his eyes.

Except she wasn't a bike to be ridden. She'd done the riding. And it was glorious. He was glorious.

He stopped just inches from her, the soft smile on his face almost too much to endure. "Did I say thank you?"

She gave her head a tiny shake then made a sound she didn't know she could make as his hands settled on her waist. His palms were scalding through her—no, he'd slipped her sweater up so quickly and smoothly she hadn't realized until they were skin-to-skin.

"I really do thank you. Best night of my life." His voice had gone rough. His eyes looked lazy. But as he drew her in by the waist there was nothing remotely calm about the heat swirling between them.

His cock, half ready to go, was nudging her groove. She felt the letdown of wetness in answer as he playfully poked and prodded, enjoying the dance before the dance.

She opened her mouth to protest. But his mouth sealed the words inside. He was kissing her with the focused intensity she'd felt in surprise the morning before. But that time there'd been at least an edge of anger in his kiss. This time, it was all sexual allure and persuasion and hope. Oh God, what he was promising her.

Her knees unlocked but he was there, hands sliding down and behind, grabbing her ass and lifting her up onto the counter beside the sink. Her knees fell open naturally and he moved in like a man on a mission. Hard hairy thighs brushed the inside of hers as the kiss went on and on, one melting into another soul-burning kiss.

They hadn't really kissed last night. Even in the midst of the shattering climax when they'd been skin on skin, him buried to the balls inside her, their lips hadn't met. Now she knew she could come from the feel and taste of his mouth alone.

Shattering.

He groaned against her mouth, whispering, "Shit." He lifted his head. "No condom."

"Doesn't—" She grabbed fistfuls of his hair and pulled his mouth back down to hers. This wasn't going to happen again between them. Not ever. She wanted, this once, to feel Kye inside her. And then she stopped thinking.

She scooped forward and lifted a leg to wrap it behind his thighs.

He expelled a breath of laughter into her mouth. And then he was moving his hips in slow circles, his cock bumping against her lower lips until he was wet with her essence. Her body opened and tightened in anticipation. His hands slid forward to tighten on her hips, his thumbs digging into her inner thighs to part her and make his way easier. The head of his cock touched her sweet spot and she gasped.

He sucked in her lower lip, nibbling on it without pain until she was gasping again and again. His tongue delved in behind to lick pleasure from her. Tongue and cock each nudging her toward a climax. Then he paused, took a breath, tightened his grip, and with a frank sexual roll of his hips shoved into her sleek heat.

She was trembling now, and sweating. Yet he paused and held her, the fit snug and smooth and tight. She could feel him inside her, pulsing and filling her to capacity, his body arched over hers. For this moment there was only the two of them.

The world stopped.

His hips rotated slowly, as if he were moving to a primitive beat only he could hear. That rhythm pulsed with the urgency of life, the downbeat coming as a thrust that speared straight into the heart of her. She didn't try to hold back, be an adult. An experienced woman. A sophisticated being. She let go, opened her mouth, dropped her hands to his buttocks, and gripped him hard. Her head fell forward against his shoulder and she simply held on as if her life depended on it.

He had it, the rhythm, the beat, the heat, the push–pull of lust in perfect sync with her need.

He came hard, lifting her off the counter to ride the gush of desire jetting out of him.

"Damn, Yard. You feel . . ." He took a breath. "So damn good. So good."

He looked so happy. So very happy.

That's when she lost her grip, sliding down more than his sweat-slick body into the depths of shame. She's just had sex—oh, please. It was more than that. She'd just offered every bit of her physical self to a man she couldn't have.

She slipped sideways from his splendid body and looked away with more regret than she would have expected. "I really could use that coffee." And an ice bath. Why had she thought she was cold?

"Yes, ma'am." He offered her an intimate smile, so tender and happy it made her feel like the greatest cheat of all time. Then he ran his hand lightly down her spine, making her arch in spite of herself. He cupped a butt and gave it a gentle squeeze. The whole time his caramel eyes, soft with the aftermath of satisfaction, held hers.

In the mirror she watched him walk away. Treacherous eyes taking in every inch of his shoulders, back, and butt. It was a glorious ass, firm and full with shallow dimples on either side. She'd betrayed David for that butt.

"Oh Lord." She felt a flicker of unnamed panic flare inside her. She could still feel her desire for Kye pounding in all her pulse points.

If there was a heaven, she was going directly to hell for those last minutes. She couldn't lie that it wasn't her idea.

The first time it had been all about her. She owed him a session where he had his way. But Kye in charge didn't feel in any way like giving up anything. It felt like a bonus ride on the craziest sex machine ever. But he was more than fine manly parts. He wasn't in his own head getting off for his own pleasure. He was there with her, every second, making it personal, important, and precious.

"You okay?" He'd whispered those words several times in the throes of their wild ride. Against her mouth, against her ear, against her breasts. He'd wanted to share. And take care of her. He'd wanted her to be satisfied. It was personal.

She smiled, despite her fraught emotions. The immature young solider she'd met a dozen years ago had matured into one helluva man. This was someone she didn't know. Or rather, was meeting for the first time. She could admit it now, when it couldn't mean a thing, that she liked him.

There was a strong streak of the protector in Kye. Not the macho I-got-this show-off style she saw on display among K-9 handlers from time to time. Competition was a natural result of putting aggressive, streetwise cops or battle-ready soldiers together in a learning situation. To work with a dog, the K-9 officer needed to be something of an independent who preferred to work on his own with little or no supervision. Occasionally that competition spilled over into their personal lives, with men more interested in scoring against other men than in making happy the women they might be with. Not Kye. For all his laid-back surfer style, he was a man, strong, tender, and caring. He'd turned out to be one of the good guys. If only.

She glanced back down at her phone. No reply.

She caught a breath and held it, trying to steady her suddenly galloping heart. She was caught, between new experiences and old. Where did her loyalties lie? Could one night negate a year? No, that was crazy. She'd just made some terrible decisions. That, to be honest, she couldn't find it in her to regret.

But now there was David. Still in her life, if uncertainly.

It had been her idea that she and Dr. David Gunnar purchase phones with numbers only they knew so that their relationship could have the privacy they both craved. Neither wanted their very public lives to spill over into this most personal connection. They even went so far as to trade semi-coded texts about where to meet, like children with a secret. David had a thing for pop standards from the '40s and '50s, music popular long before either of them were born. At various times over the past year she had received messages that read:

That's Amore. Free to share a pensione in old Napoli?

April in Paris. I forget the lyrics. Bring them to the Madison Hotel.

Georgia on My Mind. Outer Banks paying good dividends.

This one was different. And caller ID was blocked.

David had never done that before. Yet the text could only be from him. Only he had this number. Perhaps he'd lost his original phone, or it had stopped working and he couldn't replace it until now.

This message meant that he was okay. And that he wanted to see her.

Still, her sense of relief came mixed with a splash of anxiety as she reread his text. *Do nothing until you hear from me?* What did it mean?

"Coffee's on." Kye was back. His lids slid low over his gaze, taking in her bare legs. His smile held the warmth of a Pacific sun. "Should be ready by the time we've showered."

Yard couldn't miss the invitation in his gaze. It gave her a hot flush. "I don't have time. You go ahead."

She saw the humor drain from his expression at her tone. "Something's going on, okay?" She held up her phone as if that would make her point for her.

"It's not serious, I hope?"

"I don't know yet." But she did. It was very serious. Only she wasn't certain what to do next. "Can you check the heater? It really did go out during the night."

"Is it cold? I hadn't noticed."

She believed him. His erection was in full bloom again, fired by the same urges that made his gaze burn as it met hers. "I'll check it out." He turned, taking his fine ass and swaggering cock with him.

As soon as he was gone, Yardley started the video

again. This time the second line of the song caught her attention. *Pay no attention to what's said.* Was David telling her to discount whatever well-meaning friends or family might have said about his disappearance? They didn't know anything about each other's family and friends. Would he think she would tell anyone about them? Had he told someone? She didn't think so. Or did he mean the FBI and the DEA?

They'd told her he had applied for a permanent work visa to some unnamed country overseas. He might be texting her from Outer Mongolia, for instance. But she didn't think so. She had the feeling he hadn't left the good ol' U.S.A. Otherwise, why would the FBI be involved?

It didn't add up or make sense. She didn't have any information to go by. Nothing, except the intuition that had her left leg doing the River Dance all by itself.

David was in trouble. Probably in hiding. Unwilling or perhaps fearful of drawing her into whatever trouble he was in.

She shut off the song and thought about the kind of trouble that brought the feds to one's door. It wouldn't be some local or isolated problem. This was something serious, and it remained to be seen whether David was on the right or wrong side of it.

She met her reflection in the mirror and was startled by it. Her lip was still swollen. A bruise fattened one cheek. The opposite eye was now ringed red and deep purple. The patch above it itched. But the reason for her appearance, Stokes's attack, had been momentarily forgotten in the light of the last few hours. Too much had happened.

Kye had happened.

She glanced guiltily toward her bedroom doorway. She could hear him moving around upstairs. He was whistling. He was happy.

She had been happy, too. For six short hours her world had righted itself.

Do nothing until you hear from me.

There was nothing she could do. She had no way of knowing where David was. But he was still in her life. The text confirmed it. And he wanted her to wait for him. There was a promise in those song lyrics.

There was nothing more she could do but wait.

No, that wasn't right. What she must do was get rid of Kye.

Her stomach cramped with feelings of guilt. If she'd just stayed in her own bed. If she'd just not felt all the feelings that had come stealing in on her last night. If Kye hadn't been so kind. So able to deal with her craziness. If he hadn't been so *Kye*.

That was the thing. From the very first time they met, he'd had a sixth sense about how to talk to her. She might be the K-9 guru, but Kye understood her.

But he wouldn't understand David. And David wouldn't understand Kye.

She couldn't blame either man for that. She didn't have an explanation for what had happened during the night and again just now in her bathroom. It made no sense, even to herself. That didn't mean it wasn't real, all the feelings swirling through her, whispering wicked secrets about what else she and Kye might do together and to each other. But she knew better than to listen.

Feelings were just that, feelings. You didn't have to give them the space to rule your thoughts. She certainly wasn't going to act on them, again. She was going to use her brain and think her way out of this emotionally hot-blooded female mess she became when Kye touched her.

She did have some hard reality to help her deal.

Number one. No more touching. Not her touching Kye. And mercy no, not Kye touching her. Those big talented hands of his were definitely mind destroyers.

Number two. She'd made up her mind before Kye arrived that David was the man for her. Nothing had changed. Good in bed was not a commitment.

Number three. All those feelings she was feeling were because Kye had come to her at a low moment, when she'd just given up hope on David and was in need of comfort. Her pride was cut up. She'd put herself out there and thought she'd been dumped. She flinched. She hadn't exactly used Kye. She disliked people who used others to make themselves feel better. But she hadn't had the strength to hold them apart. Her bad.

She'd let old feelings, memories, and sentiment cloud her vision. She never did that. She was always reliable. Steady. Ready to make the hard decisions. The path was always clear for her. Choices clearly defined and labeled. She'd made her choice. David, not Kye.

So why was she hoping there was another choice, like door number three?

Forsaking all others.

She hadn't made that commitment yet. But just a week ago she had been prepared to do so, if David contacted her. She'd let Law and Georgie, and especially Kye, sway her away from her gut feelings.

But now she knew David still cared. She'd heard from him again. Why didn't that knowledge feel like a victory, a triumph, or even simple relief?

Lily came in, carrying something white. She chewed

a few times and then deposited the soggy cloth at Yard's feet. It was Yardley's PJ bottoms.

She picked up the destroyed garment. "Really? That's your judgment of me?"

Lily turned and walked out.

"I'm not trying to take him from you." Yardley rolled her eyes but then caught back a sob. Now even dogs were turning against her.

She needed a shower. A long hot shower followed by a cold one and then some other excuses to keep her from facing Kye. She'd give her hair a deep moisturizing treatment, pluck her brows, and maybe even paint her toenails. Anything that would give her time to regain her balance before she talked with Kye.

CHAPTER FOURTEEN

At least he was dressed. She doubted she could keep it together if Kye had still been nude.

He was sitting at her kitchen table with a cup of coffee in one hand and a mini laptop balanced on one knee. She wondered if he'd been in touch with Law but decided not to ask. If he had, there was nothing she could do about it now.

He had showered and wore jeans and a black hoodie with the Hawaiian Warriors' crest stenciled on it. His dark hair was still spiky with dampness. His bronze cheeks had been shaved, glowing as smooth as his butt— no, not the image she needed in her head at the moment. Lily lay at his feet. She gave Yardley a questioning glance but didn't raise her head. For some reason the toller didn't like her.

Kye looked up. "Hi." His gaze took in her black leggings and hoodie. "I've already walked the dogs. Fed them, too. I think Oleg and I have reached a truce."

"Thanks." Yardley folded her arms across her chest as she same through the doorway. She'd taken a long shower during which she'd decided how to handle the situation. All she needed to do was put it into action.

"I forgot to say thank you. Last night." She saw his eyes darken. "I mean, you letting me blow off steam. I was pretty much a basket case before the boxing session."

"No worries." He grinned fully and her toes curled. "What about earlier this morning? Guess I should be thanking you."

She shrugged a shoulder as she moved toward the coffeepot. "Not necessary."

She saw his smile slip a notch just before she turned away to reach for a cup. He'd read her state of mind, just like that. And he wasn't happy about it. She really wished he was a bit less attuned to her. It would make this easier.

When she had poured a cup and added milk she turned back to face what had become a strained silence.

He was standing now, the long solid strength of the man unfolded for her observation. He didn't need a scowl to add force of personality. The reality of him, present, was enough to set her pulse thumping.

She could see him thinking about what to say next before he spoke. "Yard, don't do this. I know what happened this morning. It's scary. But let's not run away from it. Maybe there's something here we missed the first time."

She shook her head and took a gulp of java before replying. "Don't make this more than it is." She lifted her gaze to his because it was impossible not to look at him. "It's a good time."

"That's all?" His expression warned her but still the

words stung. "The great Yardley I-must-be-in-charge-at-all-times Summers got laid so all's right with the world?"

She looked away from his expression. She'd forgotten that because he played nice most of the time, he had a hard-ass streak. But it hurt to have him wield it against her now.

"What did you expect, flowers and chocolate? We got off together. It was good. Okay, great. But I don't need or want anything from you."

"That's not what you said four hours ago."

He was closer now, and moving closer than she was comfortable with. He stopped before her and lifted a hand slowly to shift a swatch of her damp hair back from her shoulder. His hand settled in a light caress on her shoulder. *Uh-oh.* She could handle hard-ass. Sexy seductive Kye was much harder to defend against.

He smiled again, and this time it had Yardley hearing the familiar intro to "Aloha 'Oe" played on a lap steel guitar. "Last night you said you wanted everything."

She certainly had. Now she'd had very physical proof of his everything, twice, and it still didn't feel like enough. His fingers went wandering up the side of her neck in little light strokes, and she felt sparks of a desire that weren't dwindling embers. They were ignition sparks.

She stepped back from that touch, feeling a little desperate. But he mustn't know that. She had to be cool, keep-it-together tough. "I meant in bed."

She took another sideways step and lifted her coffee cup, speaking to him over the rim. "Let me spell it out for you. I'm not interested in anything long-term. You're safe. You can go home to whatever and whoever's waiting for you."

She saw his expression go funny and wondered, just for a second, what that was about.

His jaw hardened. "You want to hear about my love life?"

"No." She didn't. She really, *really* didn't.

"Because I'm happy to share."

"I said no."

"You'll enjoy it." He folded heavy forearms across his chest. "She made a complete fucking idiot out of me."

Yardley slanted him a glance behind her cup. "Then maybe I'm a teeny bit interested."

"Let's start with the key part. I was married. We divorced four years ago."

She tried to harden her heart against the sadness edging his tone. "She threw you out?"

"I walked. She was preggers when I got back from my last tour of duty. It wasn't mine. Heard enough?"

Not nearly. How awful. Damn. "Go on."

He settled hips against the kitchen counter and crossed his legs. She didn't glance at his package deliberately. It was an ocular accident.

"She was a local girl named Healani. We married between my tours of duty. It wasn't fireworks at night or anything. We'd known each other our entire lives. After a while you stop expecting . . . crazy kinds of love." He didn't look away. He was being more honest than he needed to be.

"I was happy. And then the big news came via Skype on my last tour. She even had this blurry photo of a blob as proof." His gaze shifted away from her. "I'd always thought I'd be thrilled to hear the words, *You're going to be a dad*. Nothing. I felt zero." He shook his head, as if still unable to believe it.

Yardley bit her lip, winced. "What happened?"

"She was pretty far along by the time I got home. Two weeks after I returned stateside, the boyfriend calls, tells her he wants her and the baby. That's when she confesses the truth to me. Baby's not mine. It was Christmas Day." He looked back at her. "That's when I finally felt some emotion."

Crap. He'd been really hurt. She could see the lingering effects of it now in the tautness of his mouth and the tightness around the eyes. "I'm sorry, Kye."

He shrugged. "The hardest part was dealing with everybody else. She left the island with Baby Daddy without a word to anyone. Not even her family. Everybody'd bought us all this baby stuff for Christmas, in preparation. I gave it all back. I haven't been back to Hawaii at Christmas since."

Yardley didn't know what to say to that. He was sharing his most intimate pain but she wasn't ready to share David. It wouldn't change anything, for either of them. She changed the subject. "I heard you tell the sheriff you served with Law in Afghanistan. Is that where you met my brother?"

Kye nodded but his eyes hadn't lost that old-wound pain. "I was there the day he was wounded. Haven't seen him since. He's rejected my calls and messages for the past four years."

"But he sent you here. Why would he do that?"

Kye looked like he wasn't going to answer. "Law said I was the only one he trusted."

"Why?"

"He knows I'll take care of business." He made full eye contact. "After they were attacked, I'm the one who had to shoot Law's K-9, Scud."

Stunned, Yardley tried to digest that, in all its implications. The death of Law's military police K-9 had figured greatly into her brother's PTSD issues. "Law said Scud was wounded, too, and went a little mad trying to protect him from even his squad members."

He nodded slowly. "Tried to bite the medics who needed to get to Law before he bled out." There were a lot of emotions vying for dominance in Kye's expression. "It was Scud's life or Law's."

The gruff pain in his voice raked up her spine. He wasn't cutting himself any slack for that decision, even after all this time.

She touched his crossed arms with the gentlest of touches. "It was a fucked-up situation, Kye. No good options. You did what you had to do to save my brother's life. Thank you."

His gaze shifted to her hand where her thumb instinctively brushed along his forearm in comforting strokes. Then it rose to her face. "You Battises try to have the world your way. Even your friendships occupy little compartments in your minds that you open and close when it suits you. It makes it hard for those of us who care about you."

Those of us who care about you.

The words echoed inside her mind. Jori, Law's new lady friend, had said something similar when dealing with Law. An hour ago she would have been happy to hear that hint of caring in Kye's voice. Now it only made her feel worse. There were other considerations. There was David.

She almost reached for the phone in her pocket before she stopped herself. She would have known if there was a message. It would have pinged and vibrated.

She turned and reached for the coffeepot to refill her still mostly full cup. "Don't start rearranging reality, Kye. Law is the reason you're here, or you'd never have come back. It's been twelve years. Where was the interest in me for those twelve years?"

"Hawaiians have a saying. *Aloha mai no, aloha aku.*"

She glanced over at him. "What does that mean?"

He gave her something short of a smile. "Look it up."

"Right." Yardley nodded. On autopilot because, suddenly, she wasn't certain any longer about anything.

She couldn't feel for David what she did and make peace with her actions with Kye this morning. That had been too intense, went too deep, had gotten past all her barriers. Even ones David never touched. What a mess.

She'd thought love would make every other man a shadow in her thoughts and feelings. It's what everyone said. *You'll know. Without a doubt. When you're in love.*

Maybe she didn't have the capacity to love that way. Perhaps she wasn't able to love the way other people did. Full-on and completely. Perhaps David had felt it, too. And that's why it had taken him so long to reach out again. She'd hurt him. Just as she was about to hurt Kye. But she owed him honesty. She owed him in return for his revelations of his private life.

She turned to face him. "You must know there's someone in my life."

"Dr. David Gunnar. Law told me."

Hearing Kye say David's name gave her a jolt. "What else did Law say?"

"I know you guys were hot and heavy for a while. Law mentioned something about a possible wedding."

"That's never been in the plans."

"Whatever." But the edge of his lips curved enough to let her know she'd been played for information. He reached out and touched her again, this time with warm possessive hands on her upper arms that felt wonderful even through her clothing. "He's been gone three months. He has nothing to do with us."

"He has everything to do with us." She backstepped but he held her in place without exerting any effort. This wasn't going the right way. By being nice, he was seeing weakness in her. And that panicked her. She needed to be strong.

She tossed back her head. "I was pretending last night. Pretending you were him. That I wasn't alone." The moment the words were out of her mouth she wanted to take them back.

Instead he pulled her toward him. Until inches separated them. "When you're scared you say things you don't mean, Yard. I don't think you could do what you did last night if you didn't have feelings for me. That wasn't just sex last night. I've had a lot of 'just sex' in my life. That wasn't it."

"Maybe." Her voice sounded suffocated. "But it doesn't matter. I'm not like other people. I don't know how to be in a relationship. My father—"

"Was an abusive asshole." He paused to let her recover from the shock. "So you—what? You decided you'd hide in relationships with unavailable men so you don't have to commit?"

"How—?" *How could he know that?*

But he was looking at her with those golden-brown eyes that saw more than any man had a right to see. His hands held her in a hard grip but his voice turned soft and low. "I know you, Yardley. We didn't know each other long the first time. But we knew each other when our emotions still rode the top of all we said and did. Then somewhere, as the years passed, you got so busy trying to prove yourself that you've lost touch with who you really are. Last night wasn't about this Doctor David guy. It wasn't even really about me. It was about you. What are you afraid of finding out about yourself?"

She tried to twist away. "Stop."

"Sorry. No. Next argument."

"If you don't stop I'll sic Oleg on you."

"No you won't." He was smiling at her in a strangely tender way. "Besides, he likes me now. I've walked him twice. We bonded. Over poop. So, you know, it's serious."

He was being nice, and kind and funny. It scared her to death. Losing David hurt. Losing Kye just might kill her.

She jutted out her chin, trying not to notice how it brought her mouth even closer to his. "I will call your tutu."

"My grandmother?"

"Yes. You said she taught you that to dishonor a woman is to dishonor one's self."

"You remember that." His voice had a funny hitch in it. Then the aloha heat of his smile was back. "You like me, Yardley. Maybe I'm not *the* man, but I'm proof that this doctor's not the one, either. He's gone. Move on. Let's see what we could have."

Reality dropped on her with a thud. "I've heard from Dr. Gunnar. This morning."

"Nice try. Third ploy."

She reached into her sweater pocket and pulled out her phone. She held it up between them. "This is why I wanted my phone back. Only David has the number. He sent me a message this morning."

Kye looked at the phone as if it were a grenade. "Show me."

"Not that you deserve to see it but here." She punched the buttons to bring up the message.

He squinted at it. "It's a music video."

She shrugged. "This is how we communicate. We use song titles to plan meetings."

She saw him shut down. Nothing to see there. And then she remembered, he'd once been military police, in law enforcement like nearly every other man in her life.

When he'd heard thirty seconds of the song he looked at her with a serious expression. "This doesn't say anything. Not where he is. Or what he's been doing. Or even when or if you'll see him again."

"It tells me he's alive." She sounded defensive. She felt defensive. "He's okay. And he doesn't want me to worry."

Kye snorted. "What a guy. After three months of silence you get music from a dickhead. So what? You're going to sit on your hands some more and wait until if and when he condescends to get in touch again?"

"You sound like he ghosted you, instead of me."

That brought him up short. "He let you stew for months, Yard. You were worried enough to contact the feds. Does your precious doctor know or even care about that? Or is he so wrapped up in his world, whatever it is, that he just fits you in when he can?"

"Don't say things like that. You don't know him."

"He's no paragon, Yard. I've bailed on women before. I'm not proud of it but I know that when a man doesn't make it his business to stay in touch, it means he's not attached in any serious way. He saw you as a target of opportunity."

The angrier he got, the calmer she became. "Dr. Gunnar is nothing like you. He's a serious man. He's a professional who doesn't play it safe. Unlike you, who spends his time guarding holiday vacationers from avalanches that never happen. Running around playing ski bum. Probably hitting on girls young enough to be your daughter." She saw him flinch and kept throwing verbal jabs. "David save lives every day in scary places. He's smart and educated and passionate and committed. He's everything—"

"—but here. He's not here. I am. You're with me."

He kissed her, hot and deep, not waiting to see if this was what she wanted, but knowing instantly it was what they both needed.

Yardley didn't think of resistance. The heat licking through her was still too strong, the memories of half-light lovemaking too new and fresh to resist the wonder of losing herself in the embrace of his lips.

His kiss was so needful all she could do was hang on and ride. And he took her everywhere, the stroke of his tongue on hers as persuasive as the sexual tension of his body, braced for action but not actually touching hers. She locked her own body into a rigid posture, fighting with everything she had not to give in to the so-easy need to melt into him, fit her body to the harder contours of his. But letting nature take its course would completely derail any self-respect she had left.

Think of David. Think of— Think.

When he lifted his head, Kye looked as hot and confused and needy as she felt. But a whole lot more certain about what exactly he wanted, and how to get it.

He brushed a finger across her mouth. "Your head and heart aren't saying the same things."

She curled fingers into his hair though she had no idea

when she'd snaked her arms about his neck. "You mean my head and my body."

He shook his head, looking more serious than ever. "Your body, like mine, isn't to be considered trustworthy. It's about your heart. Because when I tune your words out, Yard, what your eyes say isn't even close to the trash talk."

She slid her arms from his neck. She wasn't going back to bed with him. No matter how much she ached to do so. And she ached.

"You don't know me that well."

"I'm trying."

He rubbed a hand down his face. "I know some of what's made you so tough. But surviving has changed you. And not all for the better. You'd make a great drill sergeant. But you know shit-all about being a woman." He saw the stricken look on her face. And it stunned him. "Look, I didn't mean it like—"

"No. You meant it." She backed up a step, forcing herself not to bolt. "And that's okay. We're done." She turned and walked away.

Kye let her go because what he was thinking was insane. What was trembling on his tongue was the admission that he liked her just the way she was. Thought she was the sexiest, most female woman he'd ever set eyes on. Tough made her better. The challenge to get her coal-black eyes to smolder with sexual surrender called to everything male in him. Gave him a rush of primitive satisfaction. He liked her as much as he had the first time.

Hell. If he was being honest with himself, he liked her more now.

CHAPTER FIFTEEN

Agent Jackson stared at his breakfast on the desk of his D.C. office. It was a ham sandwich from the night before. It was cold. It was thin. It was—no other word for it—sad. A stingy smear of mustard formed an adhesive that after refrigeration tore the center out of the piece of white bread he lifted to inspect the sandwich's insides. No lettuce. No tomato. No fresh cranberry relish. Worst of all, no crackling bits that made a fresh ham sandwich worth eating.

Jackson's assistant poked his head through his boss's doorway. "Sir, we've had contact with Dr. Gunnar."

Jackson dropped the sandwich, forgotten before it hit the foil it had come wrapped in. "Where?"

"He called the U.S. marshal's office in Phoenix. They're on line two."

Jackson wiped his hands and picked up the phone. "Tell me everything."

"Dr. Gunnar called just after five a.m. local time and identified himself."

"You're sure it was him?"

"He gave us his safe word."

"Did he say where he is and why?"

"No, sir." The officer on the other end of the line made shuffling-paper sounds, no doubt checking his notes. "Dr. Gunnar said he 'felt claustrophobic and had to get away.' He went on to say he'll be returning to custody shortly."

"Sounds rehearsed." Jackson glanced at his clock and did the math. "Why did you wait an hour to notify me?"

"We're a bit busy here tracking the call." The deputy marshal finally sounded annoyed. He must have had about the same amount of sleep Jackson had had. "We just got confirmation that the call came from a prepaid phone he purchased here in Phoenix. It may take a few hours but we should be able to trace it. We do know he's not in the immediate area."

"A search won't help you. He'll have dumped it after that call. Have you checked to see what other calls he made before he called your office?"

"There was only one other. An unlisted number in Virginia."

"Another burner phone. I need you to keep a tight lid on this. Oh, and if Dr. Gunnar should call again, patch him straight through to me. Only me. Got it?"

When he'd hung up Jackson squeezed his right eye shut, the better to concentrate. Virginia was where Yardley Summers lived. Coincidence? He'd bet a month's salary it wasn't.

He smiled when his assistant appeared in the doorway a second time. "Get DEA agent Glaser on the line. The Summers woman has just become a person of interest."

CHAPTER SIXTEEN

Fine ice particles sifted through the midmorning air. More shards than snowflakes, they stung Yardley's face as she and Oleg made their way across the field where four inches of white stuff had fallen during the night. Judging by the tinkling sounds of the iced branches of distant trees, the temperature was well below freezing. The sun was up, barely. Its light and potential warmth were being shouldered aside by slate-blue clouds bringing the promise of more snow. Not that the weather was ever a factor in the decision to train at Harmonie Kennels. K-9 teams needed to be prepared to work in all weather, all conditions, at any time.

They weren't doing endurance today but as her boots crunched through the layer of ice beneath the snow, she wondered how Oleg would handle the change of terrain. Dogs, even well-trained K-9s, were notorious for not wanting to do their poop duty on snowy ground. Often they had to be taken out hourly after the first snowfall until they adjusted to the idea that the only options until the thaw were slick and cold.

She bent and unleashed him then gave his coat a good scrubbing with her gloved hands. "*Va porshed.*"

Uninterested in her affection, Oleg danced away from her touch after a few strokes and bounded off a few yards, kicking up the fresh snow as if it pleased him. Then he turned, going perfectly still, and gave the distant stand of trees his full attention. She wondered with a shiver of remembered fear if he had known, as she now suspected, that Stokes had been hiding there watching them the day before. If so, she'd failed to pay attention to his alert. She didn't do that now. Despite the fact that she knew Stokes was in the county jail, she stared at the tree line with her full attention. Nothing stirred in the blue shadows beneath winter-bare limbs that the snow had thrown into sharp relief.

After a few moments more, Oleg turned back and with a sharp high bark bounded toward her and grabbed at the leash dangling from her hand. He was stronger than he looked and almost pulled it out of her hand. He growled and released it before she could correct him. Then he ran behind her and play-attacked her from behind, growling and using his teeth to tug at her coat hem.

As Yardley swung around in surprise, Oleg grabbed her sleeve and tugged then released before he danced away.

"Oleg—" She stopped herself. She didn't want to give him a hard command because she sensed he wasn't really attacking her. But he was moving quickly around her, growling and jumping against her as if he was testing her for vulnerable spots. He growled and snarled but did not sound angry. He hadn't done this before with her.

Yardley suddenly laughed in understanding. He was playing. The snow seemed to have invigorated the Czech wolfdog. He was practically prancing across the frozen earth like a pony.

She tucked the leash away—a serious tool for serious training—and took several strides away, pretending to ignore him.

Oleg stopped, checked the terrain for a few seconds, then came after her, leaping up repeatedly as he soft-mouth-grabbed at her coat from behind.

She dropped to her knees and began pushing him away with a straight arm and the flat of her hand each time he leaped on her, snarling and growling but only barely nipping at her with his teeth. Even so, he played rough, thrusting his full muscular body weight against her. More than once he almost knocked her over.

He continued scrambling around her to throw her off center. Then when he had found a weak spot, he'd nip in and grab her coat or hoodie and tug in a kind of catch-and-release tag. Her coat would be in tatters if she allowed him to continue. But his playfulness was a good sign. The first from Oleg that signified that he was adjusting. She was becoming more than another alpha he was trained to obey. They were becoming friends.

Determined to defend herself in a playful way, she grabbed up handfuls of snow and packed them into a ball to toss at him.

Sensing this was a new game, Oleg leaped up to catch the snowball in his mouth. It disintegrated and he was left switching his head left and right, as if he expected to see it bouncing away. She quickly made a new one and tossed it. Again Oleg stretched up in a graceful leap to snatch it out of the air. This time it hit him full mouth and shattered, pasting his muzzle in flakes. He shook it off and barked, ready to go again.

She threw three more before he went still and swiveled his head, listening. After a second, he turned away from her, tail curving up and ears going forward.

Yardley paused to follow his gaze. This time he stared at the bunkhouse. She frowned. Kye had been prepared to bunk there the day before but had ended up sleeping beneath her roof. And she in his bed.

Just the thought gave her a hot rush she had to work to ignore. *Not now*, she told her unreliable emotions. She needed space from all things Kye.

She glanced back at Oleg. He was growling, low. The ridge hair on his back had lifted. High alert.

She glanced back toward the house. Instinct told her to go and get Kye. She slapped the instinct down because she was certain that it was more about an excuse to be near him again than it was about the need for help. She'd never hesitated to walk her property before. She wasn't going to ask for help now. Not when she had Oleg with her. "Oleg. *Knoze!*"

He assumed the heel position so that she could reattach his leash. But he never fully broke concentration on the bunkhouse, glancing from her to it and back, waiting for a command to search. A rill of anxiety snaked up her spine. Could there really be something going on there? Occasionally hikers cut through her property when they thought no one was about. Once, when all the staff was away, local teenagers had broken into the empty bunkhouse to drink beer and party. She'd returned to find a dozen underage drinkers being held hostage by two of the Belgian Malinoises who'd freed themselves to patrol the kennel grounds. K-9s were nothing if not resourceful.

She hadn't trusted Oleg yesterday, to her regret. But Oleg was in stealth mode now.

Feeling the first pump of adrenaline, she patted her pocket for her phone. It was there. If she needed help, it was a speed dial away. She could do this, inspect her own property. Meanwhile, no trespasser, if there was one, would get past Oleg to her.

She found the main door to the bunkhouse unlocked. Another bump of excitement pumped up her heartbeat. She wouldn't have thought Kye was the type to leave a door unlocked. But perhaps in all the excitement of the night before he had forgotten. She ran a gloved hand over the latch. It did not feel jimmied. She pushed the door a little wider.

Oleg was there before her, wedging his strong lean body through the opening. Unlike a police K-9 who would have announced his presence with ferocious barking, Oleg simply simmered on low growl. Covert on alert.

Czech wolfdogs didn't protect property. They would watch a thief steal everything in a house, empty but for them. But if a wolfdog perceived ill will in someone sneezing in the direction of his handler, the sneezer might need a lot more than a tissue to mop up the response. Oleg was reacting to someone. Not something.

Yardley kept a tight grip on the leash he was straining against. Along with her growing anxiety she realized she felt a rush of excitement. Though she'd taught hundreds how to, she'd never actually cornered a suspect in real life. *Those who can't, teach*. What a stupid cliché.

She could so do this. She needed this. After Stokes, she was determined to prove to herself she could face anything, when prepared. Oleg's presence would be enough to hold an intruder at bay, if need be.

I've got this.

In some unexpected kind of way, the night before was spurring her courage now. She was nervous but that didn't mean she would live in fear. It wasn't her style.

Oleg pulled her toward the door of the first bedroom, stretching as far ahead as possible, silent now but riveted on the room beyond. She saw why before she reached the doorway. Alarm zipped up her arms. They weren't alone.

A man was propped up on a bunk against the far wall. His denim-clad legs were half sprawled off the mattress. Melted snow mixed with mud dripped from heavy boots onto the planked flooring. She knew it was a man by the shoe size and the heavy corded thighs pulling tight against his denim. She couldn't see his face. His head was in shadow against stacked pillows. He was still. Very still. Asleep?

She took a step forward, trying to see who he was. Oleg had bared his teeth, sharp fangs glistening in the meager light. He barked once, high and sharp.

The man jerked, caught himself in what sounded like a painful choked-off cough, and opened his eyes. A pale gaze met hers from across the dim room. And then his tight mouth stretched and his teeth showed. "I knew you'd find me."

Yardley froze, uncertain that her eyes weren't playing a cruel trick on her in serving up the sight of the man she'd been longing to see for months. "David?"

"God. It's good to see you." He paused, seeming to

need to catch his breath. Yet so far, he hadn't expended as much energy as needed to sit upright. "You didn't bring your boyfriend along, I hope."

"Who?" Her confusion seemed to please him, for his smile deepened.

"I'm asking if you came alone?"

"Yes." The shock was wearing off, leaving Yardley a little dizzy with joy, but something held her back from launching herself at him.

Are you alone? That kind of question was asked only when it mattered. If it mattered now, it meant he was in trouble. And that made her hesitate.

She stuffed away the feelings of relief and joy that had come bursting out of her at the sight of him. None of those thoughts and feelings were helpful at the moment. Not until she knew why he was here. For her, or for another reason?

"You can call off your dog. I promise I don't bite." His teeth gleamed in the dim light. "Much." His voice sounded stronger now but he still hadn't moved.

Yardley glanced down and double-fisted the thick leash that Oleg strained against, eager to put himself in charge of the encounter. "*Lehni!*"

The K-9 didn't so much as glance back at her but ceased straining against the leash. "*Pozor.*"

As soon as Oleg lay down facing the doorway to guard it, she dropped the leash, assured that they wouldn't be disturbed without warning.

She turned back to David, still ten feet away. Her feet wouldn't move forward. Details and context, that's what she taught her handlers to stay prepared for when working a dog. She felt like a K-9 herself, all senses on alert as her gaze roamed the man she'd been searching for against everyone's advice.

He wore a cheap puffy jacket, plaid shirt, and jeans. Nothing like the casual but expensive clothing she'd most often seen him wear. The hard angles of his jaw and slash of dark brows were the same. As was the shock of choppy hair streaked blond in places by the sun. There were changes. The pleats around his eyes and mouth were etched more deeply. But it was his eyes that made her draw careful breaths. They weren't the same. The once clear-sky-blue gaze of a man accustomed to making life-and-death judgment calls with confidence was clouded. Something significant had changed. It electrified the space around them.

"Did you get my text?"

She nodded and made her voice sound casual, as if he'd just dropped by without notice and rung her bell. "Why are you here, David? What's going on?"

He frowned. "Aren't I welcome?"

"Of course. But it's weird. Three months of silence and suddenly you show up here. Why the silence? Where have you been?"

"Come closer." He held out his hand to her, seeming to sense her reluctance. "You're not afraid of me?"

She crossed her arms and cocked a hip. "You haven't answered my question."

He patted the mattress with his left hand. "I'd rather not shout."

That's when she noticed that something dark streaked the red-and-cream-striped coverlet on his right side. Then her eyes homed in on the dark-rust-red spill from a tear in his jacket's right sleeve above the elbow. Blood.

She gave up the pretense of indifference and came toward him. "You're hurt."

"*Shhh.*" He lifted his good arm and pulled her down beside him. "I'll survive."

Yardley didn't think of herself as squeamish but at the sight of his bloody arm things took a nasty turn in her mind. All of them translating into danger. A dozen questions rushed to mind. Who wanted to hurt him? And why? Why was he hiding? Because, obviously, he was hiding. Most of all, why had he come to her? But that couldn't be her first consideration.

She glanced with a troubled expression toward the doorway that Oleg was guarding.

His left arm slid across her possessively to hold her by the waist as she perched on the edge of the mattress. "I thought you'd be happier to see me."

Yardley pinned him with a stare that made even marines follow her orders. "Tell me what's going on, David."

He seemed surprised by the hardness in her tone, which made her regret it. She should be worrying about him. She touched his face. "You're hurt. I need to know how to help you."

He closed his eyes and turned his face into her caress, his stubble tickling her palm. "It's nothing. I was just in the wrong place at the wrong time." His voice had begun to get sketchy again, as if breathing was a chore. He frowned suddenly. "What happened to your face? Jesus! Have they already been here looking for me?"

He began to sit up but she stopped him with a hand on his chest. "No, David. I'm fine. But you're not. Let's talk about you. Who's looking for you?"

"That's not important. Now."

Not happy with his answer, Yardley glanced again at Oleg, who had stood up but made no move or sound. "Could you have been followed?"

"No. I made certain of it."

When she looked back at him David smiled at her, and a familiar tide of longing rolled through her. But she'd spent her life around men and women who knew how to prioritize needs over feelings. "How can you be sure of that?"

He grimaced, definitely in pain. "I just know. Like I know there's a man here with you. Who is he?"

Yardley's turn to be surprised. "His name's Kye Mc-Garren." She felt herself blush as she mentioned Kye.

David didn't relent. "Is he responsible for what happened to your face?"

"No. He actually— I don't want to talk about a few bruises. I want to talk about you. I thought something had happened to you." Her gaze strayed again to his bandaged arm.

"I'll tell you everything. But first." He scooped a hand behind her head and brought her head down to his.

At the touch of his mouth heat shook through her. His mouth was hungry and hard, as if he were imprinting her with his taste and touch. Or reminding her why he was here.

Familiar passion surged through her. After all, they'd been together for more than a year. It was a good kiss. It was what she'd been waiting for, everything she expected. What she'd been hoping to recapture, needed desperately to make things whole again. This was it. The real deal. But it felt strange, all the same.

Something had changed. She had changed.

His eyes were heavy as he gazed at her, blue eyes now

harp and bright with desire. "God, I've been waiting to do that for three months."

"Me, too." The words came automatically but felt false on her lips. She hoped he wouldn't notice. Because it was no longer true.

She was good at many things but she wasn't a good liar. Even that much had her conscience squirming as she pulled back from him. Because somewhere in the middle of that kiss, Kye's face had slid into view behind her closed lids.

Confused and more than a little off kilter, she shifted her gaze to the blood on his jacket and winced. There were more important considerations than her feelings at the moment. "You're bleeding! What can I do to help?"

"I need to know a few things first."

He was watching her intently, as if looking for a tell if she'd lie. This was a new side of him, but one she suspected was necessary in the world in which he worked. "Has anyone been asking about me?"

He wouldn't be put off this time. "Yes. An FBI agent and a DEA agent were here yesterday asking questions about you. But that's because I called them first. Weeks ago," she added when his eyes widened. "You were missing and I was worried."

His eyes narrowed until his blue irises looked like chips of ice. "What did you tell them?"

"The truth. That I hadn't heard from you in three months."

"What did they tell you?"

"Nothing, at first. And then about a week ago I got a call saying they had learned that you had applied for a visa to leave the country permanently. Is that true?"

"No. It was a cover."

"For what?"

When he didn't answer immediately, Yardley glanced down at the makeshift bandage around his right biceps again. It was oozing, which meant the wound was still bleeding. She glanced back to catch his expression as she voiced her worst fear. "Did someone in law enforcement do this?"

His brows rose. "Are you hoping your guy's turned romantic outlaw?"

"Don't joke, David. This is serious."

"You're right." He touched her face very gently with his left hand, rubbing his thumb lightly across her lower lip. "Those bruises are less than a day old. Are you certain you're okay?"

She grabbed his hand to still it. "I'm not a fragile flower who has to be distracted from reality, David. Tell me what the hell is going on."

"I was just about to ask the same question."

Both she and David turned toward the doorway at the sound of Kye's voice.

CHAPTER SEVENTEEN

"Kye. I'm glad you're here." Yardley scooted off the bed but the man on it refused to release her hand. "We need your help."

"Who's we?"

"This is Dr. David Gunnar."

Kye stood stock-still. Concern had sent him looking for Yardley when she didn't immediately return from her walk with Oleg. They could have been working in a classroom because the weather had turned nasty, as expected. But after all that had occurred within the past twenty-four hours, he wasn't taking any chances.

Now he wished he'd come looking for her a lot sooner. *Dr. David Gunnar. In the flesh.*

He took in the guy on the bed in a glance. Male. Fit. Probably what women would call dreamy. Kye hated dreamy. In fact, instantly, everything about the guy irritated him.

The doc's teeth were too white in a face weathered

by the elements. Even the squint lines around his light eyes seemed calculated to attract. His light hair, streaked almost platinum in places by the sun, made him look ruggedly handsome. His dirty and mud-spattered clothing should have ruined the effect. It didn't. Well bred in rustic clothing, the doc looked like a blond David Beckham.

"What the fuck are you doing here, Doc?" He added a hard glance for Yardley. She offered one right back but kept silent.

The man struggled to a seated position. "Who are you?"

"We'll get to that when it becomes relevant."

"It's okay." Yardley reached for the doc's hand. "This is Kye McGarren, a friend of the family."

Kye's attitude took a further nosedive. *Of the family, my ass. I was the guy moving hot and heavy between your thighs not three hours ago.*

He shoved that thought aside as less than helpful at the moment. He pointed at the man's bloody sleeve. "What have you got there?"

"He's injured," Yardley said tightly.

Ignoring her, Kye pointed again. "Mind if I look at it?"

Gunnar gave him a hard man-to-man look. "You know first aid?"

"MP. Two tours. Afghanistan."

The doc jerked his head once in the affirmative.

Kye produced a Swiss army knife from his pocket. "Cutting your sleeve is the most efficient way to get to the injury. Sorry if it ruins your *ensemble*."

Doc gave up a ghost of a laugh.

Kye frowned. Sense of humor. The annoyance factor with this guy just kept ratcheting up.

Kye slit the sleeve before untying the bandage and slowly peeling it back. It was stiff with blood. He was more interested in the shape of the wound it covered. He pulled in a breath at the sight that was at once familiar, but shocking when discovered at Harmonie Kennels.

He locked gazes with the doc. Confirmation was there in those steely blue depths. "He's not hurt, Yard. This man's been shot."

"Shot?" Yardley turned to David.

The man's expression went remote as it locked with Kye's. "I need to talk with Yardley. Alone."

"Not going to happen." Kye leveled him with a cold blast of distrust and pulled out his phone. "I'm calling the sheriff."

"Excuse me." Yard's voice was sharp enough to cut through the testosterone standoff. "Last time I checked this was my property. I make the decisions." She looked down at David. "You want the police involved?"

"We need to talk first."

She glanced up at Kye. "No police."

Kye rejected the first two, maybe three, thoughts that came to mind. Every one of them would be something he'd later regret. It was her eyes that won him over. There was a plea for understanding. Well, he didn't understand. But he didn't need to hurt her because of that.

"Right. You two have a chat while I find something to bind up the doc's wound. But don't take long. It's snowing like fuck out there."

"Wait. I'm coming with you. You don't know where anything is." She gave David a reassuring smile. "I'll be right back. Don't worry. Oleg will protect you."

Kye waited until they were both beyond the bunk-

house before turning and blocking Yardley's path. "V
the hell, Yard! When were you going to tell me he w
here?"

She jutted out her chin, the bruises smudging the lush beauty of her face but not dimming it. "I didn't know. I had just stumbled upon him."

"You weren't holding back earlier about your text messages?"

"Why would I lie to you?"

Kye ran a hand through his hair to dislodge the salting of snowflakes lighting there. "It's fucking obvious he's on the run, Yard. From something bad."

"I know that." She swallowed, blinking snowflakes from her dark lashes. "He was about to explain what's going on when you barged in."

Kye reared back. "So this is suddenly my fault?"

Yard brushed snowflakes from her face. "Can we do this indoors?"

"Fine. But I'm not going to back off." She wasn't listening to him, she was plowing ahead, leaving him to follow in her wake.

Harmonie Kennels' state-of-the-art facilities included, among other things, a fully stocked veterinary clinic where the needs of their K-9s could be taken care of. The small space was equipped with everything a small-animal vet might need, including an examination table, bandages, and a small fridge full of medications.

Yardley began grabbing bandages and surgical tape off the shelves.

Kye reached up to block her with his body when she reached for more. "It's an arm wound, Yard. You've got enough stuff to make a mummy out of him."

she looked up, her face flushed. Something had changed; this was no longer only about them.

The truth was there in her eyes. So alive in a face she too seldom allowed its full range of emotion. She wasn't an enigma. She was just very careful. Too careful for her own good. But now her expression was revealing every emotion running through her thoughts. There was fear. And the fierce need to protect. And affection. It just ate him up inside that it was caused by a man that wasn't him.

"What do you really know about this guy?"

She didn't answer, just started raiding drawers for tubes of ointment.

He hip-checked her reach for the stethoscope hanging on the wall. She turned a blazing glance on him that nearly set his short hairs on fire. But at least he had her attention.

"You two had a thing. I got that. But you know nothing about him but what he's told you. He disappeared for months without any explanation. Believe me, you don't know who he really is or what he really does."

"I know enough."

The reverberations of those three words made Kye sway on his feet. Law had warned him. This was the man Yard thought she wanted to marry.

He and Yard had always had a volatile history. They were like oil and vinegar. Shake them up and they became a delicious blend of emotions to satisfy their sexual appetites. But when things settled out, they were once again divided in every way that mattered. To argue otherwise would be stupid, pointless, insane.

Still, he wasn't going down without a fight.

He went toe-to-toe with her, bringing his body against

hers without laying a finger on her. She didn't back away. "Then add this into your calculation. Men don't get shot at without reason. Someone wants him dead. Do you understand what that means?"

Yard's eyes grew wider but she came back at him like a tiger. "It means David needs my help."

"And you need mine." He could feel the warmth of her breath on his cheek. It was killing him not to touch her. He reached out and pushed a lock of hair from her cheek. "The doc's in no position to argue. I'm calling the sheriff or the FBI. Take your pick."

Outrage had never had a more beautiful canvas than her face. "You'd do that to me?"

"To save your sweet ass? In a heartbeat."

She stared at him as if he had morphed into a troll. Then she shoved her armload of supplies against his chest. "First you need to finish what you started. Don't drop anything. And try to keep up."

"I like the way you say *Please, oh please, don't abandon me, Kye.* Yep, when you plead for help, it just goes all over a guy in a warm and fuzzy way."

She tossed the middle finger over her shoulder at him as she moved on to the next room to get antibiotics. But he would swear he caught the edge of a smile on her face as she turned the corner.

"I can do that." Yard was watching Kye slit the rest of the sleeve of the doctor's flannel shirt in order to get to the rear wound.

"You're emotionally involved." Kye didn't look up from what he was doing. "Don't-give-a-damn trumps emotionally involved. If you want to help you can boil water."

"Screw you. I'm staying."

David looked back and forth between the pair. "You sound like an old married couple."

"Do not," they replied in unison.

Kye scowled at his patient. "If you can't take the pain, let me know."

He levered the doctor's arm high to check the back of his biceps. Then he pulled out a penlight and bent close for a better look at the injury.

By the time the examination was done, Gunnar was sweating, and it wasn't from the temperature. But his voice was steady and his gaze direct. "How bad is it?"

"You know more than I do, of course. But I'd say it's an ice-pick injury."

"Ice pick?" Yardley looked confused. "I thought he'd been shot."

"It means the bullet passed through my arm." David reached out his good hand to her. "I agree. I did a preliminary examination first chance I could. I could tell by the blood flow that the bullet didn't sever an artery. And the bone's not broken."

"Still, it did damage, Doc." Kye tried not to stare at the way Yardley was smoothing the hair back from the man's face. But he was jealous. So green he made the Hulk look jaundiced. "You've got a lot of swelling, and judging by the heat around the wound, infection could be an issue really soon."

Gunnar was swearing softly by the time Kye finished rebandaging the arm. And his complexion seemed to be draining away behind his deep tan. He needed liquids, and probably some kind of sedative. But he wasn't complaining.

"Think you can scare up some painkillers from the

clinic, Yard? I figure Dr. Gunnar will know which he can safely take and at what dose." He glanced at his patient. "Of course, you won't get the cherry flavoring."

Yardley passed a worried glance between the two men before she turned to leave.

"Take Oleg. For safety."

She nodded, grabbing the dog's leash. Lily had long ago curled up under the bunk the doc occupied.

When she left, Kye turned to David. "Start talking and make the words count."

Gunnar watched Kye for a moment, and Kye knew he was weighing his options. "How long have you known Yardley?"

Kye glanced at the door. Yardley would make that the fastest trip possible. "I trained under her father about a dozen years ago."

"Why do you call her Yard?"

"All her friends do." The doc was getting exactly one more question before it was his turn again.

"You're more than a friend."

Kye held the man's gaze. He knew what he was asking. "We've got a lot of shared history. First her father. Then I served with her brother in Afghanistan."

The doctor blinked. "I didn't know she had a brother."

"If you want to know more about Yard, you'd better ask her."

A sketch of a smile appeared on Gunnar's face. "She's a very independent and private person. It's one of the things I like best about her."

Kye flicked him a look. "Let's cut to the chase. I haven't called the authorities because she asked me not to. But I don't trust her judgment about you. You put her through hell. So you don't get to come here with your wounded-warrior act and lean on a woman whose only real flaw, in my opinion, is her weakness for you. You need to tell the truth about what's going on. Then let her decide if she wants to be part of your bullet-dodging world. Do we understand each other?"

"That's a lot of talking for an uninvolved man."

"Yeah. I work alone a lot. You should ask my dog Lily about how I can chatter on."

"You have feelings for Yard."

"Well, I'm just a touchy-feely kind of guy."

"Does she know?"

"If it mattered do you think I'd be talking to you instead of hauling your ass out of here?"

Gunnar gave him a long look. "I haven't done anything illegal."

"Tell Yard the whole truth. She's a big girl. She can deal. If she wants to. If she doesn't, I'm going to be a bigger problem than anything you've got going now."

Yardley came back then, moving in a hurry, Oleg at her heels. "I found several meds that might work. But we need to move David to the house. It's freezing in here. And the weather is getting worse."

CHAPTER EIGHTEEN

Yardley sat beside her bed watching the handsome man propped up on her pillows. How many times during the last three months had she lay in this bed wishing David could be here with her? Now he was. Yet all she could think about was being overheard by the man on the other side of the closed bedroom door.

Maybe that was because what David had explained to her so far about what lay behind his sudden disappearance was a long way from reassuring. The fake drug industry, that's what David had set himself against. He was a witness in a government task force to take down traffickers in bogus pharmaceuticals. She didn't have to ask if it was dangerous. He'd been in protective custody, waiting until he could give testimony in a trial. And when he left, he'd been shot. She had a thousand questions but he was very weak, and getting more so by the moment. There was one, at least, that demanded an answer.

Her gaze strayed to his wound. "You haven't told me who shot you."

"The less you know the safer is it for everyone." His expression was strained by pain since she and Kye half carried him to the house. He was gray-faced by the time they got him into bed. He had rallied a little after sips of Gatorade, green tea, and a couple of the heavy-duty pain meds she'd found in her bathroom cabinet. She'd kept them after healing from a muscle pulled while demonstrating how to rappel down a thirty-foot wall with a K-9 strapped on.

"You've got to give me something, David." She locked eyes with him. "Why did you come here?"

"You." His smile winked in. It didn't have a firm perch on his lips.

"I never gave you any personal information. How did you know how to find me?"

"The FBI." He closed his eyes, the effort to speak taxing him. "They told me you had come to them for help finding me." His eyes opened again, searching hers with a seriousness she'd never before seen from him. "Is that true?"

She nodded, feeling acutely uncomfortable. "If that's the only reason you came, you shouldn't have."

His smile turned tender. "That's my Yardley. Prickly as a cactus and still as intoxicating as tequila shots." He sucked in a long breath. "You were looking for me. Why?"

Yardley stood up, began straightening the things arranged for him on her bedside table. Anything was better than sitting next to him feeling as she did. "I needed closure. When we parted at the airport, you could have just told me then that you were going away and not to expect to see or hear from you again." She paused to look at him, her gaze direct. "I'm an adult. I would have handled it."

"That's not what I wanted to say to you."

"Then what?"

"I love you." He laughed at her expression, a coarse hollow sound cut off almost instantly by a grunt of pain as he clutched his side.

She moved quickly back to him. "David, what's wrong?"

He hissed in a breath between clenched teeth. "Your bodyguard wasn't as thorough as I would have been. He missed diagnosing my bruised ribs."

Yardley nodded slowly and brushed the hair back from his forehead, trying desperately not to let her feelings get in the way of what she was hearing and needed so badly to understand. He was hurt more badly than he'd told her. "What can I do?"

"Love me?" He said the words carefully this time, a grin forming.

She smiled back but shook her head. "I think that's the painkillers talking, David."

"No." The word was harsh. "You were right about the last time we were together. I intended to break up with you." He took another shallow breath, but the blue of his eyes blazed a path right through her. "I knew it wouldn't be safe." He swallowed, his lids fluttering. "But that was before."

"Before what?"

Once more he seemed to rouse himself and she realized he was fighting the medications she'd given him as well his pain. He gripped her hand. "You aren't safe. That's why I'm here. You aren't safe, Yardley."

* * *

Headphones on, Kye had had two hours to do some soul searching while the doctor and Yardley were locked behind her bedroom door. At the end of the first hour, he'd used up all the reasons why he wanted to drop-kick the good doctor from here into the middle of next week. Reality began to reassert itself shortly thereafter. The upshot was, he was being a douche.

The reasons why the doctor disappeared, had gone silent, and then miraculously reappeared were none of his business. Even who'd shot him and why. Only Yardley's business. He had no right to an opinion, or to try to influence hers. He knew coming here that what Yardley wanted was to find the man who'd gone missing from her life.

Now the doc had turned up. It didn't matter what his story was. How weak-assed or un-fuckin'-believable his story was. He'd seen the look on Yard's face when they'd lowered David Gunnar onto her bed. She was totally absorbed with the man. Those where the facts. For everything else he'd have to work around them.

As for anything else that had been going on in his own mind since dawn, that was strictly his problem. Sure they'd slept together. How could he blame her for seeking a little solace after the night she'd had? Damn. She'd fought Stokes thinking that he'd abandoned her. The realization made him feel a little sick each time he remembered it. He wouldn't be able to live with himself if he hadn't shown up in time.

Kye glanced at that closed door, trying like everything not to imagine what could be going on behind it, and failing miserably. He knew what would be going on if he were in Gunnar's place. He was jealous.

No. He pushed away any wording in his thoughts that made it her fault. She'd come to him for security reasons the night before. She'd needed to feel safe. And she'd come to the only available safe place. If she'd decided that his protection included participating in the life-affirming need to merge bodies then, hell, he was one lucky sumbitch. But that didn't give him any rights or sense of ownership over Yardley Summers. He'd lost the opportunity to build on the perfect union of bodies. For a few precious hours she'd been his again. And it was her idea. Her way.

"Fuck." He hurled the magazine he'd been half reading for two hours across the room. This was not good. He was feeling things he shouldn't be feeling about a woman that he could in no way lay claim to. Because, much as he didn't want to feel this way, he could feel it eating away inside him. He was jealous as hell of David Gunnar.

He itched to call Law but he could imagine what he would have to say about recent events. He'd sent Kye here to be his sister's protector. Not his finest hour, leaving her to deal with Stokes, innocently or not. Still, nothing had changed now that his responsibilities included Yardley asking him to protect her almost-fiancé.

He looked around the living room that seemed cold despite the pile of logs snapping and hissing in brilliant flames in the fireplace. There was nothing here for him but a sorry-ass assignment that he wished he hadn't taken. Curiosity, hell! He was feeling way too many things than was good for either of them. He was only going to get his head handed to him on a platter, again.

Kye shook himself like a dog, causing Lily to lift her head and bark.

"*Shh.* Sick people inside."

She gave him her famous huff and laid back down.

Even Lily thought he was out of line.

He wagged his head and turned his music volume in the headphones up to eye-bleed territory.

Kye almost missed the knock on the front door for what it was. The person was knocking a second time when he reached the door. He flipped on the porch light and peered through the small window set in the plank door at eye level. Yardley's eye level. He had to stoop.

Beyond the door, a man in a baseball cap was bouncing on his toes and shivering. His hands were shoved in his jean pockets. He looked cold. Which made perfect sense since he wore only a corduroy jacket unbuttoned over a T-shirt advertising a microbrewery. He was lean, almost wiry, not carrying much insulation.

Kye opened the door six inches, bracing a booted foot firmly behind it. "Yeah?"

The guy flashed him a grin, revealing a gap between his right front tooth and incisor. "Hey, man. Sorry to bother you but my truck broke down back on the road." He pulled a hand from his pocket to hitch a thumb over his shoulder. "I'm Purdy Hollister, by the way. I called a buddy who lives over this way to come get me. But he says the roads are so bad he don't know when he'll get here. I been waiting over an hour and freezing my ass off in the truck. Now I'm about outta gas. Last time I leave Georgia without checking the forecast first. Friggin' Yankee weather." He paused, waiting for Kye to respond.

"You want to come in to warm up?"

"Hell yeah. If that's cool with you. Not disturbing the family or anything."

He reached for the door but Kye held it firmly. "Where's your truck?"

The guy grinned wider and pointed in the general direction of the road. "Just back up over there." He turned and picked up a sack he had evidently brought with him. "Got some New Year's cheer, if y'all partake."

Liquor in a sack. Real class. Kye gave him his MP stare, noticing that the man wasn't as young as he'd first appeared. And his scruffy jaw and country way of talking were at odds with his haircut. A very complicated fade was only partially hidden beneath his cap. Not that it mattered. "You can get warm but you can't stay here long."

"Sure, man. Just need to thaw my balls."

Kye blocked him as he was about to enter. "Also. You can't use that kind of language here."

"Oh, sure thing. Excuse me. All due respect."

"On second thought, how about we just check on what's wrong with your truck."

The guy shrugged but Kye would swear he saw a flash of irritation he quickly locked up behind a chicken-shit smile. "Aside from it's out of gas, I'm guessing the flat tire."

"You said it broke down."

"I don't think so." He suddenly glanced up past Kye's biceps blocking the open space and smiled. "Evening, ma'am. I was just here asking your husband if I could come in and get warm. My truck broke down out yonder."

Kye didn't need to look back to know Yard had, finally, come out of the bedroom. He did check with the hope that Gunnar wasn't with her. He wasn't. In fact Yardley was closing the door tightly behind her. "He can come in, Kye."

Kye raised an eyebrow at his about-to-be guest. "She says okay. I say for a short time."

The man paused to wipe his shoes on the doormat before coming in. Something at least. Kye was more interested in the footprints in the snow beyond the porch.

Gunnar's still unexplained—at least to him—appearance had him edgy. It wasn't yet fully dark, but the world outside seemed closed off. On a good day Yardley's nearest neighbors were a quarter mile away, by the road. In the glow of the NightWatcher light coming to life on the utility post nearest the house, he saw only one pair of footprints coming up the drive. The snow was swirling thickly now, filling in the imprints even as he noticed them. He guessed they were getting close to six inches. Heck of a walk for a man in a corduroy jacket. He would close and lock the gate after the guy was gone.

"Would you like coffee?" Yard's gaze flicked from the man to Kye. "I'm just going to make some."

"I'd purely love anything hot, ma'am." He moved forward with a kind of quick, jerky movement and held out his hand to her. "I'm Purdy, like I told your husband."

That was the second time he'd referred to Kye as a husband. He wondered why.

Yardley took his hand but didn't offer her own name. "I'll put that coffee on." Kye smiled at her in approval. She got it without him saying it. They needed to be careful, with everything and everyone. He needed to talk to her. Maybe she'd learned something useful.

"Take a seat by the fire, Purdy. I'll be right back."

The man had already moved to the fireplace. He reached a hand down to Lily, who had been dozing. "Hey there, puppy. How you doing?"

Lily jumped to her feet and gave a "toller scream," a series of squeals pitched in a key that could peel paint.

"What the—fudge!" Purdy jumped back, stumbling over a floor pillow.

"Careful. She's a killer." Kye barely got the words out before Lily dived behind his legs, still squealing like she'd been stepped on.

The man wiped his mouth with a hand, watching Lily as if she were rabid. "I don't suppose I could use your facilities?" He jiggled from foot to foot as if needing to emphasize the reason why.

"Top of the stairs. First door on the right."

"Right. Appreciate it." He moved quickly toward the narrow staircase back near the front door. As his foot hit the bottom step, Oleg ran up and hit the door of his kennel with his full weight followed by a blood-chilling growl.

The man sprang back from the stairs so quickly he almost fell. "God almighty!" He recovered quickly, meaning he was in good shape, and backed up a few more steps before turning to Kye. "That's some kinda crazy dog you got here."

"He's the shy one." Kye smiled. "Didn't you see the sign over the gate? This is a professional K-9 kennel. The mean ones are stashed upstairs. They've been known to tip their kennels and escape. Just keep to the door on the right and you'll be okay."

The man glanced up the stairs, seeming to measure the need of his bladder versus the need to keep his skin intact. "First on the right. Got it."

Kye watched him take the stairs, checking him for anything besides his haircut that seemed out of place. And there it was. His jean leg had hiked up, probably when he stumbled over the pillow, revealing a Ka-Bar ankle holster. Kye glanced away before the man noticed him watching.

Mouthing a curse he didn't want heard, he backpedaled toward the kitchen. It had been five years since he'd been military police. He was rusty. He should have just shut the door on the bastard. Could be nothing. Could be that the trouble he'd been wondering about had just boldly walked up and knocked on the front door. And he'd let the devil in.

Yardley came out of the kitchen just as he reached the doorway. "Coffee's—" She paused at the expression on his face. Her eyes went wide as they moved left and right past him.

Kye put a finger to his lips and made a pushing motion with his other hand to move her back into the kitchen.

Before she could backpedal, the door to her bedroom opened and David stood there, his face ashen with pain as he leaned heavily against the door frame. He locked gazes with Kye. "I know that man."

CHAPTER NINETEEN

Every hair on Kye's neck came erect as he heard a toilet flush overhead. There were only a few seconds before Purdy would appear again. No time to ask questions. Still, it didn't take a lot of brain math to put together the two and two of danger he represented. Even so, Kye's brain was calculating double-time.

Gunnar recognizes Purdy.

Someone shot Gunnar.

Someone followed Gunnar here.

Most likely candidate? That would be Purdy.

He locked eyes with the doctor. "Gun?" His question went out in a mere whisper of sound.

Gunnar barely nodded, his grip on the door frame slipping.

He pointed at Yardley, then the doc, and indicated that they should both move back into the bedroom.

Yardley gave him a defiant look, as if she had something else in mind. But he narrowed his eyes beneath lowered brows, in no mood for a standoff with her.

Gunnar swayed and moaned ever so slightly. It was the barest breath of pain, but it was enough to galvanize her.

As she moved toward Gunnar to help him, Kye leaned in. "Lock the door."

Yardley nodded and scooped an arm around Gunnar's waist. Gunnar let go of the door frame, shifting his weight onto her, and threw his good arm around her shoulders.

Kye watched them in a combination of frustration and anger sprinkled with jealousy. He didn't have time for number three on his emotional Top Ten. Once he'd pulled that door closed behind them it was about a would-be killer and him, and him without any form of protection.

The squeak of the bathroom door opening sent his thoughts snapping back to attention. A spike of adrenaline sharpened Kye's senses, pouring information into his hypersensitive brain. Even the irrelevant details came pouring in. The asshole hadn't bothered to wash his hands.

The creak on of the second-story floorboards announced that Purdy was in the hallway, about to head downstairs. Then silence. Had Purdy paused, listening before he revealed himself?

Kye's stomach flipped as he heard a soft moan from inside the bedroom. Gunnar might have done himself some damage struggling to get out of bed alone. That knowledge gave him a sense of just how desperate Gunnar was to warn them. Or at least warn Yard.

Yardley. She was now depending on him, too.

Just the thought her being subjected to more violence after what she'd been through the night before brought every instinct to protect within him roaring to life. He pushed down hesitation and brought up his army MP training, mentally dusting off the cobwebs as footfalls sounded on the steps.

Whipping around from the bedroom door, he lifted his arms and arched his back to stretch as he let out a big yawn. Something to cover himself as he scanned the partially hidden stairwell.

He glanced over in time to see Purdy's pant legs descending the stairs. The right one had been rearranged to cover the knife. Was Purdy wondering if he had seen it? Or was the knife now somewhere handier, like in his pocket? It had been a while since he'd had to disarm a man. Best not to let it come to that. Act first. Control the situation.

By now most of Purdy was visible on the stairs. His corduroy shirt was buttoned and tucked in. Less material to grab in a fight. And then his grinning face, lean with suspicious eyes, was staring at him. Coyote eyes, hungry and feral, and without compassion for its prey.

"You got a nice place here."

Kye smiled. "It goes with the job. If you like dogs."

The man gave Oleg's kennel a sharp glance and stepped off early to avoid going past. The dog was watching their guest silently with slanted eyes. "Actually, I don't."

Lily had made herself scarce. Tollers didn't like strangers or confrontation. Definitely not a fighter.

As Purdy wandered back to the fireplace, Kye wondered if he could free Oleg before Purdy realized he was about to be wolfdog bait. However, if Purdy got to his knife before the dog got to him, he could cut the K-9 to ribbons. He'd seen what a knife in practiced hands could do. A man mortally wounded before he even knew he'd been cut. No. He wouldn't risk an animal like that. There were potential weapons everywhere. The household was full of them. His mind began ticking them off.

Guns. Handguns?

Yardley must have a firearm about the place. Personal handgun in the bedside drawer, maybe. Not a good option from here. At all costs he wanted to keep Purdy from Yardley.

Shotguns. Rifles. Flares. Flash bangs.

Harmonie Kennels used guns to accustom K-9s to the sounds of pistol and rifle fire, and other things they could be exposed to on the job. But he knew that those guns were kept in the locker in the classroom building on the other side of the bunkhouse. They might as well be in Mumbai for all the good they would do him at the moment. He was going to have to get the drop on Purdy before Purdy realized he'd been made.

"Heard from your friend?"

Purdy wagged his head and half reached for his phone. He was right-handed. Good to know. "Shit— oops. He ain't answering his texts. Hope he ain't got himself in a ditch somewhere on account of the snow."

Had the man's accent changed to more folksy than before? Maybe he wasn't even a southerner. Not that it mattered. A hired killer's point of origin was fucking useless knowledge, at the moment.

"Interested in the game?"

"Sure. Who's playing?'

"Damned if I know." Kye moved with a deliberately easy stride to turn on the TV. It would cover more sounds of movement coming from the bedroom. Every shift or sigh from within scraped along his nerves.

He reached for the remote. Punched it on and then turned up the sound louder than need be, as cover.

Purdy remained by the fire, as if his whippet body could never absorb too much heat. Kye's gaze ranged beyond him.

Stacked logs. Fireplace poker.

He supposed he could say something like, *Excuse me. Need to stir the fire.* And then grab up the iron poker. But he wasn't sure he could carry off a strike with enough power to disable Purdy with one blow. A man with a gun and a Ka-Bar wasn't going to give him many chances to get it right.

Overwhelming force. That's what he needed. And to give Yardley warning time to defend herself, if need be. Please, God, let there be a loaded gun within her reach.

"That coffee smells ready. Still want a cup?"

Purdy looked up from the TV, all easy manners. "I surely do. Thanks."

Kye hated to turn his back on the man. But he called over his shoulder. "Come on in."

"Where's the wife?"

When Kye glanced at the man coming into the kitchen arch, his expression was still mild. Had he mistaken the edge in his voice?

"Primping." Whatever the hell that meant. "Have a seat. Cream and sugar?"

"Black. Thanks." Purdy sat down at the kitchen table, spreading his legs wide and resting an arm on the table-top as though he didn't have a care in the world. But Kye noticed he'd positioned himself so he could see back into the living room.

Kye eyed the knife set as he looked in the drawer for spoons. Knives weren't his thing and if Purdy saw him draw one out, he'd guess it wasn't for cutting cream.

A faint cry of pain, cut off in mid-voice, managed to penetrate the sounds of a cheering crowd on the TV. Pretending he hadn't heard a thing, Kye set a mug in front of Purdy and began to pour.

A second deeper groan—unmistakably male—jerked Purdy's head in the direction of the kitchen door. "That doesn't sound like—?"'

The shit had just gotten serious.

Purdy moved an arm as if to reach behind himself. That action had only one possible purpose. Gun.

No time to think, Kye swerved the stream of hot steaming fluid into Purdy's lap.

Purdy cried out as the scalding coffee soaked his crotch. Before he could jump out of the way, Kye swung the full metal pot up, catching Purdy just under the chin, a fully caffeinated uppercut. As Purdy grunted in pain Kye threw his full weight on the man, letting the force push the chair over as he used both hands to grab Purdy's right wrist.

They went over in the chair together. The crash splintered the chair back. Purdy cried out in pain. Maybe the broken wood had gouged him. But the man wasn't going down easy. He was a seasoned fighter even if he'd been caught completely by surprise. Kye delivered a fist jab to his throat. Purdy got in a blow of his own, to the face, smashing cartilage. Kye felt his nose give. Hot stabbing pain shot through his facial bones. Not enough to stun Kye into freeing his opponent but enough so that for a split second Kye saw that black dark sky twinkling with stars that people write about. He swallowed and tasted blood. It didn't matter. He grappled with the man beneath him, the difference in their weight alone enough to keep the man pinned. If only he could find the damn gun. But he couldn't let go of the man's arm or Purdy might beat him to it. Kye knew his advantage. He was bigger, heavier. All he had to do was keep the guy's hands off his weapons until he wore himself out.

He heard voices as if from a distance. Had Yard called the sheriff? Fuckin' A.

"Stop it! Stop moving now or I'll set my dog on you!"

Yardley's voice at Kye's back came as a total surprise. He hadn't heard the bedroom door open or her footsteps but when he turned his head slightly he saw her crouching in the doorway holding a thick leather leash with two hands. At the other end, straining like hell's fury itself, was Oleg.

The military-trained K-9 growled and jumped repeatedly against the restraint of the thick leather leash, almost yanking Yardley out of her squat. His lips were peeled back over sharp fangs in a mouth with jaws spread wide to take a full-mouth bite of his target.

"For the love of fuck!" Purdy kicked out in Oleg's general direction, panic making his eyes bulge. "Call him off!"

"Stop fighting me and turn over on your belly."

"Fuck that." Purdy tried to head-butt him. Kye ratcheted one of the man's fingers back until he heard it snap. Purdy didn't make a sound. Hardcore. But he had leverage now. He grabbed another finger. "Over on your belly. Now."

"Can't. You're sitting on me."

"Figure it out. I got nine more opportunities to persuade you."

Cursing like he was trying to win a profanity contest, the man struggled onto his side under Kye's considerable weight, and then flopped belly-down on the kitchen floor. "Fuck you" ended the tirade.

All the while Oleg was lunging and growling, sounding like the soundtrack of a monster thriller. Even Kye was beginning to feel the stress, but he didn't have time to own it or even look behind him. "Yard. You okay?"

"Fine." The word came out of her like a shot. Clearly, Oleg was taxing her, but she knew not to call the dog off too soon. The snarling rampage of canine fury at the end of the leash raised the blood pressure of every person in the room to astronomical levels. It proved too much for most civilians. They gave up. But there was still every likelihood Oleg would have to bite Purdy before he gave up.

Kye pressed his knee harder into the man's back, his right hand gripping his arm back at an angle designed to dislocate it if Purdy struggled. Then he leaned in against Purdy, applying pressure to his arm until he groaned. "I'd stay still if I were you. That Czech wolfdog's new here and not all that reliable."

Purdy craned his head around to stare at the dog. "I hear them dogs are bred to kill men."

"Is that so?" Kye leaned harder. "Yeah. He does look like he needs to bite something really bad. If you upset him it won't be me. Got that?"

Purdy nodded.

With his free hand he began to search for weapons. He found the bulge of a concealed carry over his right hip and pulled out a Smith & Wesson Shield. In a pocket he found an extra clip. He placed them both behind him and scooted them across the floor in Yardley's general direction.

Kye looked over at Yardley. She was sweating, her eyes narrowed as she monitored Purdy while her arms trembled from holding the powerful wolfdog in check. "Yard, pick up the gun."

She nodded then barked the command in Czech to call Oleg off his prey. "*Pust!*"

The wolfdog glanced back at her as if he couldn't possibly have heard right, but then he quickly returned to her side when she didn't speak again.

"*Hodny*, Oleg!" Her praise was bright and girlish but she didn't reach to pet him—the wolfdog was still on the job, hackles raised and gaze still locked on the pair of men on the floor.

Kye watched Yardley work to calm Oleg with more whispered words of praise until he seemed to work back from high find alert. Only then did she free one hand from her two-handed grip on the leash and reach down for the gun Kye had shoved her way. She picked it up carefully but confidently and looked at Kye for direction. There was fear in her gaze but resolution, too. She would do whatever he asked next.

"So now we're armed. That's a good thing." He grinned at her. "I need duct tape. Lots of it. But first secure every door."

"Right. I'm leaving Oleg with you." Yard made a motion with her hand sending Oleg into the down position before releasing his leash.

The Czech wolfdog lay down immediately but continued to growl, his teeth on display as he kept absolute focus on the pair of men on the ground.

She looked back at Kye, not asking the question in her gaze.

He nodded once. "I got this. But hurry."

"You beat your woman, big man?" Purdy snickered. "That why she moves so fast when you speak?"

Kye realized he was talking about the marks on Yardley's face. He'd stopped seeing them. But he supposed that like David, Purdy was seeing her as cowered by the bruises. Not in his eyes. In his eyes she was beautiful and strong, and sexy as hell. They'd missed the stubborn glint in her gaze that said she was ready to do whatever needed to be done.

Yardley disappeared into the living room and reappeared after a moment with a roll of max-duty silver tape. "I'll put us on lockdown."

Kye took it and wrapped several turns about his prisoner's wrists and then up his arms until his elbows were tightly pinned together behind him.

"*Ow.* I think my shoulder's dislocated. You're cutting off my circulation."

Kye jerked the tape tighter while Purdy began to struggle. "You were going to try to kill me. If I were you, I'd be grateful this is all the pain I'm dishing out."

Oleg came up a bit, nails scrambling on the floor as he assessed the situation. Both men shot wary glances over their shoulders.

"Lie still. That dog is going to bite the one he gets to first. I swear I'll be yards behind you if you so much as twitch again."

Purdy went flat on his face, as if his bones had liquefied.

When satisfied his arms were immobile, Kye scooted back slowly to where he could bind his ankles, and then removed the Ka-Bar with its sheath. Then he patted Purdy down, finding a wallet, keys to a vehicle, and a cell phone. He shoved them all into a pocket of his jeans.

Finally, Kye flipped him onto his back and straddled him again. "Let's start at the beginning. Who the hell are you?"

Purdy spat in his face. "Fuck this! You're screwed."

"Maybe. But not by you, you piece of shit." Kye tore off another short piece of tape, ignoring the blood dribbling down his face onto his shirt. "Are you really expecting backup?"

Purdy, or whatever his name was, only stared at him with an ugly grin. "Broke your nose, pretty boy. I fuckin' screwed you."

Kye blinked. "I'll take that as non-compliance."

As he reached forward, the man's bug eyes practically popped from their sockets. "What are you doing?"

Kye glanced at the tape strip hanging from his thumb. Did Purdy think he was going to tape his nose to torture him for more information? *We judge others by what we would do ourselves.* He'd heard that somewhere. Okay, this was a level of fucker he really didn't want to deal with.

He slapped the tape over the man's mouth, sealing it tight with the palm of his hand, and then quickly shifted off him on his knees on the floor, needing to put distance between them.

"What are we going to do with him?"

Kye glanced up. Surprise zipped through him. Yard stood there, tall and resolute. In the midst of the struggle to control his own emotions he'd nearly forgotten her.

"The doors are locked. Windows, too. No one else in

the house. I checked upstairs." She held Purdy's pistol pointed at the ceiling.

Kye rose to his feet, muscles and joints protesting the punishment they'd taken. He swallowed more blood before he found his voice. "You have a basement?"

She shook her head. "Cupboard under the stairs has a lock."

"Let's stow him there until the sheriff gets here."

She moved in to help him carry the man. The look on her face gave him pause. And then he realized that she was looking at his face. His nose felt like a bloody pulp that he could barely breathe through. "I'm okay."

Her dark eyes remained a moment longer, taking in the damage, until her lips thinned in a way that was painful for him to watch. But she nodded. "You're good."

At their feet, Purdy had begun to struggle a bit until Oleg sidled up alongside him. One look into the K-9's yellow eyes and he went slack.

Kye bent and gripped him under the arms while Yardley moved to his feet.

"Wait." Pulling Purdy's body up against his chest, Kye said, "If you kick that woman I will lock you and the wolfdog up in the closet together. That's not a threat. It's an absolute certainly."

Kye went first, taking most of the man's weight as they did an awkward backward dance into the living room and then to the stairs. Once Yardley opened the under-stairs door, Kye dragged Purdy into the narrow space half filled with boots and jackets and other gear.

He looked down at the bound man. "The next person to open this door will be the sheriff. Until then, you'd better be the quietest mouse in this house."

Purdy jerked his head but his eye were brimming with hatred as Kye closed the door.

Yardley waited until he had turned the key in the lock and stepped away from the door before she spoke softly. "Who is that man?"

Kye weighed his options, wanting to tell her how fucked up the situation had become now that Gunnar had arrived. How they needed law enforcement like yesterday. How lover boy had screwed up royally. How her paragon of virtue had been thinking too hard about himself to really consider the position he was leaving her in when he disappeared into protective custody. Or when he busted out, only to land on her doorstep.

He could have said that, and a lot more, and felt pretty good about destroying her illusions about Gunnar. But he didn't. Because it wouldn't do them any good. And it wouldn't make her feel better or safer. And right now, Yard was all that mattered to him.

"I can smell the rubber burning from here." Yardley crossed her arms and cocked a hip to one side. She looked determined and resolute, but her left leg was doing that nervous jig it did when she was pissed. "When are you going to stop thinking and start talking to me, McGarren?"

"Not until I get some answers myself."

Kye moved quickly past her and opened the bedroom door, his eyes fastening on the man propped up on the bed.

"What the fuck is going on?"

CHAPTER TWENTY

"Huh." Kye wiped the blood from his nose with a wet cloth then slapped the bag of frozen corn Yardley handed him against the back of his neck and angled his head back to try to stop the bleeding.

Lily entered the bedroom where he sat listening to Gunnar explain the circumstances that had brought him to Harmonie Kennels. She climbed up in his lap, doing her kitten impersonation as she curled into his stomach. She seemed to understand he was in pain. Added bonus, the warmth of his body. The thermometer hadn't crawled past freezing today and night was coming on.

Yardley, who refused to sit, stood with her back to the wall, her arms folded, the dangerously sexy curve of one hip jutted toward him in an artless invitation he knew she wasn't making. That didn't stop him from remembering the feel of her naked hips in his hands as he'd buried himself in her. Was that only this morning? It seemed like a week ago. Looking at her face, he revised.

A lifetime ago. Her gaze was sharp and focused on the man on her bed. He wished he could read her mind. Her expression was giving away nothing but serious attitude. Enough to make the room hum.

Oleg was at her side, sitting alert in his handler's pheromone cloud as his slanted eyes continually surveyed the terrain of her room. Not even an ant crawling on the floorboard was getting past him unnoticed.

Angling his gaze, Kye refocused on the problem at hand. Gunner's narrative of his good deeds and selfless attitude was giving him a headache. The man had some, if not all, of the responsibility in the danger he'd brought to Harmonie Kennels. The gnawing in his gut told Kye it probably wasn't over.

Finally Kye broke in, pain and inaction making him impatient. "So far you haven't mentioned the guy we've got stuffed in the closet."

"That's my fault." Gunnar licked his lips, his eyes dull with fever. "Before coming to see Yardley, I hired a security agent I'd dealt with overseas." A ghost of a smile laced with affection sketched his mouth. "I wanted to be certain she was protected, whatever happened."

Kye stomped on the temptation to say that her brother Law had already taken care of that by sending *him*. He needed to hear the doctor's side. "What went wrong?"

"We were on our way here when he pulled out a gun and told me there was a bounty on my head that he intended to collect."

Yardley gasped. "You didn't say that earlier."

Kye moved on before they could turn this tidbit of information into a lovers' tiff. If that happened, he'd need to gag them both and stuff them in next to Purdy while he went to see the sheriff. Because, though they seemed in doubt, that's where this was headed. He just wanted his facts straight first. "Did he say who set the bounty?"

"No, but I can guess." David sighed through some pain. "You won't like it."

"I haven't liked anything about this so far."

"Most recently I was acting as a go-between for a counterfeit drug ring and Interpol. I can identify names on both sides that their employers would like kept secret."

"Thanks for narrowing it down." The grimness in Kye's voice registered as frowns on his companions' faces. No need to say it. Their situation was becoming more and more like a plot out of a James Bond movie.

"So, Purdy." Kye hitched a finger in the general direction of the stairs. "He's your boy?"

David's gaze sharpened, the resentment in Kye's tone cutting through his own daze. "I'm sure I recognized his voice. But that's not the name I knew him by."

Kye pulled out the wallet he'd taken from Purdy. The driver's license was issued to Pruitt James Hollister. It was a good fake, if one didn't look too closely.

He handed it to David. "Is this the man?"

David took the ID, his hand a little unsteady. As he looked at the picture a "fuck" escaped through dry lips. He really needed medical attention.

"I know him as Harold Prosett Jr. He's based in Texas. Private security. He'd done work for DWB overseas. I thought he'd be trustworthy."

"They all call themselves private security for a reason. Many are no more than mercs working for hire. Their loyalty is fluid. It goes to the highest bidder. Obviously you weren't it."

"I've known some reputable men in that line of work."

Yardley said the words tightly, giving Kye a hard look as she crossed the room. She bent and picked up something and put it in Kye's hand. "Ice pack. Put that on your face."

Kye shrugged but did as he was told. She was trying to take care of him. He was just too angry to be grateful. "What else should I know about this Prosett guy?"

"I didn't tell him who I wanted him to protect or where she lived. Once he agreed to do the job, I told him I'd meet him in Richmond, Virginia. He hired the car. I couldn't exactly use my ID. I gave him directions on a turn-by-turn basis. After we entered the mountains, he suddenly turned off the road and pulled a gun on me. He said there were people in Atlanta who wanted to chat with me. I waited until he was distracted by making a turn and jumped from the car."

"Moving vehicle?" Yardley sounded shocked.

David's gaze shifted to her, a tender smile forming on his mouth. "He shot me. I was not going to win by staying in the car."

"Gutsy move, Doc." Kye sounded impressed. "How'd you get here?"

"I hitchhiked. After I crossed the highway. I took the gamble that Prosett wouldn't want to shoot me with witnesses."

"How did you explain your wound?" Yardley sounded appalled.

"I told the driver I'd broken my arm when my car went into a ditch. I needed to get home so my wife wouldn't faint when she got a call from the police or hospital. She's not good in a crisis."

"He bought that drivel?" Yardley sounded offended for all womankind.

"So how did Prosett find you?"

The doctor looked pained but, again, he didn't give an inch. "I left my cell phone behind when I bailed. Didn't know it at the time." He looked at Yardley. "This is all my fault."

"Just so you know that." The icepack muffled Kye's voice but not his anger. "You might as well have drawn a bull's-eye on her back."

Yardley rounded on Kye. "That's hardly fair or true. Everything David's done, he's done to help others. He didn't have to take on the fake pharms. He could have looked the other way, like I'm sure so many others have."

"Got it. The doc fronted a worthy cause." Kye hitched a shoulder and got a twinge in his back for it. He was going to be sore all over in the morning. Not the biggest problem right now. "But maybe you should have thought about how it would affect the people in your life before you dragged Yard into it."

She shifted against the wall. "I'm standing right here. I can speak for myself."

Gunner's gaze sharpened. "She knew nothing. That should have protected her." His eyes shifted to Yardley, his expression softening. "I had no idea that you would look for me."

"Then you don't know Yard." Kye surged to his feet, tempted to block his view of her with his body. The urge was primitive. "When Yard wants something she goes after it. Nothing gets in her way."

Her back came away from the wall. "Still here. Talk to me, dammit."

David spared her a half smile. "What's why I took her at her word when I asked her to come with me—"

"—You did that?" Kye couldn't keep the surprise out of his tone. His gaze moved from the bed to Yardley, who refused to meet his eye. "You asked her to go into hiding with you? What did she say?"

"That's enough!" Yardley swung away from the wall and faced Kye. The look in her eyes had backed down men twice her size. "What I said is none of your damn business, McGarren. You're sticking your nose in where it doesn't belong. You think it hurts now? Do it again."

Kye almost smiled. The old Yard was back online. She'd been so subdued since he'd packed Purdy in the closet, he was beginning to wonder if she was afraid of him. She only knew the laid-back happy-go-lucky Kye. She'd never met him on the job.

"He has a right to know, Yardley." David shifted his gaze left to Kye. "I never got that far. My time ran out. The feds picked me up and took me into protective custody the next day." His gaze softened when Yardley turned toward the bed. "You'll never know how sorry I am I didn't just ask you then and there."

Kye's stomach muscles contracted, hard, as he wondered what her answer would have been. He turned to her, hoping and fearing the answer was written in her expression now.

Her expression said *Go to hell*. But that was okay. She hadn't jumped in to say she would have gone with the doc. Kye let out a slow breath in relief.

Yardley moved to the bed and brushed the hair back from David's brow. "You're exhausted. We'll talk later, privately. Right now, we have decisions to make."

Kye realized the conversation had just moved on without him. He was the third wheel in a lovers' quarrel.

Something hard and heavy was solidifying in his chest. He'd been outmaneuvered. It sparked his competitive spirit.

He lifted Lily from his lap and approached the bed. Oleg turned to face him, ever on the alert.

Kye didn't as much as glance at him. "Great plan, Gunnar. But you didn't stop to think that maybe the bad guys already knew about Yard because she was looking for you. Maybe they've been watching her all along, waiting for her to uncover your whereabouts? Perhaps her inquiries were what was protecting her? They couldn't do anything to her without bringing the feds down on them."

David rallied, anger shining in his feverish eyes. "Easy for you to say. I didn't know who to trust. That's why I came myself."

Abandoning Lily, Kye leaned his fists on the bed and said in a low but menacing voice, "Right now I'm all that's standing between you and Yard, and some very bad people. That's why you're going to trust me."

Yardley turned her head to glare at him over her shoulder. But he noticed something else in her eyes, a dark tide of fear rising. It acted like a splash of ice water over him. He didn't want her frightened. He wanted her safe.

He stood up and focused on his would-be rival. He was sweating, feverish, and clearly in pain. He felt the urge to lay a reassuring hand on the man himself. Getting him medical help had just become goal *numero uno*.

"I'm calling the sheriff. And I don't give a flying fuck who in this room thinks that's a bad idea. Purdy didn't know we were on to him. But he might have called for backup after he lost Gunnar. That person will come looking for Purdy if he doesn't hear from him."

Yardley nodded. "I agree. We need to do something with Purdy and I don't need to tell a doctor that he's in need of medical attention."

David didn't argue, just stared at Yardley in a way that made Kye want to smash his face.

Instead, Kye turned and walked out.

CHAPTER TWENTY-ONE

Yardley followed Kye out into the living room. He was pacing with Lily right by his side, who was taking hurried steps to keep up with his long stride. He looked awful. Blood still dribbled from one nostril. His face was swollen and red in places. His eyes were bloodshot. And his poor nose. It hurt to look at it. He needed medical attention, too. This was her fault. She should never have let him cross her threshold yesterday.

He glanced at her, looked as if he was about to say something, thought better of it, and continued pacing.

"I know you're upset, Kye."

"Upset isn't even in the neighborhood." He paused and ran a hand through his hair, making it stick up at all angles. "I just had to take down a professional killer with a coffeepot. A goddamn coffeepot!"

Yardley forced herself not to relive all the fear she'd felt for him when she'd heard Purdy cry out and then the thud of bodies hitting the floor. She'd slammed out of the bedroom and gone straight for Oleg's kennel. If she hadn't been afraid Oleg might mistakenly bite Kye, she would simply have set him free. Precious seconds were lost attaching his leash, but she needed to control the situation.

Looking at Kye now, still so angry she'd swear she could see little puffs of steam rising from him, sent a flood of gratitude and affection and concern rushing over her. She wanted to thank him for protecting her and David. Wanted to say how much it pained her to know that she was the reason his beautiful face was a mess. But she knew he was in no mood to accept anything from her.

She'd seen how he looked at her when she'd touched David. She'd felt like Delilah must have felt after shearing Samson. The horror and shame of what she'd done to an undeserving man. A man whose bed she'd shared. She'd betrayed them both, and herself. And she didn't know how to climb back from a single second of it.

Because, deep inside where she supposed most people never wanted to look at themselves, she didn't regret any of it. She'd fallen for David. Yet she didn't regret climbing into Kye's bed when she thought David was past tense in her life.

If only Georgie were here to talk with. Far from being unable to feel too little for a man, she was suddenly brimming with so many emotions she couldn't sort them out. As much as she liked David, it took only a kiss from Kye to plunge her back a dozen years and an emotional lifetime ago to when she believed she was in love.

The rush of self-knowledge that she could feel this way surprised and exhilarated her. But was it real?

She took a step toward him, but the heightened

wariness in his gaze stopped her short. "I just wanted to say I'm sorry, Kye. About everything. Law and I should never have brought you into this. This isn't your fight."

He blinked, seemingly surprised by her words. "That doesn't matter. I'm staying with you until this is over. And, just so you know, I don't like losing."

She nodded, touched by words that weren't exactly lover-like but so Kye. "Your poor face."

He looked down at his shirt, which was soaked with his blood. Wincing, he grabbed the back of it and pulled it up. "Do you think you can get some tape on my nose that will stop some of the bleeding? My face hurts like a sumbitch."

She nodded, mouth going a little dry as his muscle-molded abs then pecs came into view. By the time his shoulders were on display she couldn't have spit if her life depended on it. She averted her eyes. "I'll get my first-aid kit."

"Hold up." She turned back as he reached into his backpack and pulled out a white wife-beater. *Hate the name. Just hate it.* But it looked, yeah, really good on him as he tugged it down over his too-tempting male torso.

He came toward her, hands going out to frame her shoulders. "I'm going to protect you, Yard. I promise. To do that, we need to get Gunnar to a hospital and law enforcement on our side. Where's Purdy's gun?"

She pulled it out of a pocket of her cargo pants.

He looked at it, noting the cartridge was full. "You have a gun?"

"I have K-9 protection." She glanced down at Oleg, who was practically sitting on her boots. "What do I need a gun for?"

"To protect both of you. You do own one?"

"Of course. But I don't like guns."

"You don't have to make out with it. How many do you have in the house?"

"One. Handgun."

"Ammo?"

"Somewhere."

"Seriously?"

"I work with dogs. Oleg can protect me from anyone breaking in."

"Oleg can't take down a bullet." He held up Purdy's gun as exhibit A.

Yardley folded her arms across her chest. "I don't think I could shoot someone."

Kye gave her a shrewd look. "You tried to take out Stokes with a hammer."

"That was different. I wasn't trying to kill him. Just make him stop."

"Purdy already shot Dr. Gunnar. If he'd been hurting your doctor friend or Oleg and you'd been armed, you don't think you'd have used it?"

"Maybe. The butt end. To save them." She stared at him before giving in to the most reluctant shrug he'd ever seen. "Or you."

Kye went still. She didn't have to say that. But she was looking at him in a way that, for a few seconds, took away the pain of his face. He mattered to her.

The moment spun on, gone as quickly as it was captured, as she spoke again. "But I'd rather not have that option."

"At least you're honest." He shrugged. "Get your gun."

"After what I just said?"

"It's for the doc. And to be clear, it works better with bullets. So find them."

She hesitated. "Do you really think someone else is out there looking for David?"

"We're talking illegal drugs. That means production, sellers, dealers, all with a shitload of money on the table. Then there's you." He gave her a slow smile. "Anyone else you pissed off lately?"

She smiled back. "Besides you?"

He grinned. "We're good."

Kye reached up to feel his nose, a ploy to keep her from reading the truth in his gaze. They were more than good. He was bleeding for her and would keep bleeding until he had fought through whatever was required to get her to safety.

She must have seen something because she reached out and touched his cheek. And then she leaned in and kissed him just behind the ear. "Poor nose," she whispered against his ear. "Let me get some gauze and tape. I'll be right back."

Kye watched her go. He was an adult. He could handle just about anything that came his way. He knew a person didn't get what he wanted simply because he wanted it. Or even deserved it. Relationships took two. But if he didn't win Yard, he wasn't sure what survival was going to look like.

Right now he needed her strong and ready to fight back. Any other conflicting emotion would only weaken her. That meant protecting her, even from himself.

She was back in a flash. "Take a seat." She pointed to the sofa. He perched on the arm. "This might hurt a bit but it will stop the bleeding." She began cleaning his nose with antibacterial wash.

He should have been planning a strategy to get them to safety. Instead, he teased himself with the sight of her, how she smelled, how she felt each time she brushed against him. If this were twelve hours earlier, he'd have busied himself peeling the layers of her clothing off her as she tended to him. He'd have taken handfuls of her breasts and held them up so that he could lick at her nipples until she groaned with pleasure. Only now, he was about to groan, and it wasn't from pain.

He made himself focus. She was a little pale, eyes revealing the fear she tried to tap down, her left leg wiggling like an ad for restless leg syndrome. She was vulnerable. A protective arm, a little squeeze, a kiss on the forehead. Maybe just a little more body contact—

He spread his legs so that she could get closer, only to suck in a breath as she unknowingly pressed her hip against his arousal. He shifted, giving her more access as she worked on his face. He was nowhere near do-gooder status. Nope. Not even a little.

Within a few minutes, she'd dried the blood and added antibiotic, then gently pushed rolled gauze pads up each nostril. He swore under his breath more than once but didn't stop her until he was taped up to hold them in place. Only then did he move.

"Thank you." He sounded like he had a bad cold but he didn't care. His hands came up with the intention of framing her waist. It was stupid. She wouldn't like it. But he just really needed to touch.

"What are we doing?" David was back in the doorway, looking more and more like a zombified version of a handsome man.

Yardley spun around, startled by the sight of him. "You shouldn't be up."

"We're getting you medical help." Kye's gaze switched to Yardley, his hands rising to touch his bandaged face. "Thanks. Now find Gunnar a coat, get some blankets, and dress for warmth yourself."

He was up and moving toward the door, his SAR coat snagged up on the way. "The roads aren't plowed in this area, I'm guessing. There's the possibility we could get stuck but we need to get out of here."

"I'll drive." Yard was moving toward a closet. "My Jeep's four-wheel drive."

Kye came up beside her. "Are you sure?"

She turned to him. Her gaze was absolutely clear, direct and solid with confidence. "I know the roads and I've driven in conditions worse than today's."

Kye smiled for the first time since he'd first spied Gunnar. "Yes, ma'am. Get us ready to roll. I'll be right back."

He thrust his arms in his SAR jacket then reached for a pair of leashes, called both dogs to his side, and tethered them. A moment later man and dogs were out the door.

Kye checked the availability of the compact Smith & Wesson in his pocket before stepping off the porch into the soft snow. The night was eerily bright with the salting of small flakes sifting out of the sky. The clouds, some lit by urban centers hours away, reflected light down onto the white world below, making everything unusually bright. With the ground sparkling before him, Kye could see farther than he might have on a night with a full moon.

The pleasure of the beauty of the moment lasted about as long as it took him to notice footprints being rapidly filled in by those relentless flakes. Some of them were coming toward the house. But others led away. Purdy had come but he had not left. Who did the others belong to?

Kye grabbed back the leashes as his K-9s would have charged forward to relieve themselves. "Lily, come." The toller bounded back toward him, yipping for the sheer pleasure of being out-of-doors. Oleg glanced back, curious about the toller's actions. Kye reached down and petted his partner. He did not want to give away the fact he was on to their secret visitor. But sweat popped out on his upper lip and trickled down his back. Whoever was out there was probably watching him. And the big white cross on his back might as well have been a bull's-eye. His main hope, since he hadn't been shot yet, was that the man was waiting out there to see if his cover was blown. "Search." He didn't know the Czech word for search but hoped that Oleg would pick up on Lily's posture and follow suit.

The toller lifted her head and sniffed the air. She turned her face slowly one way and then the other. Oleg, at the far end of his long lead, paused, looked back, and then his whole body came to attention. At the moment Lily caught a scent, Oleg seemed to fix on something in the distant line of trees.

Kye pulled in a careful breath as Lily yipped in delight and bounded toward Yardley's vehicle. Oleg on the other hand continued to stare off toward the distant line of trees, where shadows blacked out Kye's vision of what lay beyond.

Every cell in his body moved to high alert as Kye followed Lily to Yardley's Jeep. The aching of his face had faded away in the cold. His skin was suddenly an all-surface sensory organ as he strained for sights, the touch of the wind, anything that would give him a whisper of anticipation before disaster struck.

Oleg remained still, his head swiveling in 180-degree angles, as if completely confused by the information he was taking in. Refusing to budge, even when called, Oleg's rigid stance made Kye feed out leash to the end as Lily bounded toward the Jeep and reared up, pressing her paws against the driver's-side door.

Dammit. They weren't alone. And he had no idea who or what or how many.

Then he noticed the tires. They were flat. All four of them.

Oh shit.

Hoping not to give his new knowledge away, he called to Lily in a voice louder than necessary. "Stop farting around and go potty, Lily. Now."

She glanced at him, her eyebrows doing semaphore signals. He knew she was trying not to let him pull her off a legitimate find.

He pulled out a bit of kibble and held it out. "Here. Good girl, Lily."

Satisfied that her point had been made, she bounded toward him and took her reward. Then she moved several feet away, circled twice, and took care of business.

All the while Oleg examined the periphery with his back to Kye, silent but alert as any sentry.

It took everything in him to turn his back toward the house. He wondered as he had many times in Afghanistan if that would be his last move, having turned a back on an enemy he could not guess at. But this was the good ol' U.S. of A. Even a hired gun would want to make a kill look like an accident, not an assassination.

That wishful thought propelled him all the way up the stairs to the front door. But he was definitely in perspiration fail as the door opened and Yardley appeared.

She took one look at him and her gaze said she knew everything. Yet she waited for him to say the words.

Kye looked at Yardley, his heart thumping. His voice was a rough urgent whisper as he reached down to unleash Oleg. "Get back inside. Purdy didn't come alone."

As if he'd gotten a signal from some great canine handler in the sky, Oleg turned, grazed Kye's hand with his teeth, and then bolted away.

Yardley gasped. "He bit you?"

Kye examined his offended hand. "He barely broke the skin. I think he just needed to get away in the worst way."

"He's trained to self-deploy when there's danger."

By the time he turned to the night, Oleg was nothing more than a smoky phantom blending into the white night as he sped away toward the tree line. He looked back at her grim-faced. "You're going to have to explain that dog's skill set when there's time."

He had hoped not to give away the fact that he knew they had company. But Oleg's defection probably blew that hope to smithereens. Whoever was out there was about to find himself at the business end of one very touchy canine.

Self-deploy. Unless Oleg could take their enemy down alone, they were worse off than before, with Yardley now unprotected by K-9 power.

Heart hammering, Kye remembered that though he was trying to behave in a way that didn't alert their intruder, they were sitting ducks. He shifted his body protectively in front of hers as he grabbed her by the arm to push her back inside the safety of the house.

Bristling at his treatment she waited until he had locked and bolted the door before she got up in his face. "Tell me what's going on?"

Before he could answer the lights went out.

CHAPTER TWENTY-TWO

"Glaser here. We've got an intruder."

Jackson smiled to himself. For hours he'd been stuck in a motel room off Interstate 81 with nothing to do but stare out the window at the weather. Finally, they were getting somewhere. "Has he been there long?"

"Can't say. He showed himself about fifteen minutes ago. Reconnoitered the premises before retreating to the tree line opposite my location."

"Can you give me a description?"

"Didn't get much of a look before retreating. Male. By the posture. I'd guess he's had some military or law enforcement training. If I hadn't caught the flash off his goggle lens I wouldn't have suspected he was there until he moved into the clearing. Thought I'd better pull back before I called or he'd get the same opportunity to make me."

Jackson thought fast. It didn't sound like Dr. Gunnar. "Keep an eye on him. If he makes a move toward the house or the people inside, contact me immediately for further instructions."

"There was a visitor to the house. Came along thirty minutes before I spotted the second one. He knocked on the door about an hour ago and was admitted."

"Hellfire, son. Why didn't you start with that?"

"I was told I was to report only suspicious conduct. The man came straight up the drive on foot and knocked. As he was admitted, I assume he was known to those inside."

"Jesus. That kennel is busier than a corner dealer handing out samples. What did he look like?"

"Plaid shirt and gimme cap and jeans. No coat though it's snowing ninety to nothing out here."

"Anything else? Anything at all."

"Hold on. Looks like we've got a situation developing. The lights on the Harmonie Kennel property just went out."

"Shit." Jackson automatically reached for the reassurance of his non-government-issued weapon on his hip. "Sit tight. I'm coming to you, and calling for backup."

CHAPTER TWENTY-THREE

The darkness lasted only for a few seconds before lights flickered on again, dimmer than before as the emergency generator kicked in.

Even as Yardley moved to begin turning off non-essential lights, Kye was on the move, too. "Call Sheriff Wiley now. Tell him we've got a guy tied up in the closet who tried to kill your boyfriend and that there's a good chance he has a partner close by who slashed your tires. He'll believe that bullshit story if it comes from you." As he talked, he headed for the back door.

Lily followed on his heels. The sudden darkness had been enough to excite her into doing a great imitation of a hysterical person. Her unnerving toller scream was a shrill-screech match for a victim in slasher movie. The high-pitched keening went through everyone within hearing, like fingernails on a chalkboard.

Kye paused and looked down. "Lily, no."

Lily paused and looked up at him, prancing in place,

as if she knew he intended to leave her behind and she wasn't having it.

"No screams. No barks. No sound, Lily." He made the *closed mouth* sign.

The calm deep tone of her handler's voice soothed the toller. She continued to stare at him with an alert gaze but didn't make another sound.

"Good girl." He reached down, offered her a bit of kibble, and then picked her up. Holding her high on his chest so that she had physical contact, he stroked her in long smooth glides of his hand. "You can't go with me this time, Lily. It's not safe out there." After a moment he nuzzled her neck. "Be good until I come back."

He shifted his body and handed Lily to Yardley, who'd come up. "Take care of her. She'll be okay once I leave."

Yardley nodded, her eyes wide as she gazed at him. He really was an extraordinarily good handler. Pausing in his mission to calm his dog when she wasn't coming along.

"Just a second." She grabbed Kye by the arm as he made to swing around. Well, he paused and turned to her. The biceps bulging under her touch could easily have resisted her effects to stop him. "What are you planning?"

"You've got ordnance in the classroom building. I need it."

"We've got flash bangs and rifles and lots of weaponry out there." She dug a hand into her pant pocket, pulled out a set of keys, and handed them to him. "Most of it will be useless as defense because we fire blanks around our handlers and dogs. Our insurer told us it's not safe to do otherwise."

He grinned. "You know that and I know that. But

whoever's out there won't know that. Besides, a flash bang is a flash bang."

She dragged at his arm again as he tried to turn away. "You don't know who's out there."

"I know he slashed your tires and cut our power. I don't want to wait to see what he has in store next without letting him know he has a fight on his hands. If you're nervous about the gun, give it to your doc. I'm sure he's handled firearms where he's been."

She nodded solemnly. "Be careful. I don't want you to get hurt."

He turned fully to her, a question is his eyes. "Would it really matter?"

Yardley didn't misunderstand. "Of course it matters. I don't want anyone else to get hurt."

"No." He reached out and began drawing a slow circle on her cheekbone without a bruise. "I need to know. Would it matter personally to you, Yard?"

She took a deep breath but she was already nodding. "It would matter, Kye. I just don't know how that changes anything."

She could see him trying to evaluate her words as if each and every one was a puzzle to be solved.

Muttering a curse word, he moved suddenly into her and grabbed the back of her neck as his mouth swooped down on hers. His one-arm embrace crushed Lily between them but the dog didn't struggle to get away. It was a hard kiss, as if he was trying to brand the impression of his lips on hers. Just as quickly, he dropped his hand and backed away. "Finishing the task before me. That's where I am. After that . . ."

After that what? He would fight for her? Did he see David as a rival?

While those thoughts chased one another, he turned and slipped out the door with a whispered, "Lock it."

Only when she had locked the door and turned away did she notice David standing in the doorway. How much had he seen, or heard? Impossible to tell. His expression was composed only of pain.

She felt her neck flush but her tone was brisk. "I'm calling the sheriff. Kye needs backup. We'll talk later." Though she hadn't the slightest idea what she would say to him about what he'd just seen, maybe heard. It was impossible to make decisions when the sky was falling.

David braced himself against the door frame. "Kye looks like a man who can take care of himself."

She nodded. "I sure hope so."

David offered her a probing stare. "About that gun you were discussing earlier."

Ooo-kaaaay. He'd heard a lot. She nodded and went to get it, pulling out her cell phone to call the sheriff as she climbed the stairs to the second floor.

She reappeared from an upstairs bedroom less than two minutes later, Glock and bullets in hand. David was perched on the arm of her sofa, his mouth a firm line of pain. "The sheriff says he'll get someone out here as soon as he can. There's been a pileup on the main highway and the state police pulled in all available law enforcement personnel to help. Meanwhile we should find a safe place and hide."

He looked at her dubiously. "Where would that be?"

The lights flickered and went out. Their enemy had gotten to the generator.

Please let Kye be safe. That was the only thought in Yardley's head as she stood rock-still, waiting for who-knew-what.

"Yardley?" David's voice was no more than a breath.

"I'm okay." She puffed out the words into the silence.

She strained so hard for sounds from outside that her head began to ache. But all that happened was her eyes gradually became accustomed to the light source beyond the room—the security light on the telephone pole out front. It was connected to a separate line from the one that ran to the house and generator. The light bounced off the snow, making it eerily bright as it seeped between the gaps of the curtains at the window.

"I can't sit by and do nothing. Kye won't know where things are in the dark. If he uses a flashlight, it will make him a sitting duck."

"You aren't armed. Yardley, don't do this. I know you care for Kye. I understand. But it isn't safe."

"It isn't about that. I wouldn't leave you, or my brother Law, or any of my trainers to face God-knows-what while I hid. It's not in me to let someone else fight my battles."

He nodded. "Got it." But his expression said he understood a lot more. And none of it in his favor. "Take this." He handed her the loaded gun.

"I don't think—"

"Don't think. Just do what you have to do."

She stared at him. "Could you shoot a man who came through the door?"

"If he was trying to hurt you, in a heartbeat."

"That's why you get to keep the gun."

Giving up, he pulled her close and kissed her. He was hot with fever and trembling. "I want to be your hero. I'd follow McGarren out there in a heartbeat if I could."

"I know. I know." She cupped his handsome face in her hands, trying not to let him see that she knew how every breath was taxing him. "You're already trying to save millions of people. Let me try to help out one Hawaiian dog handler."

Keeping to the shadows, Kye made his way, boots sinking to the ankles in fresh drifts, to the back of the bunkhouse before the lights went out a second time. He knew the generator was right behind the bunkhouse because it had been revving up the night like a lawn mower on steroids. Suddenly the motor coughed, sputtered, and died, leaving the shock of silence. The house and all the buildings on Harmonie Kennels' property went dark.

Heart slamming against his ribs, Kye turned with gun in hand expecting to encounter the saboteur who'd shut down the generator. But nothing moved in the cold, blank darkness. Even the snow could no longer be seen, only heard as it whispered past his face. He pressed his back against the building and waited for his eyes to adjust. As he expected, gradually a light source appeared in the twenty-yard space between the main house and the guesthouse. The security light was still on in the front driveway. It swept a clean white arc through the snow, stopping just short of the tree line where the ground began to climb steeply to the hillside not far from the back the house.

He waited, listening so hard he heard the blood roaring in his ears, for any sign that he had been spotted. There was someone out here with him who wanted very badly to keep them contained. Why? Was he waiting for reinforcements, as Purdy had been? Or was he taking precautions to keep them off balance until he could determine how best to attack?

Nothing. Silence. Only his heartbeat for company.

Kye glanced back at the house. He thought about going back to protect Yardley. But the three of them penned together inside a house they could not adequately protect wasn't a good idea, either. He needed supplies, something to fight back with. A stun grenade in hand sounded better and better.

He sent his gaze sweeping over the dark ridgeline, looking for any sign of a presence there. He'd seen the utility road halfway up the ridge this morning. But nothing penetrated the night.

After what seemed like forever but was only minutes, he forced himself to begin moving again. This time the crunch of ice under his boots sounded as loud in his ears as an ax splitting wood. His only protection was the dark. But he wasn't a stealth panther prowling on silent paws. He was more like a buffalo stumbling along. The ground was uneven behind the bunkhouse, icier than where the new snow was accumulating.

Breathing through his mouth had several drawbacks. Not only was it unnatural—a mouth breather he wasn't—but the icy air was drying out his mouth and his throat had begun to ache. *Shit fire.* He hated cold. He'd had enough already this season to last him a good long time. *Skiing, my ass.* He was going home, maybe to stay. At least until he was flambéed by the sun over every single inch of his body.

Finally he reached the end of the bunkhouse back wall. The shadows beyond were deeper where the Night-Watcher security light was blocked by the building. Twenty feet ahead was the corner of the classrooms, his destination. He leaned out cautiously to check the side of the building for intruders.

And then he heard it. The sound of a door opening.

Behind him. He whipped around and waited. He was certain he'd stopped breathing by the time a shadow appeared opposite the bunkhouse. The figure moved cautiously but much more quietly than he had. Long. Lean. Something familiar in those movements.

Well hell.

He ducked back behind the side of the bunkhouse and waited. Just in case his eyes were fooling him. He wasn't dressed for the weather. Already his hands were beginning to ache from the cold. The gun in his hand burned his palm, the cold steel giving the false impression of warmth. But he didn't pocket it. Not when he didn't know who or what was out here with him.

As the figure came even with the edge of the building, he grabbed and slammed his follower back against the wall, simultaneously pressing a hand to the mouth as he jabbed his gun into the middle. It took only a second to confirm what he suspected but could not trust. He had Yardley jammed between the wall and the weight of his body. He dropped his hand.

"Fuck." It was all he could think of that was appropriate as he stared into her frightened face.

"Kye?" Her breath came back unevenly. "Thank God."

He pulled the gun out of her middle and pushed her back into the dark shadows behind the building. And then he found his voice again.

"What the fuck are you doing here?"

"Helping you." He couldn't see her face any longer, but he didn't have to. He recognized that squinty-eyed tone anywhere.

"Help—" He was at a loss for words again. Finally, Yardley had struck him dumb. He peeled his body away from hers slowly, looking back past her shoulder, as if expecting she had brought along company. The long strip of darkness was empty. Beyond, fresh swirls of snow tumbled more thickly than before in the broad white expanse of the security light.

He felt hands cup his hand, fingers like icicles after just a few minutes of exposure. She leaned in against him, her height making it easy to bring their faces close. "With the lights out, you won't be able to find things. I know where everything is."

She spoke so quietly, her words were mere puffs of warm air in his ear. But he welcomed every sweet whisper, if only because her lips kept brushing his lobe. Even so, half of him wanted to throttle her for taking the chance. The other half wanted to stuff her in his pocket and head for the trees and safety.

He leaned in close, using a hand to embrace her by the waist as he pressed his lips to her ear. "Did you call the sheriff?"

She nodded, rubbing her cheek along his. "He and his officers were called to a bad accident at the junction of Highways 81 and 64 up near Staunton. He says hold down the fort at least an hour."

Kye didn't bother to curse. A waste of breath. They were on their own. Anything or many things could happen in an hour.

"Don't speak. Don't stop. Stay close behind me. If anything happens, make for the tree line above us and hide. Stay there. No matter what happens. Until the sheriff arrives." He pushed back from her warm body, reluctantly, and grabbed her hand. He tugged, the equivalent of *come on*.

Yardley fell into step behind him. A moment later she

almost jumped out of her skin when a swoosh of falling snow dumped on their heads from a cracking tree branch far above their heads. She had neglected to pull her hood up and the ice sluiced down her neck, under her neckline, and down her spine, making her gasp and shiver.

Kye's head swung around, tossing more melting snow from his hoodie into her face. "You okay?" At least that's what she thought he said. Between the dark and the danger she wasn't sure he'd even spoken aloud.

He pulled her in close by the wrist. "Move fast."

All at once he was sprinting across the open space between the bunkhouse and the classroom building. She wore combat boots, the same as he did, and this was her property. She knew every rut, stone, pothole, and scrub. But snow and fear were making it all seem unfamiliar, alien, even hostile. Twice she slipped, her footing almost giving way beneath her, but Kye didn't slow his speed, pulling her along by his momentum so that she just stumbled forward, her face colliding with his back as she scrambled to right herself.

It was only thirty feet but it seemed like fifty yards as they ran straight out for the deeper darkness on the other side of the open ground. She could hear Kye's sharp breathing, remembered how he was hampered by the swelling and bandages of his broken nose. But it didn't seem to affect him. He moved strongly and confidently over strange ground until, finally, they slipped into shadow in the rear of the building. Only then did he turn to her, hands going to frame her shoulders.

"You okay?"

She nodded. No need to tell him she'd turned her ankle a bit. It wasn't that bad. Nothing she couldn't walk off. "The keys." She placed her hand against his chest so he'd know where to put them.

He handed them over and she turned, feeling her way along the back of the building until she came to the first door. All the classrooms opened to the outside. A center corridor gave access from the inside. With K-9s needing frequent breaks, this arrangement came in handy. It also meant that one key fit many locks. She felt along the key ring in the dark, counting the number and then choosing one that felt most familiar. Like trying to read Braille, she ran her hand over the door until she found the lock, using a fingertip to locate the keyhole and then pushing the key in.

She swallowed a little *ta-da* of achievement when the key turned. He had needed her. This wouldn't have been so easy otherwise.

They pushed into the dark of the classroom smelling faintly of dry eraser, wooden desks, two-week-old stale air, and the ever-present whiff of K-9, an earthy, not unpleasant musk she loved.

"This way." She was whispering, though once the door closed behind them she thought they were probably safe enough. She grabbed his wrist this time, the thickness and heat a welcome reminder of his presence, and led him through the configuration of the room. In her mind's eye she pictured the long desks with chairs pushed in. Much easier to navigate a room with indoor obstacles used to teach K-9 techniques. Once in the corridor she turned left into the utter darkness of the interior space. She ran a hand lightly along the wall, counting doors until she was past the third classroom door. The corridor formed a T. Straight ahead was the cafeteria/

social room. To the left was the supply room containing ordnance.

She tugged Kye left, strong and solid, reassuring at her back.

She wasn't certain in what order she heard things. It was as if the night suddenly wrecked itself, like a car crashing.

A shout. Shots fired. A scream.

Kye's voice sounded strangled. "Lily!"

Jackson was watching his windshield wipers make fan patterns as they swept the snow from side to side on his windshield and feeling pretty good around himself. He'd seen a few wrecks since he'd gotten on the road. But his vehicle was equipped to deal with snow and ice. Nasty night. Not a good night for man nor beast. But he was FBI. The post office had nothing on an FBI agent on the job.

The chime of his cell phone lit up the panel on his four-wheel-drive vehicle.

"Jackson."

"Glaser hasn't called back in, sir."

Jackson gripped his steering wheel. Maybe the shit had hit the fan. "How far out are the people on their way down here?"

"That'll be difficult to ascertain. A major pileup at the intersection of Interstates 64 and 81 has all area roads backed up for miles."

"Find a way to scramble them. I got a bad feeling about tonight."

CHAPTER TWENTY-FOUR

"David!"

Yardley turned and tried to push past Kye.

He didn't yield. He gripped her shoulders and pushed her back into the darkest corner against the wall, holding her there with the weight of his body.

Her hands came up, palms braced against his chest as she pushed, her voice adamant. "Let go of me, dammit."

"No, Yard. Think." Kye spoke quietly, a tone at odds with the thunder of his heart under her right palm. But he knew the best way to manage fear was to slow things down. Think and act methodically. "Where's your gun?"

He couldn't see her face but he felt her stop struggling. "David has it."

"Okay. Good." Kye was thinking as fast as he could. So far, no more sounds. That was neither good nor bad. Just knowledge. "Maybe David was scaring off an intruder."

"He's so weak."

"He's tougher than you think. He got this far, didn't he?" Strangely, he meant those words. It didn't make him like the man any better but he did respect him. He was beginning to understand why Yard chose him in the first place.

He heard Yardley draw in a long breath. Felt her shudder and then release it. She was trying to get command of her nerves. "What about Lily?" She was whispering but it sounded to his ears like a shout. "Oh, Kye, do you think she was shot?"

"No." He struck away the image of Lily being wounded. "More likely she's under a bed upstairs." The gunshot alone would have been enough to frighten her into emitting those cries. She was trained to track and save, not to hunt. Without her handler to reassure her, she would be confused and worried. When anxious, a toller hid.

"David's protected and Lily can take care of herself. We need a plan before—" He swallowed the last of the sentence. Before *he* moved one step back toward the house. He didn't want her anywhere near the fight to come, whatever shape it took.

She stiffened. "Where's Oleg?"

That was a good question. One that Kye had been considering when he'd gone out the back door of the house. The self-starter Czech wolfdog might not separate friend from foe, or even care, if he was frightened or "self-deployed." So far the K-9 had been lying low, for what purpose Kye couldn't begin to guess. But he was out there, in the mix, somewhere.

"Would he track an intruder, Yard?"

"If he'd picked up on my anxiety about him, certainly. On yours? I don't know."

Kye thought about that. He and the wolfdog hadn't exactly come to a meeting of the minds. But Kye had been sweating bullets once he saw the footprints in the snow. And Oleg had been right there beside him, staring at something even before that. Now that he thought about it, the trained K-9 had seemingly divided his attention between two points in the distance. Maybe Purdy had brought more than one snake to the hunt.

From far away a sound broke the silence, something between a grunt and a groan.

"Kye?" Yardley twisted against him, trying to free herself from his grip.

"*Shh.*" He leaned harder against her, stilling her urge to push him away. It wasn't exactly the best time to notice things like her chest rising and falling rapidly under the pressure of his. The last time they'd made contact like this, there were no clothes between them. Just her lush soft skin on his.

His dick stirred. No. Not the right time at all. Next time. If there was a next time.

He levered away from her and dropped his hands. "Go and open the ordnance room. Bring me half a dozen flash bangs. Then we'll take the fight to them."

"Them?"

He could feel her breath on his face. And for the life of him, despite the danger and thrill of the fight rising in him, all he wanted to do was kiss her.

Reward for deeds done.

So far, he'd earned nada.

With that thought he shoved all personal considerations aside. People were depending on him. Besides, he'd heard her whisper Gunnar's name in the wake of the mess that had just gone down outside.

That snapped him back to attention. There'd been no more sounds after that first outburst. No more shouts or even barking from Lily. WTF was happening outside?

He released Yardley. "Go."

Her fingers curled into his parka. "Don't leave me behind this time."

"I won't." One of the first things he learned in police academy was how to lie convincingly. He was just sorry he had to use it on her.

As she slipped sideways away from him, he turned toward the cafeteria area that led to the front of the building. Across the room slices of light from the security lamp cut through the glass panes of the double doors with push bars, illuminating twin wedges of wall and floor.

He stayed in shadow as he approached those slats of light, not wanting anyone looking to see him cross the windows. He heard a door open behind him. Good, Yard would be busy trying to locate things by touch alone. That would make her slow and methodical, her senses totally concentrated on the task before her.

He hunkered down and moved forward in a squat position to slip free the bottom door latch. Now he needed to free the top one. Above waist height, the closed doors provided only about eight inches of door frame between the glass inserts. He doubted even sideways he was a slim eight inches thick. His coat made him even bulkier.

He slipped off his jacket and then rose up just enough to peer over the bottom edge of one narrow glass panel and froze. Behind him he heard Yard opening a cabinet. Ordinarily he wouldn't have noticed so slight a sound. But with his every sense online and straining for information, it sounded like she was prying up floorboards with a crowbar. He needed to move, and quickly, before she realized he'd left.

He went back to surveillance of the world beyond the door. The security lamp threw its bright-white light in an arc around the parking lot, making the snow a brilliant carpet embedded with diamonds. His vehicle and Yard's were thrown into high relief, with stark sharp shadows angled behind them. In one of those shadows something moved.

Kye held his breath. Something or someone was on the ground. It looked like a big sack. But he suspected it was a living being. No way to tell if it was man or dog. The noises they'd heard earlier had had consequences.

Time to act.

He extended an arm straight up over his head and then inched his body up the door, trying to keep himself inside the protective span of the frame. The effort to move slowly and keep his body perfectly erect had his calves burning by the time his fingers touched the bottom of the latch. He pulled down hard and twisted.

The sound echoed through the cafeteria but he didn't have time to worry about that. Gun in hand he pushed through the door to the outside. If he didn't move now, Yard would try to follow him. If he wasn't there, instinct would force her to be more careful and go back the way they'd come. By then, with any kind of luck, he could have a read on whatever the hell was going on.

He skittered along the wall, in full sight of anyone who happened to be looking toward the classrooms. He hoped against holy hell that whoever had fired that shot was riveted on the house. Not looking for phantoms in the snow.

He'd never moved faster in his life with the gun out in front of him, fisted in both hands as his boots churned up the ankle-deep snow. His goal was the back of the bunkhouse that lay between the classrooms and Yard's home. If he made it that far, he could duck into the shadows again, with the relative safety of the building to shield him.

It struck him as he made the nearby wall of the bunkhouse that he'd forgotten something. His SAR parka lay on the floor in the cafeteria. No wonder he'd moved so easily. And now he felt the wind and snow in every part of his upper body. He was wearing nothing but boots, a pair of cargoes, and a sleeveless undershirt.

Way to go, Honolulu Boy.

At least he'd lost the big fat white cross marking the back of his bright-red coat.

Small mercies.

A bigger issue was getting his breath back when he had to gulp air through his mouth. If he got a chance he might go back and break Purdy's nose, just to even things up. It slowed him down to have to breathe this way. Any exertion made his face throb.

He reached halfway for the tape before he changed his mind. Bleeding all over himself wasn't a better solution. And the cold would make his sinuses burn like a sumbitch. Acknowledge then disregard. He dropped his hand.

His instinct from years ago was kicking in. Once it had been second nature to not only run toward trouble but neutralize it. In many ways, he had adjusted to civilian life better than men like Law who carried daily the scars of war. He'd switched from MP force and protection mode to search and rescue fairly smoothly, thanks

to his business partner Oliver. He preferred saving lives
to threatening them. But now he needed those predator
skills to survive and overcome. The hunted needed to be
a hunter.

Motivate. Devastate. Incapacitate.

He moved toward the back of the bunkhouse. By circling to the rear, he would be protected by darkness and
closer to the back of the house when he reached the other
end. Perhaps from that angle he could tell who or what
was down in the front yard.

He moved as quickly as the ground allowed. In coming out this way, he'd been sinking footprints into un-
touched snow. But now, in keeping close to the back wall
as he retraced his steps, his boots sank several times into
uneven holes already made by his first passage. Some of
them must have been Yard's, too.

Snapping sounds brought his head around several
times. But there was nothing to see either behind him
or up the incline behind the building where the terrain
made a sudden climb as it became the foothills of the
eastern range. He remembered the road on a ridge halfway up. Perhaps Purdy's henchmen had come in that
way. No way to check without revealing himself. And
he needed to know what lay on the ground near Yard's
vehicle.

By the time he came even with the back corner of the
bunkhouse he was breathing heavily again. His chest
hurt from the rush of icy air in and out of his lungs. All
the way up to the top of his throat, his breathing felt con-
stricted, as if his windpipe had begun to freeze. He
brought his lips together, sipping in air as if from a straw.

How much time had passed since Yard had called the
sheriff? Could have been an hour or fifteen minutes. His

internal clock was on high alert status, everything coming in as either speeded up or painfully slowed down. Was an hour all the time he had to burn up before help arrived? Or more likely, with snow still falling, would it be a very long wait? Best to plan for option B.

This time as he prepared to turn the corner and look, he pulled his weapon in close to his chest, both hands on it to steady his aim.

He did a ninety-degree pivot so that only half his body was exposed as he looked toward the parking lot and cars.

His angle of view was better, as well as closer. It was clear from his first glance that a human body lay in the shadow of the Jeep. Cussing up a blue streak in his head, Kye made himself stay exposed as he did a perimeter check, looking for other casualties. Perpetrators. Animals. Nothing stirred. No Oleg. No other human being. Nothing.

He pulled back and swung away, planting his back against the back wall of the bunkhouse in shadow. The icy sting of the siding felt good. It was a reminder that he was still alive. Still making plans to devastate and incapacitate whatever dickwad was out there. Because he knew, without confirmation, that whoever lay prone in the snow wasn't Kye's target.

Kye made himself recount what he now knew while his hammering heart steadied itself. The man down wore a wool coat and he'd seen a trouser leg and the soles of trainers, not combat boots. Not in uniform so no officer of the law. Bad guy?

Purdy had come dressed to deflect suspicion. He doubted his partner, or partners, would have bothered.

They'd come to clean up a mess. Probably dressed to disguise themselves, including masks.

Gunnar couldn't have made that shot from inside the house. Or if he'd been able to open the front door and gun down an assailant, he would mostly likely have shouted for help the moment he saw the man fall. More likely, the doc was crouched in the dark, feverish and only half alert, waiting, as Kye was, to see what came next.

He checked his perimeter again, willing himself to slow his thinking.

So who was shot? Purdy was private security. That meant his partner, or partners, would be anything from ex-police-officers to former black ops, and every scary thing in between. One thing was certain. He would be a hunter, a predator, at the top of his particular food chain. The thrill of the hunt would urge him on even when the odds began stacking up. Adrenaline junkies, the lot. The man on the ground might be playing possum, pretending to be hurt to get the drop on whoever came in answer to the shots.

Like a hum beneath the wind, he could almost hear his enemy thinking, too low to register as sound but felt all the same in the deepest part of his chest. What would the fucker do next? What should his own next move be? He couldn't stay out here in his undershirt forever. Already his muscles were beginning to ache from the cold.

I effing hate snow!

He waited. Listening. Hearing nothing but the wind and creaking trees and the faint tingling drift of snow through the air. Finally, far away, a dog barked.

After several excruciating seconds he thought he

heard something else. Was that a siren? Or was the cold making his ears ring? He slid to the edge of the building and peered around the corner toward the front of the house. He kept staring, as if by looking long enough he would be able to pinpoint the source of the sound he'd heard. Finally, he realized what his brain was trying to show him. The person by Yard's Jeep was gone.

Kye bit off a curse and slipped the safety free on his pistol. But it was only a precaution. No way could he make a clean shot at this distance in the dark.

He heard a soft swoosh of sound in the distance at his back. *Yard.* She would have realized by now that he had deserted her and was probably mad as hellfire about that. Had probably decided to come after him.

He spared a look over his shoulder, almost positive he saw her shadow take shape in the gloom of the building to his rear. He wanted to yell for her to stay back but he didn't dare utter a sound.

And then he had bigger problems.

He caught the wisp of a human voice on the wind, undeniable this time, and turned his head in time to see a faint glow behind the window curtains in the kitchen. Was it a penlight? Too small and weak to be a flashlight. Or maybe it was a cell phone glow. Was Gunnar making a call? Didn't he know that light made him a target?

The back door of the house opened and two figures emerged. His blood ran cold. The two carried a third slumped between them, head hanging limply down, with an arm draped over the shoulders of each of his captors. It was Gunnar. And Purdy. The third had to be his partner.

* * *

"Shit. Shitty shit shit *shit*."

Yard whispered the curses as a stun grenade canister noisily rolled away from her in the dark. She'd safely pocketed two before the slip. It was so dark she couldn't see her hand six inches from her face. She would never find what she dropped.

Something she hadn't considered was that the familiarity of the storage room would vanish in a zero-visibility environment. It had taken her forever to find the right key, awkwardly trying to fit each one into a hole she had to locate by touch. Besides that, adrenaline was making her hands shake, which wasted valuable seconds as she fumbled around. Her clumsiness made her impatient.

This was a stupid idea. Why was she bothering to load up with flash bangs anyway? What were they going to do with more than—?

The soft click of a door opening sent her spinning around as she gritted her teeth to keep from calling out. Her heart went into overdrive as every sense strained for more information. Kye was here with her, she reminded her strung-out nerve center. He would have heard whatever she heard. He was armed. So was she, with flash bangs. They would be okay. Even so, she'd have felt much safer if Oleg was with them. She knew dogs. Weapons, not so much.

The question was, had someone come in, or gone out?

Moving silently to the doorway of the armament room, she pulled a flash bang from her pocket, fitting it in her hand so the spoon pressed against the web between the thumb and forefinger of her right hand, and the ring of the pin draped over her fingers.

That's when she heard the distinct click of a hydraulic door closer pulling a door shut. The sound echoed in the silence like a physical presence.

Swallowing the hysteria crawling up into her throat, she made herself consider where the sound might have come from. The devices were only used for outside doors. She'd helped install them herself. The sound had been nearby. That meant the cafeteria doors had been breached. Kye was headed that way when she came here.

Kye. He'd left her.

Heart thundering in her ears, Yardley stepped into the hallway, the forefinger of her left hand curled into the pin of the flash bang. If she went down, she'd take someone down with her. At least for the moment. Flash bangs temporarily stunned, blinded, and made victims deaf.

It look a few seconds for the light to gather in her eyes, trigger the cones that sent impulses to her optic nerve. And then she saw, in the light coming through the twin glass panes in the double doors, something hunched on the floor.

She bit off the cry that erupted from her and rushed forth, expecting to find Kye wounded. But the lump didn't move as she called out softly. And when she went down on her knees before it and stretched out a trembling hand, she realized it was too small to be Kye. She touched the parka, a dark dull red in the semi-dark.

Empty.

She glanced at the door. Saw that it was unlocked. Kye had left her behind. After he promised he wouldn't.

Relief made her weak as she slumped over the coat and gathered it tightly to her chest. Kye was okay. He wasn't hurt. He was out there somewhere. Trying to protect her and save the day. Like some lunatic Lone Ranger.

Son of a B.

Anger replaced fear, burning through the terror of the last moments as she pushed her arms into the oversized coat for its warmth. It was still warm inside, and smelled faintly of Kye, that warm aloha sun, slightly salty sea smell that was his alone.

Don't leave me behind.

I promise.

Kye McGarren had lied to her face.

She wanted his balls on a platter.

After they were safe once more.

She scrambled to her feet, put her unused flash bang in a pocket of his parka, zipped up, and pushed through the door. Two could play Rambo.

CHAPTER TWENTY-FIVE

Yardley had never felt more exposed in her life than when she pushed through the cafeteria doors. Suddenly she was enveloped in illumination that was klieg-light-brilliant, or so it seemed after the tomb-like interior of the classroom building. Blinking and hiding her offended eyes behind an upheld hand, she fell back into the darkness and let the door close.

No way could she force herself to be exposed like a deer in headlights. Every cell in her body screamed *Take cover.*

Before the more cerebral parts of her brain caught up, her lizard brain's self-protective tactics had moved her back across the cafeteria and into the classroom corridor. Lizard brain was taking her back the way she had come. It knew that way was safe. At least, it had been safe before. At the moment, nothing sounded better to either parts of her brain than "been there done that."

It was a kick in the seat of her pride to realize that all

she wanted to do was climb under her desk in her office and wait until daylight. She wasn't going to do that but it made more sense than what she was about to do. Being afraid was getting to be a habit. First Stokes. Then finding David shot. Finally the realization that the man who'd shot David had brazenly entered her home to do more damage.

If not for Kye.

And that was why she was going out into this very unfriendly night. Because of the three of them, he was the innocent party. He was here because of her. She had to help him any way she could.

As for all the other feelings sloshing around inside her, they'd have to wait.

Nerves on high alert, she very carefully pushed open the same door she had unlocked for Kye to enter earlier. The deep shadows at the back of the building seemed almost friendly. But she was taking no chances. Her vision had yet to clear the blank blackness that followed exposure to her sodium security lamp out front.

Using her left hand as a guide along the wall, she moved for the corner of the building as fast as was safely possible. Once there, she paused to catch her breath. She hadn't been able to see a thing. But as the door behind her finally clicked shut, her vision came online again, minus the floaty black spots still blanking places. She looked down for three seconds then up again.

Kye was up ahead, at the far end of the bunkhouse. She knew it was him because, despite the fact he was only a vague upright outline, she doubted anyone else was out in these frigid temperatures without a coat. His back glowed faintly, as if his torso were radioactive, his white undershirt eating up the merest rays of light.

Relief flooded her, making her stumble. A moment later another sight arrested her movement altogether.

Beyond the outline of Kye, figures emerged from the back of her house.

Her blood ran cold. The two carried a third slumped between them, head hanging limply down, with an arm draped over the shoulders of the men on either side.

David! Dear God.

Yard slapped a hand over her mouth. She hadn't actually cried out, had she? The wail was so vivid in her mind she couldn't be certain. Until she realized no one had reacted.

Heart thundering, she forced herself to concentrate on the men moving across her yard. They were headed toward the rear. At fifty feet out, the ground suddenly swelled upward into the foothills of the Blue Ridge Mountains. It was one of the reasons her father had never bothered to fence it off, as he had the front property. No one was going to take an easy stroll up or down that slope. Tonight it was dark and treacherous with snow accumulations. The only reason the men carrying David would head that way was because they knew it was an escape route.

All at once she understood. They must have known about the utility road up along the lower ridge and parked a vehicle up there. The road ran for miles before coming out on the Lexington Turnpike that bisected the mountains. If they got away to the east, they would have a clear shot at escaping before law enforcement could pick up their tail. Someone needed to stop them.

With that thought in mind she moved forward—only to see Kye, weapon drawn, step out of the shadow into the light of the security lamp.

* * *

When he was fairly certain that Purdy and his partner were concentrating on reaching the back of the property under cover of darkness, Kye stepped out beyond the safety of the building. He was exposing himself, especially if there was a third partner watching. But if he didn't act quickly they'd get away with Gunnar. He was certain the doctor had no chance of staying alive after they'd delivered him to whoever had promised a bounty. Acknowledged and disregarded. Neither fact slowed him down.

He put the safety on and tucked his weapon into his waistband. No way to distinguish among the three dark forms moving away from him. He could no longer even tell exactly where they were, or how they thought they'd scale the slope with a man who couldn't stand on his own feet. That wasn't his problem. He needed to get to their escape vehicle first and disable it.

He'd promised Yard that he would protect her. It was a promise he intended to keep. That also meant protecting the man she loved.

He took off at a ninety-degree angle to the building that shielded him. The bunkhouse blocked most of the security lamp's light, giving him a protected path to the embankment. The snow slowed his sprint across the darkness but it also muffled the sounds of his movement. With a little luck Gunnar's would-be kidnappers would never know he was on to them until he was in place. He came to a sudden halt as the earth rose up before him. About fifteen feet over his head a swath of light cut across the snowy slope at a narrow angle and was then lost in the tree line. For the precious seconds it took him to traverse that lit space he'd be vulnerable.

Hell of a thing.

Back in his vehicle were gloves and a balaclava, two things that would make the job ahead easier. He could feel his scalp tingling where snow had gathered in his hair and was beginning to melt from body heat. It could be worse, he thought in grim humor. It could be raining. Or Yard could be following him.

He glanced back but saw nothing in the shadows. At least she wasn't following. He hoped.

He grabbed handfuls of a sturdy-looking snow-covered limb and hoisted himself up. After the first six feet, the angle became less steep but the underbrush provided a fright-house funfest of raking branches that swiped at his face and gnarled roots lying treacherously across this path to trip him up. Not possible to move quickly. His only comfort came from the distant swearing of the two men he was trying desperately to outmaneuver.

Had they momentarily forgotten about him? Or thought he'd turned tail and run away with Yard? Or were they too intent on delivering their prize to care any longer that they might be heard? It didn't matter. He couldn't get to them any faster because they were making noises. His path was fixed.

His fingers were getting stiff with cold and his lungs felt like they'd been scoured with steel wool. Any second he expected to be back-whipped by a branch that would knock him off balance and back down the slope.

Finally, the treacherous stretch of exposure due to the narrow band of light from below was before him. Crouched just below the swath of illuminated ground, he took a moment to breathe and scan the whereabouts of his targets. As soon as he saw them he looked away before they could catch the gleam of eyes in the dark.

The men were ahead of him, already climbing past the lightened ground. But he saw enough to know why. They were using tactical climbing ladders. And they were hauling Gunnar up on some sort of harness between them, one going fore and one aft.

Kye brushed the snow off his hair and blew into his cupped hands. So they weren't just some hire-by-the-hour mercs. Someone had taken the time to learn the terrain and equip himself for this enterprise. Had this all happened between Purdy's entrance into Yard's home and the arrival of his buddy? No, probably before. Once he'd lost Gunnar early this morning, Purdy would have had to learn where to search for him. Someone had given him Harmonie Kennels.

The damn wonders of the Internet. Douchebag Number Two had probably Googled Harmonie Kennels, aerial view, and found both the property and road on the ridge. Maybe even had the trajectory and angle of the slope he was clinging to like a damn sheep, or Lily.

He spared a thought for his K-9 companion, knowing her absence was not a good sign. Lily had the agility of a mountain goat. Under other circumstances, she would have been up and over this hillside like a gazelle. Poor Lily. He hoped she was hidden well and tight. He'd make it up to her somehow.

He looked over again. Had they even expected they might be hauling a body? Maybe the bounty was for dead or alive.

That thought acted like a kick in the gut. But no, Gunnar had to be wanted alive. Or his captors would just have dragged him any kind of way up the hill. Someone wanted to interrogate Gunnar. Then his life would be worthless. That thought reinvigorated Kye.

He blew out a final breath, ignoring his fiery throat, and launched himself into the light. He moved quickly, not caring that his scrambling dislodged rocks that tumbled and fell with soft plops into the snow below. The men were busy moving Gunnar. No time for gunplay in that precarious situation.

In only seconds he was across the kill zone. He scrambled up into the tree line and into shadow once more. He could feel cuts and scrapes burning his hands and face, but the satisfaction of reaching safety without a bullet whizzing past his head was its own kind of wonderful. He didn't stop to celebrate. Once in the trees the ground was more solid, the canopy of limbs shielding it from a lot of the snow. Strangely enough, there seemed to be more light here. Snow clouds overhead reflected light back from metropolitan areas many miles away. It was almost like having a half-moon to guide him.

He scrambled up and on. He was going to beat those dickwads to their own getaway site.

He looked back only once, when he thought he again heard sirens. The mountains distorted and reflected sounds. He didn't see a single rotating red light on the road below, but a pair of headlights was turning into the property.

Shit. Friend or foe? He really didn't have time to figure that out.

He swung around and returned to climbing, determined to give those bastards the surprise of their life at the top of the road.

He almost let out a yelp of satisfaction when his fingers finally dug into a flat surface where gravel rolled beneath his fingers underneath the snow. He'd made it to the road. He hauled himself over the side and let the kick of adrenaline power him to his feet. The past two weeks of navigating the ski slopes gave him extra power in his arms and legs that had propelled him up the steep hillside. Even so, he was a bit wobbly for the first few steps. And then he veered left.

He didn't see anything on the road ahead. No one was keeping watch. The dim, almost fairy light here was just enough to allow him to move confidently and quickly. Until he heard voices nearby. He paused. The men were just below him now. He could hear them arguing and cursing. Maybe that had something to do with the car that had pulled up in front of Yardley's house.

Kye let his gaze range out to the parking lot. He saw a man step out of a dark automobile and then he heard that man's voice over the loudspeaker say, "FBI. Surrender now or you will be prosecuted to the full extent of the law."

Kye smiled. Maybe the sheriff had called in reinforcements. Or the doc.

But he wasn't about to signal to the agent below and risk giving away his position. The FBI wouldn't know him from the mercs. And he most positively did not want to be shot at if the men abducting Gunnar were stupid enough to fire on a federal agent. If they were smart, they'd just keep doing what they were doing. The FBI didn't know where they were. With luck, they might get away before the FBI located them up on this ridge.

His work wasn't done.

Kye pulled his weapon a second time. With all his old

habits in full military police mode, he moved forward deliberately toward his planned destination.

He moved only a few yards forward before he saw the vehicle. He wouldn't have known it was there if he hadn't been searching for it. It was big all-terrain truck but painted flat black so that no light bounced off it. No shiny surfaces. Even the lights must have been coated with Veil. These men were hard-core.

He moved into the shadow on the other side of the truck as the men began topping the slope onto the road. He could barely see them. In the diffuse light they looked more like twin golems crawling out of a place in Middle Earth.

Kye waited, heart hammering in a thick steady cadence for the moment when both armed men would be most vulnerable.

Purdy came first. Kye recognized him by his voice.

"Boost the package. Higher. Fuck." When Gunnar's head appeared over the edge of the ridge, Purdy bent to drag the man up onto the road by his armpits.

Kye stepped out from behind the truck, keeping the hood between him and his prey. Gun double-fisted for accuracy. "Hold it right there, Purdy."

"Shit." Purdy dropped Gunnar like a hot potato and went for his gun. Of course, Purdy couldn't see that he held a gun.

"Don't move. I'm armed."

"I am, too, you son of a bitch." The dull gleam of a barrel appeared in Purdy's hand, aiming downward. "Move and I'll blow the doctor's head off."

"That won't save you."

The crunch of someone coming toward them jerked both of their attention toward the road in front of them.

As crazy as it seemed, all Kye could think of as an explanation was that Yardley had somehow—impossibly—found them.

He yelled a warning and raised his gun to fire just as light exploded from the end of Purdy's pistol. Only then did he hear it. The low grinding growl of a wolf who'd found its prey. A streak of something dark gray crossed his vision at chest level and then Purdy screamed and fell over backward.

A second shot went off as Purdy screamed. Oleg had made his bite. Kye didn't have to worry about him letting go. The Czech wolfdog was trained to hold until further notice. By the sounds of savage snarling, he was good for the duration.

"Fuck this." By the sounds of it, the man who hadn't made it onto the road began to climb back down. But he must have lost his footing. Kye heard a cry and then the man was cursing and thrashing as he backslid down the slope.

Kye jerked open the truck door and turned on the brights and then laid on the horn. Now the FBI would be a good idea. Along with whatever was arriving as a caravan below with sirens and lights going.

Kye leaned against the intruder's truck, the area around it lit up like a movie stage set with law enforcement lighting, as he waited his turn to be looked after. Local, state, and federal agencies were now all involved. Purdy's partner had been picked up by the sheriff's deputies and taken into custody. But FBI agent Jackson was giving the sheriff an earful about jurisdiction.

Purdy was dead. Oleg had caught him high on the shoulder at the neck, fangs sinking in and tearing the jugular. Kye knew that hadn't been intentional but the canine was trying to take down a danger to someone he thought he should protect. Only later had he learned Yard had been on the road several yards behind the dog.

His heart knocked against his ribs as he realized she might have been shot instead.

He glanced at her. Her face pale and tight in the glare of the lights as she hugged herself and hovered over the EMTs working on Gunnar. It seems his abductors had drugged him with an injection to make him unconscious so that carrying him would be simpler. But he'd lost additional blood in the rough treatment and the EMTs were talking in low tones about the wet sounds on one side of his chest. A possible broken rib puncturing a lung.

He wanted to go and put his arms around Yardley and tell her everything was going to be okay. The worst was over. It would be better in the morning, and better still the day after. But something held him back. And it was more than the way she gazed at Gunnar, bending down to grasp his hand when an EMT moved aside.

He had yet to tell her that he was pretty sure not all the blood on Purdy was his own. The man had fired two shots at close range. The likelihood that Oleg had taken one of them was high. That could explain why the K-9 had run away as soon as Yard had called him off. Instead of returning to her side as he'd been taught, he'd run back into the dark from which he'd come like a feral creature.

Kye was only waiting for a chance to slip away and look for him.

That chance seemed to arrive when the first of three ambulances appeared on the utility road. One for Purdy's body. One for the FBI agent who, unbeknownst to them, had been monitoring the house for Agent Jackson.

He'd been shot attempting to stop Purdy's partner from breaking into Yard's house. He'd lost a lot of blood but he'd been able to call for help.

The first wagon was for Gunnar, who would be transported to a nearby hospital. However, Agent Jackson had already made it clear that Gunnar was under his protection as a federal witness and he would be transported to D.C. as soon as he was stable enough.

As they loaded Gunnar into the ambulance, Yardley suddenly seemed to remember Kye was alive. She came toward him slowly, looking like a kid in his coat. It swallowed her figure and hung over her fingertips. She looked so young and vulnerable. He wanted to wrap her up in his arms and carry her away to where it was warm and quiet and very safe.

But he wouldn't. She was going with Gunnar.

She walked right up to him, so close he began to straighten from his slouch, and then she was plowing into him, her face going against his neck and burrowing there.

His arms came up about her. His SAR parka kept him from feeling any part of the woman beneath. It was enough she was leaning fully into him, her chill cheek on his even colder chest. Someone had tossed him a blanket that he'd put around his shoulders. But from the moment Yardley touched him, he burst into a blazing inferno inside.

Those around them seemed to understand it was a moment more private than most, and discreetly turned their backs and went on with their work.

Finally she lifted her head, but only so that her lips were turned up to his ear. "I thought, when I heard the shots, that you were dead. And David . . ." She seemed to run out of breath.

"I know." He pressed her tighter to his body. "Didn't I promise you I'd take care of you? And him."

"But I didn't want you to die doing it." She lifted a hand and pounded her fist against his chest. "You idiot! You left me." She was so weak the pounding was more like pats.

He lifted her chin and smiled at her. "You can beat me up later. I promise. I won't hit back." Beyond her shoulder he saw the EMT signal that the wagon was ready to roll. "You need to go with David. I'll catch up when I can."

She tried to smile at him but the muscles in her face wouldn't seem to work. "You . . . you sure you're okay? Your skin's like ice. And your poor nose."

"Yeah. Well, I was too pretty for my own good anyway. Now I'll just be an average Joe."

"Liar." This time the smile made it onto her face. "You'll always be a beautiful man. The doctors will make you better than ever."

He began releasing her. "The EMTs need you to go now."

She nodded and reluctantly turned away.

"Wait." She turned back. "How did you get up here so fast?"

Yardley blew out her breath. "There are steps cut into the slope behind the kennel. Dad made some SEALs do it for him as an exercise in cooperation. I think he just took advantage of their willingness to do anything to gain his approval."

He would have done it by himself, to gain her approval. Hell, he'd climbed a hill in the snow in his undershirt for her. Pretty impressive. But he didn't say any of that. She was in love with another man.

She turned away only to spin back once more. "Here. You need this."

She unzipped his coat and slipped it off to hand it to him. "I can't believe you've been out here dressed like that."

Kye smiled. "Why? Are you cold?"

He waited until the ambulance pulled out and then approached the sheriff. "Can I borrow a high-beam flashlight and a FLIR? If you've got one."

"Sure. But why?"

"Ms. Summers's K-9, Oleg. Purdy fired on him at close range. He's disappeared and I'm pretty sure he was hit."

"Wait. I'll go with you."

Kye nodded. "I'll need to go back to the house first. I need a few things, and my K-9, Lily. She's search-and-rescue-trained and will be able to track him faster in the snow than I can."

"And get yourself some clothes, son. This ain't Florida."

CHAPTER TWENTY-SIX

Sheriff Wiley and one of his deputies who ran his hunting dog as a retriever agreed to help Kye search. First he had to go back to the house, pick up Oleg's muzzle and leash and a blanket he thought Yardley wouldn't mind him borrowing. And, of course, Lily.

He'd found her curled up on the bed he'd slept in the night before. Well, pieces of it. She had chewed up both pillows and the comforter, so that the room look like it had exploded. And then she'd had a go at a corner of the mattress itself. He couldn't blame her. Shut up all evening and half the night with strangers coming and going and gunshots. The bedroom looked like he probably felt if he had time to think about it, which he didn't.

She launched herself at him when he came in, yipping and screaming in joy. He took a few minutes to play with her. Letting her tug on one end of a sock and then giving her several treats as she performed tricks they usually practiced daily. It seemed to quiet her. The only strange thing about all this was that it was done by flash-light.

The sheriff told him he'd see to it that someone came out to check on the generator in the morning. After all, it would be Monday, the first working day of the new year. Until then, Kye would need to find a motel room. After he found Oleg. And after he visited the hospital to check on David and Yardley. He hoped he would be able to give her good news.

Once satisfied that Lily was calm and ready to work, Kye moved quickly through the warmth of the house's interior. Even in the dark, the captured heat within the house was beginning to thaw out his fingers and toes, making them tingle painfully as he quickly exchanged his soggy pants for jeans. There was nothing for him to change out of his undershirt into so he simply zipped his parka over it. He had to go back out into the cold so there was no real use in warming up. Except for the thermos of coffee that appeared in his hand.

The sheriff's wife had arrived, thinking that Yardley might need a woman's help. She'd even come prepared with sandwiches for her husband's officers.

Kye swallowed a ham sandwich in a few bites, amazed at how hungry he was. But it was eaten on the move. He had to get back out there and find Oleg before his injuries and the cold claimed him.

The sheriff drove them back to the site where other law enforcement officers were still gathering evidence on the utility road. A man had died. There'd been an attempted kidnapping of a federal witness. A home had been invaded. Shots had been fired. There would be many inquiries into the events of the night.

The searchers came to quick agreement. Lily would

lead the search. Everyone, even the deputy's dog, would stay behind her so as not to confuse the scent.

Kye carried her off onto a snowy area in front of the truck. The wind direction wouldn't be a problem since they were up in the trees. The snow, at last, had petered out. Only problem, the woodlands here were heavily evergreen. Their pungent oily scent might cover Oleg's.

But Lily was game, prancing around on the snow-covered ground as she had done on the ski slopes of Utah.

Kye bent down and rubbed her chest to get her into search mode. "Good girl, Lily. Good girl." He held the muzzle that belonged to Oleg under her nose so that Lily could catch the Czech wolfdog's scent. Then he took it away, unleashed her, and stood up. "Search. Oleg. Search!"

The toller immediately began sniffing the air. Moving in ever-increasing circles, under the arc of lights she suddenly paused, barked excitedly, and ran forward down the road.

"Go!" Kye followed Lily, who was doing some heavy air sniffing as they went along. It was but a few seconds before the deputy's hound seemed to catch a scent, too. The dog raced forward, straining at the end of his handler's long search leash.

They quickly went off road, up an incline, and into the woods. Kye could hear Lily moving ahead of them. The sky was clear now but the winter woods were murky. Only the flash of Lily's bright-red coat when she crossed the light thrown by his flashlight offered a vivid contrast with the bare branches of oak and chestnut and the blue-green density of evergreens.

Every few minutes, Lily would stop and do what he

called her wave motion, moving her head up and down, trying to find the scent on an air current to keep them moving forward. Once enclosed in woods, scents often became misdirected. Cool weather kept scents from rising from the ground.

For ten minutes, they moved between field and tree stands, heading east and then south, deeper into the woods without a track. Kye kept his gaze forward, watching Lily's back though she was anywhere from ten to fifteen yards ahead of him. It was clear she was in her element, tracking and glorying in the chase. Once in a while she glanced back at him.

He was just about to call Yardley when Lily stopped dead. She sniffed twice. Snorting and backpedaling, she began yipping excitedly and then running in circles, sneezing and yipping.

"What's that mean?" The sheriff had come up behind them.

"She's found something. Stay back." He was very much concerned that Lily had caught the scent of death.

With a heavy stroking heart, he moved forward. When he was within ten feet of Lily, he withdrew the FLIR. It was a forward-looking infrared device that would allow him to see variances in heat. Every living thing gave off heat. He hadn't wanted to use it while there was a chance he could scan a raccoon or other wild creature. Now he aimed it in the area where Lily was dancing in concern. It registered two signatures, Lily's the brighter of the two.

"Found him. Stay back."

"Heel." Lily came bounding toward him, thrilled to get the chew toy Kye pulled out as reward. He snapped on the leash and handed the end of it to the sheriff.

He turned and approached the injured dog slowly. Oleg was lying on his side and did not even lift his head as Kye approached. He was hurt and in pain.

Kye used his flashlight to guide him but held the beam off the dog's face so that it didn't blind the canine.

"Hey here, big fella. Hey, Oleg. You've had a big night, haven't you?"

Oleg roused himself to lift his head but whined and lay back down.

Kye got down on his knees. An injured dog was often a frightened one and he didn't want to get bit if he could help it. "It's okay, Oleg. Good boy. You saved lives tonight. Yes you did. You deserve a medal." Kye wished he knew some Czech phrases but he hoped his tone would convey his intentions.

"Need to get you out of here, Oleg. Going to put the muzzle on you." He held it out so that Oleg could sniff it. After a moment, the dog did just that. He bared his teeth but did not try to bite it.

"I know. I'd hate it, too, if I were you. But it's okay. Just a precaution."

When Oleg lifted his head again, Kye slipped the wire basket over his snout. When Oleg didn't react, Kye quickly slipped the straps into place and buckled it.

Using the blanket he'd brought with him, he scooped up the Czech wolfdog. He wasn't surprised by the dog's sudden growl of warning or even when he tried to snap at him. He felt the dampness of his fur wasn't all from the snowy ground.

Once he held him in his arms, he turned to the sheriff. "Let's go. Can someone call ahead to wake a vet?"

CHAPTER TWENTY-SEVEN

April, Harmonie Kennels

"*Hier.* Storm. Thunder."

The pair of four-month-old Belgian Malinoises, born on New Year's Eve, came running on Yardley's command. They were rangy and lean, like a pair of teenagers. Of the six, Yardley had determined that these two had the most drive and intelligence for law enforcement work. Taggart, her senior trainer, had chosen two of the others. The final two had been adopted by law enforcement personnel looking for companions for their working K-9s.

"*Sitz.*" They dropped butt, all rapt attention as two pairs of serious intelligent dark eyes in black-masked faces gazed adoringly up at her. Their ears stood tall and wide, revolving like satellite dishes. Too big for their heads now, but the dogs would grow into them.

Smiling, Yardley waved the ball launcher, a long plastic wand with a tennis ball attached at the end, under their noses. And then she began walking. "*Hier.*"

Eager to earn the ball, they followed her, watching the ball's every movement as she made slow sweeps through the air. As she passed a picnic table she raised the wand up so that the ball traveled over the top. "*Hopp.*"

Both puppies jumped up on the table, eager to follow the reward they knew would come at the end of the game. Much of early training for potential K-9s was about helping the pups overcome natural fears of leaping, balancing on unfamiliar surfaces, and hesitations with new things so that they gained the confidence to try new things if their handler was telling them to do something. Practicing balance and agility gave them both. Soon they would learn to go into dark places, climb ladders, and force entry through a doorway. But for today, they were building muscle memory and getting exercise.

As she moved on, they leaped off the table after her, their natural athleticism showing in their fearlessness launching themselves from the height. She jogged quickly over to the wooden railing of the deck attached to the classroom building. As she lifted the ball wand up, Storm and Thunder jumped for the narrow railing on top. Storm made the leap easily. Thunder had to scramble a bit to keep his footing. Encouraged by the moving ball, they stepped cautiously along the two-by-four, like tightrope walkers on a high wire. Yet they both jumped off this higher perch without hesitation.

Yardley went back to the beginning and repeated the skill until they both were jumping and balancing unhesitatingly on the rail. Another lesson learned.

"*Gute Hunds!*" Her pride sounded in her voice, high and girlish as she bent to love on them. The puppy pair were pretty happy with themselves, barking and wagging tails. They had already learned not to leap on a handler.

After a moment, she held up the ball launcher again. Both puppies came to immediate attention and sat, dark eyes fixated. Thunder was the first to notice that Yardley had pulled a second ball from her pocket. He glanced at her and barked.

Laughing, she reared back and launched both balls into the air. The brother and sister's heads snapped, their bodies doing a little dance of coiled energy. But neither chased after the balls.

When the balls had bounced in the thick spring-green grass Yardley cried, "*In ordnung.*" Okay, they were free to play.

The pair took off like they'd been shot from a cannon.

Both were very eager to learn, and came with a natural drive to please. Storm was a bit more courageous than Thunder at this stage. But Thunder would develop the slight advantage of male weight and size as they continued to grow.

Yardley grinned as she watched the pair. Her first breeding project was a success.

"Here you go, boss."

Yardley turned to find Taggart coming toward her with Oleg on the leash.

Her expression went serious as she watched the Czech wolfdog approach. Nothing in his stride gave away the surgeries he'd been through to repair damage after he'd been shot.

Taggart saw her frown and smiled a big toothy grin. "Stop worrying. He's doing real good, Yard. I got him up on the tires and then jumping the bales. He's leaping like a champion."

Oleg came bounding up to her, a friendly growl issuing from him.

"Thanks, Taggart." She took Oleg's leash and squatted down to scratch him softly. Oleg offered her licks in return. They'd become more than handler and K-9. They'd become a team. But she wanted to be certain her affection for Oleg wasn't clouding her judgment about his abilities. She needed to be sure he could do the things she thought he could.

When Kye had delivered him to the vet four months ago, Oleg had been in critical condition due to trauma, blood loss, and exposure. He'd taken only one of the two shots aimed his way. Miraculously, the bullet had struck his ear first, tearing a hole in it before entering his right hindquarter. It tore some muscle, but the penetration hadn't gone deep or shattered bone. He'd had surgery that night and again in the morning to repair the damage. Then came the weeklong wait to see if he would develop an infection. But the Czech wolfdog rallied, getting back on his feet faster than anyone expected.

Now all that was left of Oleg's experience was a torn ear and a tail that tended to lean to one side where a nerve had been damaged.

"Good news, boss. The sheriff called to say the court decision has come in. Oleg's in the clear."

Yardley looked up with a smile. "No more threats against him?"

Taggart frowned, his face resembling a bulldog's. "I'd like to see someone say he's vicious after looking at those photos of what he suffered."

Yardley thought the same thing. But people were

strange. The fact that Oleg's attack had resulted in a death shocked everyone, including her. But the circumstances had been extreme. He was operating in near-blackout conditions, and he taken a bullet before his takedown bite. It was pure bad luck that his teeth had severed an artery. He hadn't been trained to kill. But he was doing his job of providing protection.

Still, all dog bites had to be reported. It had taken lots of testimony by friends and experts to convince a judge that Oleg wasn't dangerous in ordinary circumstances. That he didn't really know what he'd done, other than his job to protect his handler by biting the bad guy. Yardley had had to sign papers promising that Oleg would never work as a law enforcement K-9 before the judge would agree to consider allowing him to leave the shelter where he'd been placed while awaiting judgment.

"Too bad he can't now do his job. He's more than capable."

"Thanks to you." Yardley stood up and, not allowing herself to censor her actions, threw her arms about the big man and hugged him tight. "Thank you."

He turned bright red and grinned like a schoolboy. "My pleasure, boss."

It didn't matter that he couldn't work K-9 law enforcement. He wasn't going to be a ghost op K-9 private security dog, either.

Yardley had seen to that. She had told his owners that Oleg was no longer fit for the service they had in mind. It wasn't a lie. She hadn't liked what they had in mind. They'd been much too eager to hear the details of Oleg's deadly takedown. Wanted to know if a dog could train for that particular bite. She wanted nothing to do with them. In fact, she mentioned that if the news got leaked they were training murder dogs, they'd be out of business. Then she bought him from his handlers, paying top price for a dog that would never work a day in the career he'd been trained for. But there were other jobs he'd be equally good at.

Yardley reached for a tennis ball and held it up before Oleg. Then he noticed the pair of four-month-olds fighting to claim both balls. He glanced back at Yardley. And then at the pair. She knew what he wanted. She unleashed him.

He came in fast on the pair of puppies, hitting them low and knocking their legs out from under them. They went tumbling across the grass like a pair of bowling pins after an Oleg ball strike. They rolled and were up instantly, barking and chasing their tormentor. Oleg easily outran them, only to circle back and grab one of the tennis balls. The other ball forgotten, they chased him until their tongues hung like bright-pink flags from their open jaws, and they collapsed in the grass. Only then did she lob the third ball their way. Oleg, of course, beat the youngsters to the new ball, claiming it. They, in turn, went to find the abandoned balls. After a moment, three happy dogs lay in the grass chomping on their favorite toys.

Two hours later she was sitting behind the wheel of her Jeep headed for D.C. Georgiana had asked her, as a favor, to attend some sort of reception with her since Brad was, once more, out of town. Yardley had a feeling there was more to it than that but she wasn't in a position to pry since she'd been closed up tighter than a clam in ice water about her love life.

Or rather lack of it.

Frowning, she pushed the button on her dash display and made a call.

"Agent Jackson speaking."

"Hello. Yardley Summers here."

"Ms. Summers." Jackson's voice had taken on a warm tone she had never heard before. "I've been expecting your call."

Yardley glanced at the speaker. "Why?"

"Always to the point. I've been in touch with a former colleague. He left a message for you, in case you called."

Her stomach jumped. She and David hadn't been in touch since the week she'd spent by his side under guard in the hospital in D.C. "What does it say?"

"Two words. Bonnie Raitt."

Yardley smiled. "Got it."

"Any return message?"

"No."

"In that case, I've been advised to tell you he's taking a sea voyage. Signed up for a cruise. Medical ship. Contained environment. Very secure. Limited access. Pretty good job for a doc on a mission. I'm told fresh sea air can do wonders for the soul."

"I've heard that, too. Thank you."

"So this is good-bye, Ms. Summers. Try to have a less eventful life. At least until after I retire. My wife would appreciate it, too."

After she hung up she slipped in a CD that had come in the mail weeks ago. No message. No return address. The opening notes of a piano filled the Jeep, followed by Bonnie Raitt's beautifully plaintive voice full of love and tenderness and painful acceptance in "I Can't Make

You Love Me." The plaintive cry of someone who loves but isn't loved back.

David's way of saying that he was moving on. Back to saving the world while he waited for a trial far in his future. Only she seemed to be stuck.

Yardley suddenly understood that song from another perspective. Once she'd thought that her legacy would be to never know real love. It felt strange to be on the other side. She hadn't loved David. Not enough to give up everything that defined who she was, what she was, what she had achieved. She wasn't shocked when he told her that he was going back into witness protection indefinitely, maybe for years. His mission to take down illegal pharmaceuticals hadn't altered. But it was no way to begin a life together. David's words. Even so, there'd been something in his eyes that told her he wanted her to make him a liar, and come with him.

Yardley sighed. She hadn't asked for that chance. Her feelings toward David weren't what she'd thought they were months before. Or maybe they were. They'd just been exposed for what they were: great affection, nothing more.

Kye was the reason for this revelation. He had given her something to compare her feelings for David with. Her feelings for Kye, a dozen years old and dusty with age, were the real thing. Love. Clear and bright and undiminished. Her fault if she'd figured that out too late.

Kye had left without offering her a chance to go with him.

She hadn't seen him since the morning he'd come to the hospital to tell her that he'd found Oleg, and stayed with her K-9 through his initial surgery.

Yardley sucked in a quick breath. She'd seen in his

eyes a distance that hadn't been there befor
backed away from her touch. Wouldn't even lc
hug him in thanks. He'd mumbled something at
"Four days of insanity over," and back-walked out c
her life.

At the end of the song, she ejected the CD, rolled
down the window, and, after a brief check to make certain no one was right behind her, sent it sailing out the
window. Whatever the last year—certainly those four
days—had been about, it wasn't over for her.

Maybe because Kye walking away didn't feel like closure. Even now, thoughts of him still woke her in the
wee hours, demanding her attention when she was too
weak to keep them at bay.

She tightened her mouth and glanced at her image in
the rearview. She just didn't know what to do about it.

"To strong women, handsome men, and lousy timing."
Georgie held up her third tequila shot.

"*Salud.*" Yardley clinked glasses with her, and they
both threw back their heads and drank.

"Oh my." Georgie blinked and fanned herself, her
skin bright red in reaction to the alcohol. "I don't think
I can keep up with you, Yard. My eyes are refusing to
focus."

"In that case, it's lucky I have a room here tonight."

Yardley and Georgie were almost through a flight of
tequila shots and shooters, ranging from a *blanco* to *re-
posado* and finally *anejo*. Each shot glass was rimmed
with salt and came with a shooter. The first had been the
traditional Mexican sangrita of orange juice, grena-
dine, and chili pepper. The second shooter contained a
spicy green concoction of pineapple, cilantro, mint, and

ɔ. The third, sitting before them, contained to-
juice with Tabasco and Worcestershire sauce.

ɔometimes the only remedy for heartache was girl
me and booze. Lots and lots of booze.

Georgie signaled to the hotel bartender, who had been
watching the pair in admiration.

The women, dressed casually in tailored shirts, jeans,
and heels, had drawn the eye of everyone who spotted
them. It seemed impossible to ignore the pair of redheads
at the bar. The contrast between Georgie's curly paprika
hair floating about her shoulders and Yardley's spill of
Cherry Coke hair parted simply in the middle invited
comment.

The bartender came over with a grin. "The men at the
table beyond the end of the bar would like to buy you
ladies a refill."

Yardley reached out and cupped the back of his hand.
"Tell them no thanks. Our Navy SEAL husbands are
waiting for us upstairs."

The bartender looked down at her hand. "You aren't
wearing a ring."

Yardley smiled. "That's not where I wear it."

His brows rose but she was already looking away,
reaching for her sangrita chaser.

Georgie smothered her laughter in her palm as he
moved away. "I can't believe you said that."

"Must be the tequila," Yardley agreed. She was feeling a little reckless. But not desperate. "Want to tell me
why I'm really here?"

"Only if you want to skip dinner."

Something in her tone made Yardley suddenly very
sure she wouldn't now be able to swallow that thick juicy

steak she'd been contemplating. She looked up at bartender and shook her head as he poured. "Check."

She waited until they were on the elevator alone before she turned to Georgie, a scowl on her face. "What have you done?"

Georgie shrugged. "I refused to be in the middle, okay? But the man can be persuasive."

Yardley's stomach dropped as the elevator swooshed upward, implications running wild. "If you set me up . . ."

Georgie shrugged. "Can I have the key to the room? I don't think you'll be needing it, after all."

The doors parted on their floor and Georgie beat her out. She smiled at the man waiting to get on, then turned back to Yardley. "Neutral territory. Good luck."

Yardley stared at the handsome man standing in the doorway with his dog by his side.

He looked good, better than she'd ever seen him. He was all healed and tan, strong and fit and very handsome.

She folded her arms, suddenly stone-cold sober. "What brings you to D.C.?"

"You, sis."

CHAPTER TWENTY-EIGHT

Her half brother, Lauray Battise, stood in the elevator doorway, holding the leash of a PTSD service dog named Samantha. Sam was a cutesy rust-red mash-up of golden retriever and standard poodle with an enormous curling tail.

The contrast between man and dog couldn't have been more startling. Law was tall, hard, with black hair, sludge-gold eyes, and a chin like granite. A tinge of danger seeped into the air around him, making people move aside without even knowing why.

Yardley reached out to stop the elevator doors from closing but didn't step out or invite him in. "Why are you here, Law? Is something wrong with Jori? Did she kick you out?"

Law grinned and shook his head. "Good to see you, too, Yard."

He stepped inside as the elevator chimed impatiently and pushed the LOBBY button.

"Hi, Sam." Yardley bent down and greeted Samantha before glaring at her owner. She hated being ambushed, and every instinct told her she was going to like it even less when she learned why Law had thought it was necessary. "You didn't answer my question."

"You haven't answered my texts." He smiled at her in a way that said he knew she was tipsy. Okay, maybe more than tipsy.

"What do you want?"

"Where's your Jeep key?"

"Why? Are you planning to kidnap me?"

"I'm going to drive us home." He held up a hand as she opened her mouth. "No questions. No problems. We'll talk in the morning."

"I was going to take a cab. But seeing that you're here." She handed him the key.

Yardley fell into step beside her brother as they crossed the lobby so in sync that their movements looked choreographed. Dressed alike in jeans and tailored shirts, his matched with military boots and hers with hand-tooled western stiletto booties, the Battises made a statement without opening their mouths.

She handed the valet her ticket before turning to her brother and saying in a loud voice, "You promised me a steak dinner. If you plan on having your way with me, you need to feed me first."

Law ignored the heads snapping in their direction. "Cute. Burger on the way out?"

She glared at him. "Double meat, bacon, and extra cheese."

"Geez, Yard. Anyone ever tell you that you eat like a man?"

* * *

Breakfast consisted of coffee. Black. Toast. Burnt. Attitude. Don't give a damn.

Law leaned an elbow on the mantel and gazed around
the living room shaking his head. Usually immaculate,
it looked like a tornado had blown through and parked
six months' worth of dog hair on every surface.

Yard followed his gaze before her expression became
defensive. "I've been busy."

"I can see that." His gaze shifted to the very dusty
artificial Christmas tree still standing in the corner. "You
remember how you found me about this time last year?"

"Falling-on-your-ass drunk, sunk in poor-me piss, and
about a few drinks from swallowing your pistol?"

He winced. "Yeah, something like that. Is this the female version? Because damn, Yard."

They'd always played hard off each other. Mostly
because they'd never known each other well enough to
be tender. And because their father didn't want them to.
The last year had brought them closer, but the close was
still new and tender in its own way.

She shook her head. "It's been a rough few months.
But I'm over it."

"Over what?"

"All of it. Stokes. David. Everything." She ducked her
head. She'd almost added Kye to that list. But that would
only open a can of worms that most definitely didn't
need exposure. "Like I said. I've been busy."

"You've been something. And it isn't good. You've
given up."

"Mind your own business, maybe?"

She leaned forward in her chair to love on Sam. "Hey,
Sam. Maybe you know why you're here, since Law obviously isn't going to say."

"Where's your dog?" He picked up and sifted through his fingers a tuft of Czech wolfdog hair that had settled on the mantel. "I was going to ask if you've got a new dog. But there must be whole pack living here with you."

"Just Oleg. He's at the vet's getting a check-up."

"He heal up okay?"

"Better than that." She'd told him about all that had gone on over the New Year weekend immediately afterward. That didn't explain why he was here four months after the fact.

Law moved to hitch a hip on the edge of the sofa because it was the closest seat to hers. "I've quit the state police."

Before she could stop herself, her gaze dipped to his left pant leg. A casual observer might not have noticed the way it sagged. That's because behind it lay a state-of-the-art prosthesis. The best available. But it wasn't the same as the leg Law had left with when he went to Afghanistan a little more than four years ago.

She tried to read something in his expression but his sludge-gold gaze gave nothing away. He'd lost more than a leg in the war. He'd lost himself. He had come pretty close to the status of off-the-grid crazed loner holed up in the backwoods of northwest Arkansas when she had barged in on him a year earlier, demanding that he seek help for his PTSD issues.

Getting back on the payroll with the Arkansas State Police had been the only thing that had kept him sane. He'd even passed the Arkansas State Police physical in order to go back on full duty in February. What had changed in two months?

"Does Jori know?"

"Haven't discussed it with her yet. Figured I needed to get my act together first."

"I see." The bottom fell out of Yardley's stomach. Jori was the main reason Law had been doing so well. She and his dog.

Yardley's gaze flickered to the rusty-red goldendoodle standing watch by Law's side. Sam held a world of knowledge in her gentle gaze. Too bad she couldn't share it.

Law stood up, running a hand impatiently through his unruly black hair. "The truth is I need to think about my future. That's not something I've often done. But if I want Jori in my life, I need something to show for it beside a willingness to get shot at."

He's talking about the future. His and Jori's. Yardley almost smiled but she knew better than to be obvious. "Law enforcement is an honorable profession."

"The best. I'll always be Blue. But I've stopped running. I used to think that it was best not to owe anything to anyone and for them not to need to depend on me. But that's stupid and juvenile."

He turned back to her. "Of all the people I've hurt, I've hurt you the most. And that's unforgivable because you're blood."

Yardley swallowed back emotion. "You never heard me complain."

"No. You're a Battise, which means you're too stubborn and too proud for your own good. We'll take the heat for something we didn't do just to prove to ourselves that other people's opinions of us don't matter. Especially when we aren't even sure that's what we really want."

Her eyes widened in alarm. "Don't tell me you've been converted into some sort of touchy-feely cult?"

He laughed. "No to-the-hell not. What I'm saying is, I want to start making things up to you."

"You're making me very nervous. Just what do you have in mind?"

"First, I apologize for leaving you to deal with this." He indicated the room. "I was so busy trying to kick a dead man that I simply walked out on you and left a hell of a mess."

"You mean your inheritance? But I wanted Harmonie Kennels."

He shook his head. "I heard how you almost went under the first year. How law enforcement and the feds didn't think a woman could cut it."

"You knew about all the hell I went through?"

"I did. And I didn't care. Honest to God, I think I hoped you'd fail. Ruin everything Bronson Battise had built."

"You rat bastard." Yardley jumped to her feet, feeling tears prick up behind her eyes. "You knew and you did nothing." She gasped, searching for words that she couldn't find.

He looked equally injured by his admission. "I know. I've been a selfish prick, Yard. I was going through my own hell, and I was so angry at Battise for all the times he hadn't been there when I needed him as a kid. I wanted to prove to myself that I didn't need anything from him when he was gone. I had nothing left to give you. It was a dick move. But I've learned a few things since then. Had to crawl my way back to being a decent human being. Hell, you're responsible for a lot of it. You, and Jori, and Sam. I don't deserve it. But I'm asking. Forgive me?" He reached out an arm toward her. It was all the apology she was going to get.

Yardley didn't need more. She moved into his embrace and pushed her face against his shoulder as he closed his arms around her.

After a moment, Law tugged her hair and she swatted his shoulder, and the balance in the world returned.

"So, what now, little brother?"

"We get to work on you. Aside from housekeeping, you have some emotional cleanup to do."

She folded her arms across her chest. "What, in your opinion, would this consist of?"

"You need to straighten things out with Kye."

"Not your damn business."

"You made it my business when you slept with him."

She gasped and too late saw the trap. "Damn you. How did you guess?"

"Let's just say it seemed inevitable. I was never sure about the doc. But I knew how Kye felt. That's why I sent him here."

"Now you're lying. Kye told me he didn't even know we were related until you called him."

"True. But he talked about you before that. A lot. While we were stationed together. Afghanistan was a place of interminable boredom interspersed with moments of high drama and/or terror. In between there was nothing else to do but argue, play sports, watch TV, and talk. Kye's the talkiest guy I ever met."

Yardley nodded. "He talked about me? To you?"

"Like you said. He didn't know who we were to each other. He was just a lonely man in a dangerous place with the sense that maybe his life might not have a future. So he talked about the past. And this girl he'd met when he was first starting out as a dog man. At first he just talked about the woman who got away. Most men have that story. Finally, one time, he mentioned Harmonie Kennels and I knew it was you that got away."

"Why didn't you say anything to him? To me?"

He just stared at her.

"Right." She and Law shared a love of privacy that bordered on paranoia. "It wouldn't have mattered. I know now he was married."

"There was that, too. I thought he was just trying to make sense of his life's choices. Roads not traveled and all."

"What changed your mind?"

"Jori. Finding her. Being with her. I finally saw a relationship from a woman's point of view. She made me deal with my emotions. Love is not interchangeable. It's not easy. And when it comes, it leaves its mark on a person. Sometimes you carry it to the grave. Some of the boneheaded things I said and did were because I wasn't ready. Sometimes a man isn't ready. Even when the right woman comes along."

This was all too much, coming from her brother. Deep thoughts on love and emotional trauma and love and genuine emotion and . . . love.

She had to turn it off before she drowned. "Are you going to go all proselytizing reformed man on me? Because I don't think I can stand this new Doctor-Phil Law."

"Don't worry, Sis. I still prefer boobs and beer to *Masterpiece Theatre*. But what I'm trying to say is, Kye wasn't ready back then. I can't say that about you."

"I loved him. He broke my heart."

Law shrugged. "I heard about how Bronson threatened

him. I think Kye didn't have any options. Neither did we, back in those days."

Yard's face screwed up. "I think he broke us, Law. Bronson broke us."

"He tried. But you did better than I did. You stood your ground and fought your way through. I never stopped moving long enough for anything to stick until something literally cut the legs out from under me." He tapped his prosthesis. "I don't want you to wait for your IED moment. You might not be as lucky as I was."

"So, what am I supposed to do? I can't just walk away from this and go find my bliss." She waved her arms around.

"Why not?"

"Because there are people here depending on me. A dozen or more livelihoods are at stake if Harmonie Kennels closes."

He sat down and looked his her, his head cocked to one side. "Is that really all that keeps you here?"

"Honestly? Yes." She took a deep breath. "I'm tired, Law. I've given Harmonie Kennels all my adult life. I'm—" She wouldn't say *scared*. "I'm missing my life."

He grinned. "Funny. I think I've just found mine. I've got a proposition for you."

She folded her arms.

"I'm out of a job. I'm looking for something permanent. Something with a solid future and a place to raise a family. Maybe. Sometime. If I can get a certain woman to think about it after we've been together a year. I figure that's about how long it'll take me to determine if I can be the decent sort of person I want to be for Jori. She needs an all-time man. What I'm saying is, I'd like to try my hand at running Harmonie Kennels. Of course, you'll still be the owner."

Yardley opened her mouth and shut it three times before words would form. "We could split it fifty–fifty."

He wagged his head. "I lost my right to anything but a salary from this place."

"Fifty–fifty, dammit, or you can go find another job." She came at him, right up into his face. "You think you can do the job but then stick me with one hundred percent of the headaches around here? Think again, little brother."

He gazed at her in wonder. "Are you sure about that? You'll be fifty percent poorer?"

"Only if you screw up."

With his head tilted to one side, he looked as puzzled as a K-9 given an unfamiliar command. "Honest to God, you'd do that for me? After everything?"

"I'll call my lawyer today."

"What will you do?"

Her turn to shake her head. "I don't know. I haven't had a chance to think about something else."

"You should stay in the K-9 business."

She gave him a sour face.

"Not here. And not training. Take your skills on the road. There isn't a business involving K-9s anywhere in the world that wouldn't jump at the chance to hire Yardley Summers. You've spent your life preparing other K-9 teams for their jobs. Go out and practice what you've been preaching."

"I wouldn't know where to start."

"Start with a vacation. I hear Hawaii's nice this time of year."

She gave him a half smile. "Don't you dare make any calls. If I think you've so much as breathed in Kye's direction, I'll head for Russia instead."

He held her gaze with a slight smile. "Don't be a hard-ass, Yard. Go get your man."

CHAPTER TWENTY-NINE

Kye pored over the spreadsheet on the monitor before him. It was April, tax time. "Bad news. We had our best year so far. Going to have to pay our taxes quarterly from now on."

"Ta. Cheery thought. The wankers!"

Oliver hated taxes. He hated government and regulation and laws and anything else that interfered with "my God-given right to go to bloody hell any way I like." He said it was every Aussie's duty to hate regulation. But he did it in such a cheerful fashion, it never became an issue. They had a you-pay-while-I-play arrangement.

Oliver was in Hawaii soaking up some rays while he and Kye planned the next business quarter. But mostly he was running through the local population of beautiful women. Right now he was slumped in a wicker chair on Kye's parents' patio, drinking his protein-shake breakfast at half past noon.

"Up for some fun with the Sheilas? Met a couple,

maybe it was three, in a bar last night. Said I'd catch them beachside. Too many for me. Come with?"

Kye gave his partner a sour look. "Taxes?"

Oliver grinned. "Do a sickie. Do you a world of good."

Kye didn't doubt his friend was serious about the women waiting for him. Oliver was a ripped, six-foot-four of hard body with shoulder-length sun-streaked hair that was, at the moment, pulled back in a messy man-bun. The look wouldn't have worked on a man an ounce less masculine. But the dude was blessed with Chris Hemsworth baby blues and a scruff of red-blond beard scrupulously maintained to keep his look this side of sexiest homeless man alive.

Kye shook his head. Hawaiian women might never be the same.

"Oh yeah. I forgot."

Kye looked up again over his computer. Oliver never forgot anything.

"We've got a new recruit coming in today." Oliver sat up. "Stateside female. Has some experience with dogs. Trainer."

Kye's mouth thinned. "Do we need another trainer?"

"A good one, yeah. You might like this one. I hear she's got legs for days. And she's a ginger."

"A redhead?"

"I know you're partial to gingers. Pick her up at the airport. Do you good to get your head out of the numbers."

"Pass. I'm off redheads."

"That's your problem. You come off a bad experience, you need to replace it with good ones."

"It wasn't a bad experience. It was a favor for a friend."

"That lost you the girl and got your nose flattened for the effort."

Kye reached up automatically to touch his healed nose.

"Vain, that's what you are. It healed so perfectly you can't even show off your manly scars. Surgery for an owee. What's this world coming to?"

"I couldn't breathe right."

"You lost the woman, mate. Time to find another. Your trouble is, you want the whole package. Now me, I'm a connoisseur. A pretty face. A gorgeous ass. A nice pair of tits. They don't all have to come on the same chassis. I enjoy each wherever I find it."

"Yeah. Yeah. I get it. You're a man whore."

"Jealous. That's what you are. Go pick up the Sheila."

Kye sighed. He was enjoying having his partner in Honolulu for a few days. He just wished he hadn't chosen tax week. Or his grandmother's birthday week. "We've got a luau tonight that I have to help prepare for."

"Roasting a pig for your granny? Saw the beast go in the ground this morning. Admit it. You have no excuse."

Kye ignored him.

"You're ruining my holiday with all this business. Makes Oliver a sour boy. And no one likes a sour Oliver. Say, that would make a good name for a beach drink. The Sour Oliver."

Kye glared from beneath his brows. "Out. Now."

Oliver stood up. "No worries. See you at the luau. Unless the ginger develops a thing for me on the way in."

"If she does I won't hire her."

"I'm a partner. I can hire her."

"We settled that four years ago. If you did the hiring

our SAR teams would look like Miss World runner-ups with dogs as accessories."

Laughing good-naturedly, Oliver strolled out.

Kye waited until he heard the front door close before he abandoned his computer and went to stand at the edge of the patio. Lily, who'd been dozing peacefully under the desk at his feet, stretched slowly then rose to follow him. She watched him for a moment then followed his gaze, though she didn't understand his fascination with the view.

The vista from this house was of the clear blue water and sandy shoreline of Pukoo Beach, breathtaking each and every time he came here. The human spirit couldn't grow accustomed to so much beauty. That's what kept visitors coming to these islands again and again, to make certain their senses had not overhyped their memories.

His parents owned a home in Honolulu but kept this place on Molokai as a connection to their Hawaiian ancestors. It was where his father's mother still lived. It was her birthday today and it would be celebrated on the beach with a traditional foods and music and dance.

He'd wanted to bring Yardley here. Wanted her to see the place he called home, as precious to him as Harmonie Kennels was to her. Even if he only lived here part-time, it was the place he dreamed of when he closed his eyes. But this time, something was missing. He didn't feel all here.

Kye wiped both hands down his face. Oliver was right. He was mourning. Stupid. Useless. Waste of time. The fucking thing was, he'd known going in that she was in love with another man. Nothing had changed once she realized David Gunnar was alive.

So why couldn't he get his last image of Yardley out of his mind?

She'd been bending over David, kissing him. He had been coming to tell her Oleg had been located and saved by the vet doctor. As he arrived at the door of that hospital room, David had pulled her across him into his bed.

That sight was like a boot kick in the gut. He hadn't been able to catch his breath. He hadn't even bothered to try to gloss over the blow and knock at the door and pretend the sight wasn't killing him. Instead he'd backpedaled out of there. But Yardley had seen him. She caught up with him in the unsterile noisy hospital corridor.

He didn't remember what they said. He knew he didn't look her in the eye, afraid she'd see his pain. Or that he would completely lose his shit in front of her. It was a lose–lose proposition. He just remembered the need to get the hell out of Dodge.

He found a bar and drank enough beer to make him sleepy.

He hadn't realized until he woke an hour later, with a sympathetic waitress shaking him, that it had been more than three days since he'd had more than a couple of hours of shut-eye. No wonder his emotions were surfacing through his laid-back pose. Because all he had wanted to do for the next month was break something. Hurt something. Destroy something the way the kiss had devastated him.

Kye thumped a palm on the post holding up the lanai. Lily pushed in against him, a reminder that he wasn't paying enough attention. He bent and picked her up, absently petting her as his thoughts continued in train.

After the surgery to repair his broken nose, he'd taken

the first SAR job that came up. Wildfires had broken out early in the Pacific Northwest. It was the kind of mission that required full attention all the time. Good for his mental health. While he and Lily worked, alerting residents of the need to evacuate and searching for those who hadn't been heard from, he couldn't think about anything or anyone else. He'd left there and gone to Central America. And from there to Chile. For three months he'd been a moving target for his emotions.

Now home, finally, he was breathing easier. It wasn't a mortal blow. He would recover.

He rubbed his nose. But Oliver was wrong. There would always be scars.

His cell phone rang.

"*Aloha 'auinala*, grandson."

He smiled. "*Aloha. Hau'oli la hanau, Tutu*. Happy birthday."

"You are not here with the others, grandson. You promised."

"Yes, *Tutu*. I will be there."

Yardley hung off the rail at the bow of the ferry between Maui and Molokai as it docked at Kaunakakai Harbor. Everything she'd ever seen and heard about the Hawaiian Islands was true. Paradise dropped into the middle of the Pacific Ocean. She couldn't look long enough or hard enough at the sights. Somewhere on the mountainous green island glowing in the setting sun off the bow was the man she'd come to see. But would he be happy to see her?

"Here you go, Ms. Summers." Oliver handed her the travel kennel with Oleg inside as they stood on the dock a few minutes later. "He's not much for the water, is he?"

Yard bent down to see her poor Czech wolfdog looking wobbly. He licked her hand gratefully. She could sympathize. Her stomach was still rising and falling though they were on land. "He prefers snow."

"No accounting for taste." He picked up both her bags in one fist. "Come on, then. We're late for the luau."

"Oh, Oliver, thanks. But no partying for me. I need some sleep before we talk to Kye about hiring me."

Oliver slung an arm around her shoulders. "If I was to tell you there's something waiting for you that you'd kiss me full on the mouth not to miss, what would you do?"

Yardley gave him the stink-eye. "I'd think you were trying to sell me a very cheap bit of merchandise."

He threw back his head in laughter, gathering the eyeballs that weren't already glued to the gorgeous man.

Two hours later, Oleg had been walked, engaged in a hard-and-fast game of Frisbee, and fed; he now slept gratefully in a kennel that didn't fly, soar, or bob like a cork in the bathtub.

Yardley, showered and changed, came into the open-air lobby to find Oliver waiting for her. He wore board shorts, a hideously loud flowered shirt, and flip-flops.

She looked down at herself. She wore sandals and a simple white dress with scooped neck and spaghetti straps with a single large hibiscus flower printed at the hem. She hadn't known what to do with her hair so she'd just parted it and let it fall over her shoulders and down her back.

When she looked up to see why he hadn't spoken, his drop-jawed surprise confirmed her suspicion. His gaze lingered over every swell and curve of her body, making her worry that the thin material might burst into flame.

"Too much?" She held a hand up to the scoop neck. Maybe too little. The dress didn't allow for the kind of bras she'd brought. "I bought it in the gift shop when you dropped me off. I wasn't expecting to attend a celebration."

He murmured something that sounded like, "The whole package," and then turned and walked out of the hotel.

Yardley's mouth dropped open and then she went after him, getting hotter by the second. He could just suggest she change. But to walk out?

She found him outside the hotel doorway, paying for a flower. He grinned at her, accepted his change, and then came right up to her and pushed the hibiscus into her hair behind her right ear. "That ought to do it. Come on, we're late."

Yardley heard the party before they swung around a curve and the stretch of beach came into view. Under a large pavilion several dozen people were serving plates of food. Out under the stars, dozens of burning torches were staked in the sand. Several flanked a wicker chair with a high circular back in which sat a woman in a bright-purple floral muumuu with a garland of flowers in her hair and another around her neck.

"That's Tutu. I'll introduce you later." Oliver waved at a few people and then said, "Come this way."

He steered her toward the large group of partygoers who stood listening to musicians playing traditional Hawaiian music up on a makeshift stage.

With a hand at her back, he propelled her past a blur of smiling faces toward the front of the crowd. Growing a little nervous even in a smiling crowd of strangers, Yardley turned to Oliver. '"Look, if you're escorting me because Kye doesn't want me here, I can just go back to the hotel."

Oliver swung his head toward her, an incredulous look on his face. "Do you *ever* look in your mirror?"

"You heard of the Maori *haka*? It's a war dance. This is *Kane Hula kahiko*. Hawaiian male hula, ancient-style. Some call it the muscle dance." He winked at her. "Fair warning. You'll want to kiss me."

Yardley swung her attention back to the stage. The music had ended and the musicians quickly cleared the stage. A man appeared on stage carrying what looked like a large two-lobed gourd. She'd read about the instrument in the inflight magazine. It was an *ipu heke* gourd drum.

The musician began to chant, pounding the drum against the boards and using his hand and fingers to tap out a rhythm. It began slow. The chanted rhymes were in Hawaiian but they reminded her of powwows on the reservation where she grew up. Familiar and yet new. Her feet began to move in tiny stomp steps of sympathy.

Yardley had seen women in traditional grass skirts and leis and flower garlands in their hair standing next to the stage. She expected they'd be the dancers. But as she watched the stage wing in anticipation, the women parted, revealing a line of bare-chested men and boys wearing nothing but simple loincloths with a tantalizing strip of cloth hiding their modesty front and rear.

Oliver leaned over to whisper in her ear. "Kye's *tutu* requested that all eligible male descendants dance a traditional hula for her birthday."

A ripple of excitement ran over her skin like wildfire as his meaning registered, and then ten men were moving onto the stage. Youngest in the front and more mature in the rear. All bare-chested with crowns of leaves on their dark heads, necks, wrists, and ankles. At center back, the tallest, was Kye.

Yardley licked her suddenly dry lips as the syncopated rhythm caught at her pulse. The two lines of men began moving in time to the beat. Footsteps and small precise kicks that were powerful yet graceful moved them first right and then left across the stage as the audience erupted in applause.

But for Yardley there was only one man on stage. All she could do was stare at Kye as the muscles of his powerful thighs moved him across the floor, bent knees swiveling in and out, mesmerizing in his power, grace, and strength. Arms flexing and flowing through actions even she recognized as paddling and pulling fishnets. They all wore serious expressions in concentration for the performance.

How had she ever thought the hula was a dance strictly for women? This was raw, vigorous, masculine grace on view.

The rhythm picked up as first one and then another of the dancers took center stage to show his prowess.

When Kye stepped forward, Yardley could not stop herself from gasping as lust flash-banged through her body. Then laughter erupted from her.

Too late to stop the sound, she saw his gaze roam the crowd and then catch on her face and hold. If he was surprised, it did not show in his serious face. He seemed to grow taller, the ripped muscles of his chest and arms shown to great effect by a fist on each hip, flexed. He saw her. The raw energy of the moment causing those nearest her to glance around and look her way.

And then he was moving. The rhythm slower now,

more deliberate. His hips began to move in slow circles. The suggestive undulating motion riding liquid though the rhythm was all for her. That's what his gaze said.

The rhythm increased, forcing his concentration away from her.

But it didn't matter. The raw energy of his dance belonged to her. Others might view the flick of his hip that flashed a butt cheek, but it didn't matter. He was the most beautiful beast in creation. And she wanted him, wanted him with the same urgency and power that moved his gorgeous body across the floor. When his turn was done, he fell back in line for the next dancer. It didn't matter. They were surrounded by others, but the connection between them held. The profoundly sensual experience of Kye dancing for her left her weak and aroused, overheated and shivering in anticipation.

All the things she had feared—the conversations, the recriminations, the hurt and regrets—melted away under the powerful rhythm of the visceral need to be together.

She barely heard the thunderous applause and cheers and whistles. She was moving toward the edge of the stage and the push of the crowd fell away for her. Several people patted her shoulders but she didn't have the power to acknowledge them. There was only this drumming in her soul and the need to reach Kye.

And then he was as before, glistening with sweat, his powerful chest rising and falling with the exertions of the dance. He looked at her, the raw hunger in his gaze nearly buckling her knees. But he didn't speak. Didn't touch her. So she did.

She flung herself at him, pushing through the crowd.

"That's the sexiest thing I've ever seen."

He watched her uncertainly. "Really?"

"Fuck yeah." She slapped both hands to her mouth. "Sorry."

He shook his head, thinking harder than she'd ever seen him. Then the *aloha* smile spread across his face and he grabbed her hand. "Okay. Come on."

She stumbled after him as he plunged into the crowd, cheering now his obvious conquest. "Where are we going?"

He looked back at her. "Do you care?"

Abso-*freakin'*-lutely not.

CHAPTER THIRTY

Leaves from his floral collar and cuffs littered the floor. His loincloth was out in the hallway. Her dress hadn't made it two feet inside the front door. He'd murmured something about buying her a new one as he broke the straps and let it slide off her damp body. Her panties didn't fare much better. Kye in heat was a wonder not to be missed.

Somewhere in the middle of their steps toward the bedroom, the need for a bed gave way to a more basic need. They subsided to the highly polished wood floor.

Their bodies, slick with sweat, slip-slid over each other as they grappled to bring themselves skin-to-skin and then even closer.

The kisses were just as quick and hungry, tongues licking and flicking, lapping up the taste of each other.

She breathed him in as the heat and weight of him settled over her. The floor beneath her felt cool against her feverish skin.

He pulled up. She heard foil rip. Condom. She didn't ask. She didn't care. But she wondered. Where could he have gotten it?

And then he was kissing her again. She groaned into his mouth as his tongue ravished hers. She wanted to feel his tongue any- and everywhere on and in her body, but that would have to wait. The heat coursing through her veins demanded release before it turned her inside out. It felt like life and death. Or something even more serious.

She grabbed at his shoulders, smoothing her hands over the wide expanse as she remembered how his body had rippled and flexed, much like the ocean she had been staring at earlier. The push–pull motion of the sea. That's what she wanted to feel inside her. Kye inside her. No doubts. No regrets.

He looked down at her, dark eyes glittering in a face tight with need. "It's going to be hard and quick, Yard. I'll make it up to you later."

She frowned up at him. "Quick and hard is what I need, Kye. Hurry!"

He flexed her knees against his shoulders and scooped a hand under her butt to lift her to the right angle and then he was pushing down. Her body tingled and burned in response to being filled, but even that was not enough.

She reached down and grabbed his ass, pulling him even tighter against her.

The hunger in his movements created a delicious friction, her body pulsing with every shift of muscle and cock. She closed her eyes, the better to just feel.

As he pounded into her she began to see him dancing behind her closed lids. The undulations now punctuated by thrusts of his cock that lifted her butt higher

and harder against him. It was all that she had been fe￫
ing as she watched him move, and more. This was onl￭
for her, and him.

Suddenly he was holding her hips and thrusting into
her with everything in him. Her head made little squeaky
noises against the floor but she didn't care. His breath
came quick and sharp between his teeth. She held her
breath, holding on against the moment that pleasure spun
her out over the edge, away from everything safe and secure and known.

And then she dropped, spiraling through an ecstasy
as powerful and blissful as the man above her.

He came with her, grunting his pleasure into her ear
as he slammed himself into her and held there, pumping out every drop into her.

They lay in silence for some time. The moonlight
spilled in from the double doors open onto the night.
She had no idea where they were, who lived here or
might have heard them. Gradually, she realized that she
could hear music and laughter, and smell roasted pork.
Below it all was the hiss and roar of the ocean. They
hadn't gone far from the party. In fact, they were on full
view to anyone who might happen past the doors. But
she no longer cared.

She closed her eyes, shutting out the world beyond
them.

Kye's body, heavy and sated, sprawled across hers.
This was paradise. If anyone didn't understand what had
just happened between them, she felt sorry for them.

"What's this? Tears?" Kye was leaning over her, moonlight spilling its pearly luster over his bronzed shoulders.

"Don't be crazy." She playfully batted his hand from

cheek and sat up on the floor. "I don't cry. I never cry."

He rolled up into a seated position, spread his legs, and then pulled her in between them, her back to his chest as they gazed out on a night grown quiet after the dispersal of sleepy guests. He wrapped both arms around her to hold her close as he kissed her neck.

She folded her hands over his muscular arms, hugging his hug. "I want . . ." Lord, this was hard. But maybe she'd done harder things. "I want to learn what you need to make you love me."

Something moved in his chest, something less than laughter but more than a growl. And then he was turning her to face him. And he was smiling. "*Ma'ane'i No Ke Aloha*, Yardley."

She strained to see his expression in the dark. "You said that to me before, on New Year's Day. What does it mean?"

He used a thumb to brush away her non-tear. "Love is here and now."

"Oh."

His *aloha* smile turned dangerously hot. "*Nou No Ka 'I'ini*."

"So I want to know that means . . . ?"

"Let me show you."

"Since I totally deserted my *tutu*'s birthday party before the cake, could you make it clear to my grandmother that your interest in me is deeper than lust?"

Kye was scooping cereal into his mouth. It was sunrise in what Yardley had learned was his grandmother's beach house. Amazingly, his grandmother had not come home last night.

Yardley smiled, feeling the expression slip and slide across her face as if she'd had too much to drink—drunk in love with Kye. "Why would I do that?"

"She worries. She says all that women see when they look at my pretty face is a good time. I'm a beefcake bimbo. She's says that the reason I haven't married is that women ogling me, like last night, have ruined me for a serious relationship."

"Maybe she's right. I was in total ogle mood last night."

He looked at her darkly over his coffee cup. "What about this morning?"

"You're fishing for compliments? You are *so* vain."

He shrugged smugly. "I know what you think." And he went back to drinking his coffee.

"What I don't understand is why your *tutu* encouraged you to take dance lessons. She had to know you in a loincloth was not going to be good for local morals."

"To the contrary. It's a Hawaiian tradition. She's very strong on tradition. I've been dancing since I was ten. She told my parents it would keep me off the streets and out of gangs."

"I guess it worked. Does Law know about your talent?" He scowled at her and Yardley chuckled in delight. "Oh, now I'll have leverage with you."

"Nothing new about that."

She watched for a few moments longer, wondering why he hadn't brought it up. "Don't you have any questions about why I'm here?"

"Oliver told me a woman was coming to us for a job as a handler. I'm guessing that's you."

"I need a job."

"You need to explain that."

She did, quickly, about Law deciding he wanted to settle down and making plans for marriage, and how it coincided with her desire to take a break from Harmonie Kennels.

He watched her with a careful eye, giving away nothing of his feelings in his expression. "Hm. You don't have a job? I've always been attracted to strong independent working women."

She tried to match his laid-back attitude. "That's why I thought I should sign up with a SAR organization. I've always wanted to see the world. Work alone with a dog." She sat up. "Oleg!"

"He's with Oliver. Or rather, Oliver is with him. He texted during the night and sent his thanks. He slept in your hotel room last night as payment for his dog-sitting services."

"How would he—?"

"He's Oliver. He can talk nearly every woman out of her panties. I'm sure getting a key to your room wasn't a stretch for him. Nor making friends with Oleg. He's a dog man."

"Remind me, I owe him a big fat kiss."

"Over my dead body."

Yardley just smiled.

Kye smiled, too. "As it happens, BARKS is always on the lookout for competent people. Of course, you'd have to pass muster with the bosses."

"Oliver says you do all the hires."

"So I guess you'll have to get in good with me. How about you move in and we'll discuss it?"

A cloud sailed past Yardley's blue-sky smile. "It might be too soon."

"I was thinking about those twelve years we w̶
But if you want more time."

"No."

She moved to straddle him in his chair, scissoring he̶
legs so that his erection, poking up from the towel he'd
wrapped around himself after a shower, could find her
groove. "Show me the muscle dance again."

He gazed down his good-as-new nose at her. "This is
getting to be a habit with you."

"Gee, I hope."

She scooted up tighter and kissed him, hearing the
stomp and rhythm of lust pulse in her blood. A rhythm
as primitive as time.

AUTHOR'S NOTE

Dear Readers,

Writing the K-9 Rescue Series has taken me on many adventures and introduced me to wonderful people and dogs. I work hard to portray them realistically. But, sometimes, words can't quite do justice to the research. I thought I'd share these videos to enhance your enjoyment of *Rival Forces*.

Lily, a Nova Scotia Duck Tolling Retriever, has a unique ability to scream when in trouble. It's a sound that has to be heard to be believed. Let me know if you agree.

Toller Scream:
https://www.youtube.com/watch?v=YLAipVibHSE

I couldn't write about Kye's Hawaiian ancestry without doing research. Tall, dark, and sexy, he was a natural for male hula. *Hula Kahiko* involves chanting, percussion, discipline, strength, and is story-driven. Banned for more than a century, it's roared back to popularity. Check it out. You'll understand why.

Male Hula:
https://www.youtube.com/watch?v=389wVVny2XU

Okay, one more:
https://www.youtube.com/watch?v=sm2nDzlzhu0

...t me know if you enjoyed the video links!

Ke ola maika'i!

D. D. Ayres
Ddayresftw@gmail.com

Don't miss the next book in the K-9 Rescue series
by D.D. Ayres

EXPLOSIVE FORCES

Coming Fall 2016 from St. Martin's Paperbacks!